The Author

RUDY WIEBE was born near Fairholme, Saskatchewan, in 1934. He received his early education at the Alberta Mennonite High School in Coaldale, Alberta, then took his B.A. in English (1956) and M.A. in creative writing (1960) from the University of Alberta. He received his Th.B. (1961) from the Mennonite Brethren Bible College in Winnipeg.

From 1963 to 1967 Wiebe taught in the Department of English at Goshen College in Indiana. He then joined the Department of English at the University of Alberta, where he taught for more than two decades.

Wiebe's writing is deeply shaped by his Mennonite background. Although he frequently draws his subject-matter from Canadian history, including stories of the Cree, Dene, and other native peoples, his fiction transcends nationality and locale to explore the struggles of communities and individuals to live moral lives in a world where spiritual values are increasingly difficult to observe and even to comprehend.

Rudy Wiebe resides in Edmonton, Alberta.

Rudy Wiebe

THE BLUE
MOUNTAINS
OF CHINA

With an Afterword by Eva-Marie Kröller

M&S

Copyright © 1970 by Wm. B. Eerdmans Publishing Co.
Afterword copyright © 1995 by Eva-Marie Kröller

First published in 1970, in Canada by McClelland and Stewart
Limited and in the United States of America by Wm. B. Eerdmans
Publishing Co.

This New Canadian Library Edition 1995

Canadian Cataloguing in Publication Data
Wiebe, Rudy, 1934-
The blue mountains of China

(New Canadian library)
ISBN 0-7710-3455-5

I. Title. II. Series.

PS8545.I43B5 1995 C813'.54 C94-932836-7
PR9199.3.W54B5 1995

The publishers acknowledge the support of the Canada Council and
the Ontario Arts Council for their publishing program.

Typesetting by M&S, Toronto
Cover layout by Andrew Skuja
Printed and bound in Canada by Webcom Limited

McClelland & Stewart Inc.
The Canadian Publishers
481 University Avenue
Toronto, Ontario
M5G 2E9

1 2 3 4 5   99 98 97 96 95

the knowledge of
our origins, and where
we are in truth,
whose land this is
and is to be.

Contents

Principal Characters in This Book

JAKOB (III) AND ISAAK FRIESEN: identical twin grandsons of Jakob (I) who founded the Karatow *hof* after re-settling from Chortitza, the Ukraine, where the Friesens had come in 1789 from Danzig; born Karatow 1859; Jakob deceased there 1919, Isaak in Manitoba 1933.

JAKOB FRIESEN (IV): only son of Jakob (III) and '*Muttachi*'; born Karatow 1888, exiled 1929; wife and daughters to Paraguay 1929, only son *Jakob* (V) born Karatow 1910, deceased 1929.

FRIEDA FRIESEN: second daughter of Isaak Friesen, born Manitoba 1883, married *Johann Friesen* 1903, had twelve sons and daughters: Johann, *Esther*, Kornelius, Marie, Tina, Isaak, *Anna*, Neta, Greta, Benjamin, Abram, and Johann again. Husband deceased Paraguay 1958.

DAVID EPP: born 1870 in Molotschna, the Ukraine and had, among other children, two sons: *David Jr.*, born Molotschna 1905, whose son *David* was born in the Amur region 1930; and *Franz*, born Molotschna 1907. Deceased Paraguay 1960.

SAMUEL REIMER: born Orenburg 1905, cousin to David Epp and had, among other children, two sons: *Samuel*, born Orenburg 1925 and *John*, born Saskatchewan 1939.

ELIZABETH DRIEDIGER: only daughter of Helmut Driediger, born Molotschna 1920.

ONE

My Life: That's As It Was (1)

I HAVE LIVED long. So long, it takes me days to remember even parts of it, and some I can't remember at all until I've been thinking over it a little now and then for weeks, and little Johann or Friedl ask, "Urgrossmuttachi, what is that, so cold in Canada the ground is stiff?" Then I have to be careful or I'll start making it up, they like to hear so much. What I tell I remember only through God's grace. I never wrote anything down and didn't have more than the usual Mennonite village school, four or five years between fall and spring work. Then that was very good in Manitoba, if you got it, though it isn't anything at all there now. Or even here. But the Lord led me through so many deep ways and of the world I've seen a little, both north and south. If your eyes stay open and He keeps your head clear you sometimes see so much more than you want of how it is with the world. And if you don't you can thank Him for that, too.

In the winter when I was born the wind started to blow late in October and didn't stop until April 23. I was born on April 22, 1883. My father, Isaak J. Friesen, he came from the Jakob Friesen side, village Gnadenfeld, Karatow, South Russia and came to Manitoba single in 1879, always said when I first screeched the wind knew right away it was time to make *schluss.* Our sod house was half in the ground and drifted under like a Bashkir *boud* on the steppes, he said, and the prairie all around bare to the buffalo bones. Neuboden, the village where I was born, had been measured and lotted out that summer, but nobody had plowed anything yet, except for sod. The eleven sod houses were all that kept the snow in Canada; without them it would have all blown right past on into the States somewhere. He said in spring at least our roof was mud, even if our fields weren't.

When I was six years, during harvest my mother was stooking. At noon a worker came past and my father hired him. Just before evening as I was bringing my mother a drink out of the pail a black cloud came over the end of the field where they both were working and a stroke of lightning struck the worker dead. My father hitched the horses from the binder and they loaded the man on the wagon and brought him to his family. He had just come from Germany. His name was Schwenkel and they had three little ones, smaller than me. I remember he had a wide face with a mustache that stuck out black on both sides of it.

When I was eight or nine years I went to school. Neuboden had broken up then, some had even moved to their homestead quarter, but the teacher was the poorest farmer and still lived where the village had been. The first day my mother made two sandwiches so I and my sister Marie could stay in school and eat from our pail. The teacher called me Frieda, but I said my name was not Frieda, it was Fritzchi. He looked at me and said, "Fritzchi is a boy's name," and I said that was what I should have been to help my father and also my father said I always made so many *froutzen* that I must be a fritz. Then he said, "At home you are Fritzchi, but in school you are Frieda." When my father came to get us in the evening I said right away that the teacher had said in school I was Frieda. My father laughed. "Yes, yes. You aren't home now. You aren't Fritzchi like at home and just watch out that you're *friedlich* at school, like your name."

We went to school in the *groutestov* in the biggest house left standing in Neuboden and the teacher Abram Dick lived in the room beside it when he didn't move from house to house to eat in the winter. He needed the forty dollars for teaching all year most, they said. He was a *betchla* and we farmed some of his quarter and Elias Goertzens some too. I knew his bony face from when we had our turn feeding him. They said he sure couldn't farm and the third or fourth day I said I didn't want to go to school. The teacher just sat and drew pictures with a pencil or with a stick right on the ground sometimes the whole day, and they didn't even look like anything you could see you had seen before.

"Frieda," my father said, "there is school. We pay $1.25 cash money for each child, and then some food too. Understand?" I learned to spell out letters from *Die deutsche Fibel* and then we spelled out the Bible stories and the Hymnbook. The one-times-one was harder but I had a loud voice and soon I could stand when we all stood together and yell it as loud as anybody; just watching the teacher's lips you could see enough not to make a mistake if he didn't. School was from October to April 1; in April there was too much water and we could not go, then in May there was one more month school. Every May 15 we had a picnic at Buffalo Creek. It was mostly swamp where ducks had nests in the bulrushes and the killdeers ran around silly on the mud flats, crying and crying. When we were tired we washed off our feet and sat a little; the teacher taught us a song. He liked to sing:

> *All is made new by May,*
> *Makes the spirit fresh and free.*
> *Do come out, leave the hearth,*
> *Weave a flower wreath.*

There was nothing, just bulrushes and green water there, but the tune was nice. And the bright sunshine too, warm on your face like when you open a bun just baked and put your nose into it.

We were poor. In our family we had four girls first and only then five boys, then two girls and a boy again. Marie, the oldest, was sickly so she helped mother in the house. I was healthy and worked in the barn and the field though it wasn't with me what it would have been with a boy. We moved here and there in Manitoba, even across the Red River to the East Reserve once for two years, but every quarter we had, even if it looked so good when we moved, it always seemed to have something wrong. It was too rocky on the East Reserve or on the West the water wouldn't get off in spring or there wasn't enough breaking to pay for everything when the crop was really good or it froze too late or too soon. One fall when it had been too dry all summer and we were hauling a load of poor bundles to the yard for threshing, my sister who was driving the team let one line drop and the horses were frightened and ran away. She and I fell off the rack into the stubble; I hurt my shoulder so much I couldn't lift my arm and had to go to the bone fixer near Altona twice a month all winter. The horses ran through the yard fence, tipped the rack over, and the best horse broke his leg in the wire. My father had to get it shot. Everything seemed to come so bunchy in our family and it was enough to make you think sometimes, my father said.

"But think always like this," he said, "it does come all from God, strength and sickness, want and plenty."

Gerhard J. Willms, our neighbor by Winkler where we lived then for the last two years in Manitoba, said that that was true, yes, but a man had to be ready, waiting for the strength and plenty when it did come so he could go along with it just as far as it would go, not be so far down when it came that he used it all up getting his nose over water. So, my father said, it went with him, always one could say more or less just the nose right since he was born the second son to Jakob Friesen by about ten minutes, though he had gotten enough along to start with in Manitoba and he would not complain, always just barely the nose and then it was past and you took the other as you could, as you must. That Gerhard Willms could talk, with three thick sons all in a row the oldest in the family! No, it wasn't just that, my father said; he knew how to turn things too, over and over and over.

My youth was simple and quiet. We moved more than most but my parents brought us up to be decent. Beside us in the village of Blumental, by Winkler, our neighbors on one side was an old widow Toews. Her two daughters were older than my mother and they lived from what the *Waisenamt* could give them. Sometimes that wasn't much in the hard years, but they always had something. One daughter, Lena, had a flower garden all around the front of their small house and she talked to me when I started with youth instruction in the Sommerfelder Church. I and my sister Marie often visited there in the evening. Lena would say things mostly about the flowers; she never said about anything else. How nice they were, and clean and fresh just like God had said and they had been in the garden of Eden. One night she died in sleep. At the funeral they said only three things about her life: she was born in Furstenland, Russia in 1846, she was confirmed in 1863 and she died August 23, 1902.

In 1902 after harvest, when my oldest brother David was fifteen already, my father drove to the west with other Mennonites to look for land. When he came back he said there was a homestead and another quarter near Swift Current for $300.00 and that we would move there with others in spring. I was nineteen then and working that winter for my mother's brother Heinrich B. Abrams of Ostwick. I drove on the train for the first time to get there. Our *hauptcheuik* was there and after Easter I took catechism classes with twenty-three boys and twenty girls from Elder Wiebe, the Older. On Pentecost he baptized us on our confession that Jesus Christ is the Son of God and that He has forgiven us our sins and we were accepted in the Sommerfelder Church. There were many Mennonite villages around Ostwick and there I met Johann K. Friesen of Schoenbach who also became my *velobta* that spring. He was no relation, he came from the Abram H. Friesen side, village Olgafeld, Furstenland, South Russia. We had *velobung* in our house three days before my parents moved to Swift Current with all the younger ones and I went back to my uncle to work for seven dollars the month.

TWO

Sons and Heirs

THE CELL HAD one opening: the door. Three half steps long, nearly two wide, thirteen rows of sweating stone floor to ceiling. Erect was impossible, but lying on his coat he could stretch out and he knew quite certainly when the peephole in the door shaded gray that somewhere was daylight; yellow, the guard was coming. At first he had had every sane intention; at first every day he used the edge of the stinking can to worry a scar deep enough to feel into a stone, but after a few sessions, he was sure there were only a few, he lost grip on duration, on sequence. It happened so fast; it was down the corridor and he was – could have been – there only a few times but the edges of his mind seemed exploded, all he knew ran through him like water; the very next question would drain him away. As suddenly, that was over; they left him to rot. So the day the guard bent in, yelled to come with whatever he had, the daylight was so overpowering Jakob thought surely it must be summer; perhaps two later. The GPU fiend at the desk whose face of question question question question had chiseled itself into him until he would have to know it even contorted, spitted and frying forever in hell

blessed savior make me pure that in heaven I may

did not bother to raise his head; just wrinkled his nose as usual, said it was November 12 and he was to go straight home, stay there and not leave for any reason whatever, whoever said so, understood? Now get. His mind could still do arithmetic; it had been six weeks.

Beyond imagining, he got rides. The Ukrainian carters looked once and asked nothing; they gave him a hand-up and drove on, whips curling at the rumps of their gaunt horses. One got down and lifted him over the wheel; in the evening light Jakob recognized his own fingers crooked into his bundle blanched as grubs. He slept perhaps, shaking on dry hides, the sky and stars hard as glass, and in the early morning he walked the three kilometers from the Terwoj Road crossing. There were no carts and, lurching on as he could, toward noon through the final bend he saw the gateposts gleam between the bare trees, the first *hof* in Gnadenfeld, their *hof*. He laughed aloud, hitched at his bundle, and tried to run. They had kept his boots and his feet were broken from the wet so even winding rags helped little despite the beautiful soft dry dust, but he laughed and stumbled down the slope and into the yard, the high gable facing the street and the immense sheer granary roof run green in strips of moss all there, as ever all there. Forget rags and feet and he is coming home again, completely unexpected, from *Zentralschul* in Chortitza. Unexpected! He jerked open the front door.

"Mutti, papa, I'm home! They let me out!"

The house was a black hole. Black. He would not have known he made a sound except for his throat's burn. He was shuddering before the black hall but clamped to the doorjamb to avoid collapse, the picture of the closed yard doors and the untracked driveway, the silent shrubbery where no chicken sings as it scrabbles gathering ponderously, stroke by stroke, in his mind. No one on the road, not a figure the length of the village street, not a dog barking, no team moving in the fields.

Not one movement in the sunlight. As if in six weeks everything alive had been swallowed with him and only his aching body, by some freak spasm, had been heaved back

*six weeks   the world is dead   only the GPU lives
and in its holes the grubs   every six hours kicked up
again under the naked bulb   six days and six nights
without end questions and questions six and six and
where were you born who is your father where is your
father where were you october 6 how many workers did
you have why didn't you fill the grain quota do you go to
church how many sisters do you believe the bible were you
october 6 is your name where is your father six you read
the bible in they are all gone   jesus has come again
and taken them and I am left for hell and the devil and his
angels and the place prepared   he could not find me
with the GPU   he could not take me with him and
my mother and sisters   I never confessed when I saw
the answer and wrote it down I didn't want to see it
I   the Russian girl in the water naked squatting and
rising I never confessed that I   saw my sister
when   and wet playing with   jesus has come
again he will come again will you be ready when the
trumpet sounds six times I was not ready with all my
sins he has come   only sinners and the GPU where is
your fa –*

a thud in the *sommastov* beside him; his heart leaped again and he was jawing out a sound when from the black wall bulged a forehead, nose, shoulders. Escha, the Russian worker; his mouth hole sagged and then his whole body hunched out into the sunlight split through the front door. Wearing nothing but pants, grinning violently. Coming out of Jakob's own bedroom when Russians belonged in the barn.

"Wh – what are you, here, in the house?"

"Uhhhhgg," Escha grunted, tossing his head, fists to his eyes, "Jascha? They let you out really? Yeah?"

"Yes. In my room – what . . ."

"Every proletarian gets a room, a bed. With blankets too." It rolled like a catechism.

"In our house – where . . ." The dark hall was beginning to tilt and he raised his hand against the wall.

"Yeah, *our* house, now. You can sleep here, or anywhere, who cares. Any room, and there's even straw in the loft." His laughter roared for an instant, head jerking toward the barn, and then the sound crumpled, his hairy face screwed together.

The living picture now, the day they came. His mind went back sharp as a photograph spiked on that grin. The second week in September District Party Representative, Commissar Serebro, raised the Friesen grain tax quota for the third time and Jakob's father began to understand: so maybe it was not grain they wanted. One man on the village soviet – no farm owners were on, but every Mennonite squatting on the commonland south of Gnadenfeld had worked for Friesen at some time – told him without meeting his eye that perhaps he should go while his feet still carried him where he wanted. Before sunrise next morning Jakob's father and mother left for Bamenka, where his mother's brother lived. In the afternoon there was banging on the door and when he opened on the porch stood the thick man with a head and voice like a rooster.

"Where's Jakob Friesen?"

"I'm Jakob Friesen."

A mouthful of swearing and the two soldiers stepped up on the porch. Serebro was beyond in the driveway, surveying the yard, house, barn, granary. He seemed to look hard at the gateposts, at where the arch had been torn away during the revolution

maybe the anarchy   twice six years   I was little scrolled white iron arching over the house and barn and granary this is my hof *this is mine I am eldest son this is mine I am*

"Not you, you ass!" the rooster squealed. "Your kulak father!" He boiled redder when Jakob answered as quiet still that his father was away. "Why didn't you fill your grain quota?"

"You can go up and see, there's not a kernel. The commission before harvest said we should deliver 1000 pood, and we've even bought an extra 800 besides that to deliver and there's not a kernel –"

The official's face ground to purple; cursing, waving his arms, clawing at one soldier's gun when Serebro said from the driveway,

"Shut up. Take him then."

Jakob's sisters were crying aloud, hands scratching to hold him. The commissar's tone should have been warning enough but he thought the soviet would ask a few questions; after all, they wanted his father. Great god, innocence! He knocked the soldiers' hands away and went out. Serebro's head did not even reach his chin. The commissar was looking toward the barn, at Escha tilted against the barndoor in his split shirt. Next day they were marched to K, seven Mennonites, chained tight as oxen; every time the guard kneed his horse against them, whip swinging, Jakob saw that big horse leaning in the barndoor, grinning. Propped on the doorjamb of their *sommastov*, his arm thick as a stud's hindleg naked against the darkness, now.

"Sleep where you want," Escha said again. "They all left and I'm man here. No straw for me, Jascha."

His arm was in Jakob's fist and the jerk shifted his grin a little, but a shrug was enough to shake loose. They were the same age and size but Jakob never had thrown him except with a learned hold. Now he could not outmuscle a puppy.

"All left . . . what . . . Jesus. . . ."

"No jesus, they just run to Moscow, all, the whole works – your pa. And ma and girls. Your pa running. Just not Muttachi."

"M–m-oscow . . . M–m-uttachi . . ."

"Just she's got guts," the yell followed him as Jakob lurched forward against the door of the *groutestov* and across the room. Roar off, roar off, drip down and awash in the flood, let the waters roar down like – and he snagged at the black shape in the chair by the lying bench. Tiny, hunched, wire glasses hung on her nose. Though deaf as a wall she could not help seeing him stumble to her, but her head remained down; motionless save for the small gray bumps the spinning wheel was lifting and let fall, the fingers crooked to the white thread. The bumps moved, the wheel turned on and suddenly her sing-song emerged out of its dry miaul.

"Now they let you out, and your father thought you were lost. They had no hope for you and they left, all of them, and they let you out."

He could make no sound loud enough for her to hear. The room was there; completely always; sunlight through curtains, pillows and bedding heaped on the ledge above the lying bench where Greta and Susie played house with their dolls. Even the Kroeger clock on the wall. But its bronze weights gleamed at the end of their chain and no beat swung the pendulum. Finally he shuffled a step nearer, gesturing, and she said,

"They came from Bamenka and you taken, so they took the children and put some little together and thought they would try for Moscow. Some got to Germany last month. Wiens from Steintal that left last summer, they're maybe already in Canada. The half from Gnadenfeld is gone, those that have a little backbone left. Some are back already too, with soldiers to show them exactly where they've lived a hundred years. Na. Your Vati thought you were lost, and now they let you out."

He was prone on the lying bench, her voice and wheel sing

*ten months older than I to the day the dull bronze
still   for the wedding from Grandfather she told me
long ago when I sat with her spelling from the first year
Fibel   so proud of the long red-blond friesen the
first child   son to carry the name and the family and
the hof and the land   six daughters then were
fine   fine*

". . . old one do, like me, running to hide somewhere far in
the world, from where I lived and married and birthed and
shoveled under too. Let the young run. Oh Jakob wanted me
to go, yes, and old ones must listen to sons, yes, but to run after
revolution and starvation and Makhnovski and they split my
old Jakob in half from head to stomach and your Mutti and
you and Mari under the manure in the pig shed so those who
wanted had to work themselves dry on me – what's left they
can do yet? Take, and welcome, welcome. Chase them and
split them too and sweep up the last kernel in the grain loft and
welcome, welcome everything. And now they let you out."

Sunlight on the tiles reflected upon the motto by the clock:
"He is my Help and my God!" He lunged to his feet. Lying
down, his body had beaten him into almost overwhelming
awareness of itself; he seemed to feel the complete shape and
content of his body, every cell in its own slightly differentiated
tone drumming pain from its precise location. The wheel
stopped. "Here," she said, "if we ever heard, or someone
thought he had a chance to see you." An unsealed envelope
with a sheet in it.

Our dearest dearest Son: Oh, if we could at least know
you would read this. We have no – no, we know you are
still alive and we trust God. Each time the girls or Helmut Funk – he is so kind, takes such risks – take food to
your prison they ask if we could send a little note, but
the guards are dreadful. They take the food and dig
through everything for just a scrap of paper. We don't

know if you get the food; they would tell us nothing, just like iron. Uncle Heinrich and Johann will keep on bringing food from Bamenka but we, Jascha — have to go to Moscow, if we are to have a chance at all. Papa has sent letters to his uncle Isaak, you know the one somewhere in Canada, but we don't have any address. If they let you out, and we pray, all of us, oh, how we pray for that so often every hour, come to Moscow immediately, come. There is enough in the place you know. Take a ticket to beyond Moscow – otherwise they suspect and hold you – and to our cousins, John Martens in P; they will know. We pray so hard, dear Father, let him out. Moscow is our only hope. So they say. We have had too much here ever to be left in peace – oh, the terrible riches, so terrible to be known to have a little more than some and so much more than most. We pray our Lord Jesus, spare our son, our Jascha. What will we do without him? But if we are to have a chance we must go to Moscow, Papa says. He is leaving enough, enough, if only you get out. Our God kept us through all, we believe Him still. If you can, bring Muttachi; maybe if she is alone a little she will agree to come. God take care of you so pray we, your sisters and your loving parents. Oh my beloved only son, hate upon hate and now they take it all out on you. Oh dearest God give him quick

Her letter stopped with space for several lines left on the page. The food, well, who knew where most of it caught in its long descent from the iron gate down to him; without the bit he did get, he knew he would never have limped through the door when they opened it. Why did they? There had to be some policy reason; somewhere.

"Have they got out, of Moscow?" he could finally shout to Muttachi.

She shook her head, the wheel creaking. "Who knows? Nobody. The ones coming back say nothing. Just nothing."

After a moment she continued, "That Escha stands, looks around like heir and owner, here. Sleeps in your room. The soviet wrote him out furniture and sheets, everything."

"Food?"

"He eats what's left in the pantry, maybe the cellar. And now they let you out. Now."

He had not eaten in two days, the last a bowl of gruel, but she just trundled slowly on, making no other move. He got himself back into the hall. The *sommastov* door was closed. No fire in the kitchen stove or wood in the box. In the pantry he found an ancient roasted bun to gnaw; his front teeth moved loose in his gums, but there was a little coarse-ground barley too. Scummed water in the wash-basin; that brute never washed himself of his own free will in his life. Jakob bent to the mirror and an image focused; a long nose, matted whiskers, two side teeth jagged by the brass knuckle when a few answers did

> *don't know don't know*   *how can I know he is gone*
> *was that a Tuesday he is*   *is that what they mean*
> *when they always keep asking where is*

not sit well, caved-in eyes glaring; a hideous face that bound him, staring, and heavily, heavily in its shadowy swaying it broadened, began to double in grotesque extended repetition, the double lips twisting, lengthening slowly like a water image into grin that jarred him to comprehension and he wheeled to Escha so close his shoulder hoisted him under the chin and against the table. Six weeks before that would have stretched him along the floor.

"You get some wood."

Escha rubbed his chin, grinning. "A kulak's son is not so much different, eh? I did, for myself. But who cares – there's enough. We do what we want now, big house, barn, food in the cellar, nobody to yell, 'No! No!' For fun, eh?"

"Fun!" The pain in his shoulder soaked through his body. Sometimes in the fields far from anyone they wrestled a little, their strength felt too much for mere plows or pitchforks. Escha was like every other Russian peasant working on a Mennonite farm, just a bastard; his mother in the Russian village in the hills he never went near except to tank himself over with vodka, his reddish-blond hair giving some fly-by-night father away. Probably some clown from a foreign circus stopping for a night between Kharkov and Odessa found a sheepskin warmer than he expected and stayed long enough to start heating a pot he sure as the devil wouldn't watch till it boiled over. And now his scum screwed himself into a grin before Jakob, face enough to make a cow squirt through the eye of a needle. His father had told him how Escha arrived four years before, while he was away in his last year of *Zentralschul*, barefoot in ripped pants and forearms hanging like hams, knowing one Lowgerman word: *awbeide, awbeide,* as if Friesen didn't know Russian better than he. Friesen had said, "Go clean the barn," and when in two weeks the *schlunga* had stolen nothing more than two pans of buns cooling in the pantry window and bent over to take his whipping with less screaming than standard, Friesen gave him a shirt, a blanket for sleeping in the loft, grease to rub on his cuts and said stay. When Jakob came home with his diploma his father said now they had a steady to do the ox-work and they would really start to farm.

Jakob watched those glinting eyes; thinking, we were unbelievable fools. To think Stalin would go on and on letting them take advantage of those terrified by reports and the stupid local communists into selling and running off to Canada from where earlier Mennonite immigrants sang hallelujahs in their letters. What anarchy, drought, fear left could be had for the spitting; in two years they controlled the mill, owned four farms, equipped, and managed the village studfarm where eight Cossacks worked, the biggest operation in Karatow Colony despite taxes on every knife and straw. After harvest in 1928 the whole family even took a holiday in Odessa, travelling first class on train and ship. That must have been the first thing Serebro heard when he came to take over and clean up the mess of the soviet in spring. Absolutely incredible

> is that what they meant when they asked where
> is   where

fools.

". . . fool around, *cosheet*," Escha still leaned against the table.

"Fool you," he mumbled. "You can eat it. I'm getting –"

His carelessness jolted him too late. There is momentary silence. Then, "With the rubles your pa stuck away?"

"*Nuscht*, there's *nuscht*." He placed the wood Escha dropped on the stove carefully in the firebox, crumpled the letter and watched it burn. Escha went out, returned with a pail of water. Jakob dipped some into the pot for the cereal; flames leaped from the splintered wood.

"There's a girl from Borsenko around," Escha said suddenly. "Lies right down for it. Anywhere, for a ruble. And chesty, yuck!"

Bubbles were rising; Jakob sat feet eased high on the stove bricks, exhaustion dragging at his head. "Go stuff her then."

"Yeah! Just a ruble a shot." Escha laughed, "They teach talk like that, the GPU?"

"A ruble so there's *nuscht* for you."

"Huh, that's what you know. Your pa left me good."

"What?"

"He's not dumb. If they send him back, and everything wrecked here? I keep my eye peeled, see." The warmth and porridge aroma found Jakob and he slumped back again, "Yeah, so I got her by the tail for a month, just me," Escha slurped his finger through his mouth.

"If she's here, you pig, I'll –"

"You'll shut. You know Commissar Serebro."

"Serebro!"

"Yeah, Serebro. I take care of stuff for him too. All this is the soviet's, see."

"That's nice," he muttered at last. "You take money from my – from – who fed and clothed you for three years and taught you everything, and then –"

"Ox-work for a kopeck!"

"I worked as hard as you."

"Always the light end of the log!" It was like Escha's short-sightedness that he remembered the weight he lifted today and never thought of who would own it all tomorrow

> *three in my name and already one in yours and the stud-farm in both names   more than your grandfather dreamed was left in Karatow to own   a long-nosed red-blond Friesen a son o fatherland where my cradle did stand*

and Jakob almost laughed in bitterness.

"So Serebro whistles and you lift your tail. Just like a stupid Russian, listen to their manure and muck up our buildings with some bitch that –"

"Shut!" If the fist had landed he would have been standing before the judgment, but he got under it and a butt-end of wood into Escha's gut to double him, almost banging his head down on the brick stove. Escha's fists leaped to his shoulders but the wood high in Jakob's hand relaxed him, easy, grinning again.

"You clean your stall, Jascha, I clean mine." Laughter, mouth gigantic in the dark kitchen. "If I want one here, I will. There's enough for both, plenty enough. Like you need to make a man, straighten you, stiff out after six weeks in the wet hole, eh? No pa to see the turds fly. Ha!"

Rectangles of dark and brightness spiral, contort, the stone-wall pressing into his head, squeezing him together, working in, squeezing him moist into terror and he erupts; but his feet and fists strike nothing. Soft; sheets dry with clean over his naked body; feather pillow hollowed to his head. His head against the head board. The *ackstov*; his parents' bedroom. Gradually he is entirely in the bed, in the warm ache of exhaustion overbent and finished, of healing, of sleep slept to impossibility. In that hole he had fought for hours on end, or perhaps minutes, or seconds – he could never be sure of anything, especially duration – for sleep and then, finally, at the instant of vacuity, the guard hammered at the grate. Here was warm silence; no sweating rocks; the bed pulled completely open; soft light through the shutters gave the verses on the wall, the clothes press, the great brown closet, the room world wide and his toes flexing a meridian away. But the facing wall was blank. He had been less than two when his sister was born and he left the cradle and this room, but the dark blot above him which when he grew older he knew had been, was still his grandfather with a great beard flanking his face hung irremovably in his memory. Always. Born under that face. When his grandfather was killed his father coming home had cut off his own beard, leaving only a long mustache. Muttachi, the other half of the picture, would not allow it to hang in the *groutestov*; when she wanted to remember him she came in this room and shut the door

and when thou hast shut thy door pray to thy father which
is in secret and thy father which seeth in   our father
which art in   secret   my fa

He swung his legs out of bed and fire shot up from his feet. After a moment he could stand. There were clean pants, a shirt and his old soft slippers folded on a chair. In the next room the wheel creaked; Muttachi became aware of him.

"You slept two days, one end to the other," she said in her high sing-song. "You have hunger?"

He nodded, supporting himself against the doorframe. The clean light came through a fringe of painlessness that refused to focus in believability; only his feet were convincing.

"There's barley," she said.

"Something else?"

"Na?" in her familiar query and he shouted. "No, a little barley, it's enough for me. There's still enough other in the cellar, more than Escha can have eaten yet." As he shuffled away she added, "Get some. They'll be here for it any hour."

He looked down into the black musty shaft of the cellar; no. And the narrow treads of the ladder too. While the barley cooked he sat in the back door. The orchard trunks fanned out in precise rows but the leaves had not been plowed down and not one wrinkled apple dangled anywhere. Theirs was the first *hof* of Gnadenfeld so no neighbor blocked them on that side. Through the branches were the far low hills of their valley, folded bluish where the spring ran, where the sunlight would have been warming him on the long field, drowsing him in fall plowing. He could almost smell the clean acrid sweat of the horses hoofing steady down the furrow.

There was a pot of sour milk for the porridge; a cow must still be somewhere about. He listened at the *sommastov* door. No sound; two clamps had been hammered into the wood and joined by a giant lock. From the harness room. He edged down the corridor, under the giant beam between house and barn, so black with age the "1839" axed there was better felt than seen. Great-great-grandfather Jakob Friesen built well. The barn was bright with sun, and empty. Where the horse and cow cribs faced each other across the aisle was litter trodden to dust. Old Whitey's stall looked as if she spent the night there, but the horse partitions were ripped, the cribs split to long nails and splinters; someone had helped himself to happiness doing that. A blot of greenish water gleamed in the trough by the well at the cross aisle, the back door hung on a hinge. Perhaps Whitey was nosing the leaves in the back orchard. Everything stripped; no wisp of hay hung from the feed-chutes in the loft. The door to the giant granary, opening right-angled from the barn, gone and the granary sat cavernous, empty to its dirt and litter. The double doors yawned over the threshing floor, squeaking a gesture to the air; up high sunlight shredded between roof tile and sparrows quarreled, moving streaks here and there through the narrow light. Every back door gaped as if a huge wind had raged in and gutted all to its shell while the front doors remained barred, facing the street inviolate as great-great-grandfather.

He turned back into the barn and stared at its trodden ancient earth. All around and up the smooth pillars, along the beams where the cats curled in the winter, deep scarred by their claws. The horses stirred in sleep and outside

hear hear my child the wind is wild he has no mouth but he can sing he has no wings but himself he can swing he has no hands but you can feel his cold fingers move from your neck to heel

suddenly a laugh. He wheeled around, but nothing moved. The remembered sound had a kind of total happiness, a complete contentment. There was a stir above and he moved, soundlessly, the laugh coming again and then a thick Russian curse and his thoughtless wits blundered into remembrance as he got his head above the loft floor. The sunlight from the gable doors, gaping too, wedged through the swirling dust in the corner where that *schlunga* had slept for three years, against the mound of straw heaped there and as he got his feet on the last rung, the grip in his hand, his mind asserted itself and he was already lowering his off-foot back a rung when Escha's body humped up, flying from the straw, sent by a long naked leg that held extended, delicately toeing circles in the mist before it sank gently as a feather down pale water and a voice completely out of keeping with the brute hurling force murmured,

"That's enough, now."

When Jakob could look away Escha was standing on the bare boards, seeing him, laughing. He wore a vest hanging open on the red mat of his chest, crotch, between his thighs. His mind as if exploded, Jakob saw only him: immense naked man of varied gigantic columns half-gilded, erect in the sun. But suddenly the girl's voice broke him back to the laughter and his awareness reeled over, despairing to disappear, to vanish down the hole as if he had never existed where his feet refused to move, his hands to loosen.

"Hoh Jascha!" Escha boomed, laughing. "You're too lazy, today the work's done. Today at least."

A rustle, a shape rose in the hollow, into the dusty sunlight. Dark head, long hair spiked with straw, Russian face round and full as a ball with a flash of eyes emerged, held, and with an incredible languor the girl sat up. She sat motionless and they stared at each other. Then, deliberate as sunrise, one round arm moved down and her tipped breasts stood separate in the suddenly bluish light with a great shadow cleft between them, one half-shadowed on the other. Until the arm rose and the blouse slid over the white shoulders.

"She's got some, eh Jascha?" Escha grunted. "See that."

Words finally formed in his locked throat. "I saw you kicked," he sneezed violently; beyond dust a smell he did not know was in the loft.

"Yeah, that's signal: finished today, shut off the works."

"For you," the girl said, "but not him. A nice big Mennonite."

His entire body jerked suddenly and he was screaming, screaming out of his dryness to the rafters, "Shut up shut up

you pigs you stinking naked pigs! In my father's barn you
naked –"

"No, no," Escha yelled, his back to the light, huge shadow
flapping like a spectre, "no pigs! Studs, mares you watched
when you think nobody's looking, just you peeking poking
around, eh! Watch! Who cares? Your pants tight as a hide –
look!"

"Don't," the girl murmured. "He can't help it."

The next rung was under him and he lowered, step by step.
He tried for iron in his voice but in his roaring head it was
childish, barely mustering boyhood, "Just get out. Don't ever
let me see you here again! That's all!" And Escha's laugh rolled
down through the trapdoor:

"Don't drag up here then!"

He hoisted water, the rope whistling unnoticed through his
broken hands, till the green scum slopped out of the trough;
he stripped off his shirt and thrust himself in to the waist. Ice.
Held breath roared red to violet under his clenched eyelids.
He shook himself to shivering and by then the pain also in his
feet recalled the ladder rungs. He limped into the house,
heaved the door bar in place. In the *groutestov* he dropped to
the lying bench, bare feet up, and watched the wheel revolve
its complaint, drily, the thick string tug at knobby fingers.

blessed savior make me pure make me pure

In a pause he shouted, violently cut across his thought,

"Why spin so loose? It's thick, loose!"

Muttachi snorted; her once straight nose almost infolded
to a beak. "Why spin tight?" She nodded at the little deck of
carded wool, the ball rolled by her feet. "That's all."

"What?"

"When it's spun, unravel. Everything goes to the soviet,
haven't you seen the barn? There's some big communist word
for it but in German it's 'stealing.'"

"But what about –" he gestured to the clock, the pillows.

"It was the barn first and now the house, any day. Jakob took so little, the Brauns beside us didn't know for two days they were gone. They left too, on the third."

"Do they – ours – have enough, to get out?"

"If they can hide it." The wheel began again. "One hundred fifty years in Russia. One hundred thirty years Friesens live in Gnadenfeld, build this farm, and now just to get away we're runners and hiders. Na!"

"What was that Mutti wrote about a Uncle Isaak in Canada – Uncle Isaak, Canada?" he shouted.

"Your father's uncle. Not yours, your papa's; your grand-father's brother. My old Jakob's twin brother. Oh, that was such a story, yes." The wheel went on until it seemed to have whined her to sleep. "Na, what do you know, you last Jakob Friesen?"

"He went to Canada, long ago?"

"Yes, that was a going. Over fifty years, long before your papa was born, just when we were married, my Jakob then only twenty and Isaak that too, but younger by a few minutes; your great-great-grandfather Friesen, all those years with only one feeble son to that son's big two, said, 'Just one son gets the farm; Jakob is marrying and the other goes.' So Isaak went, your great-grandfather Friesen said not one word, just gave him money and *atje*. Maybe he would have gone to some new colony here or in Orenburg, but then we heard he went along with some that were going away in the seventies because of new laws coming in Russia. They were Furstenlander and wouldn't change. From a *hof* like this to a mud house with the Indians in Canada."

His eye had found a hair-crack in the ceiling, followed it from the door across to the yard window. "Why?"

"Why? Because your great-grandfather was a mouse. A soft quiet mouse, every few generations the red-blond Friesens have one. Great-great-grandfather built this house and barn and slept in the *ackstov* till he died there at eighty-seven and your great-grandfather still in the *sommastov* at sixty. In one year they were both gone, but we, my Jakob and I, were already in the *ackstov* and there we waited ten years through four daughters for a son, and then your papa was born. Not a mouse Friesen. Nor you."

"But I was born –"

Her tiny eyes poked at him an instant. "Yes. You were born in the *ackstov*. Your papa did that. No one in Karatow Colony had ever heard of such a thing with the parents living, but he did. Then he didn't move out till the *Militz* called him to hospital duty and when he got back in '19 there was no need to –" her voice stopped. "He was no mouse Friesen."

"But the picture?"

"They took it along to Moscow."

"I mean, it was in the room when I –" he flung his arm, gesturing at her look.

"He couldn't get everything out of the room, even if he got us. My old Jakob was no mouse, not like Isaak." The wheel almost stopped. "But he could help you laugh."

"Laugh?"

"Isaak. Like you never heard it in this house. About a cow leaning sideways against the wagon from eating mash or two old ones in the street both yelling each other something so important that after not one knew what the other had said. Na yah." The wheel started again. "Maybe it helps to laugh if you want to start in Canada."

To Canada in 1878 or 9. He had heard of Isaak Friesen just enough to know such a person existed and once during the mid-twenties when every other Mennonite in the Ukraine was working the faintest contact to get an exit permit out of the "communist paradise" and Abram Funk, the minister, had urged their entire village move, saying there were some from

Gnadenfeld in Canada already who could sponsor them. Like
Isaak Friesen. But his father, face black with rage, said he was
not moving, let the whole village run if it would. He would

> *let them run   can't fit in when a little changes or some*
> *stupid communist says don't preach so much let them*
> *run   won't take this from me   they can't do any-*
> *thing without me and they'll have to keep   exile pooh*
> *I'm no preacher*

buy it up and run it all himself. He almost had.

"Did – father – really write a letter – a letter?" Jakob
shouted.

"He had no address; maybe they're even all dead in
Canada."

"Didn't he ever write, from Canada?"

"Only that he married a Furstenlander, one of those that
wouldn't change here. Fifty years now." The old woman had
bent forward to her wheel, untangling a strand of dead white
wool. When she straightened she muttered only, as she had
begun long before, "One hundred and thirty years and now to
get away we're just runners and hiders and liars. Mouse
Friesens. Na!"

The wheel's sound churned Jakob's stomach. Runners and
hiders and liars. There was lying here she had no inkling of,
thank god. Everything seemed acrawl in him; control of mind
and body he had fought for and he thought held, sometimes
so very precisely in that stinking cell seemed now, when he
placed a finger against it, almost moldered away that he was
home in this huge, empty, house. He had been trained well, a
good Mennonite boy; learned quiet joy and denial and
prayers, sat between parents in church or, later, in front with
the other boys, decently and quietly; had been taught his sins
and cried over them and asked the Lord Jesus forgiveness, and
his parents too; been baptised to calm happiness, knowing
evil thoughts lead to evil actions and therefore are worse than

they. His teachers in village and *Zentralschul* had said if only they had more pupils like Jakob teaching would be a joy and a Christian's pleasure. Even before his last return to Chortitza not three years ago his mother had knelt with him beside his bed and prayed. He prayed also, as always, as always all he had pushed aside and gotten around though he knew it wrong, rose in the praying blacker and heavier than sin and he asked forgiveness, crying. There was such comfort in cleanliness. Runners and hiders; liars.

The Kroeger clock stood at nine minutes after eleven. He lifted himself up, pulled the weights to the top, and went. The lock still hung on the *sommastov* door. He went out through the kitchen into the orchard and slumped against an apple tree. The ground was black and familiar. Between the trunks he could see the white shape of the cow, hear her rustle among the dried leaves. Behind the folded hills the sun was almost down. Touch of gold to a penniless day.

Long after dark there was a tap at the *ackstov* window; when Jakob got to the back door, Helmut Funk's innocent face peered through the crack. The dogs were beginning to howl in the village and Jakob shut the door quickly behind him. Son of a day laborer and floor sweeper in the Friesen mill, unable to struggle through village school, three years older than Jakob with four children opening their empty mouths to him every morning, Helmut fitted the village soviet perfectly. And for keeping everyone informed. Two families had returned from Moscow that day, the men signing voluntary papers they wanted nothing so badly as to return once more to their beloved commune in the Ukraine. No persecution, no. Each family was getting two horses and one cow, like everyone else, and several rooms in their old house, depending on family size. They just sat now, Helmut said, not saying anything, not unpacking. No, they had said nothing of Jakob Friesen, though he had asked specifically. When everyone was back from Moscow every family in the village would be equal;

exactly the same in everything: animals, machinery, rooms, sheets, even the number of potatoes in the cellar. The plans had all been made exactly, Helmut said. It was the new age. If his father would stop acting like a kulak and come back he and everyone could live and work in peace and quiet. The soviet would take care of everything. They let him out, hadn't they, without hurting him? Well, his feet, but that was just the damp cell, some old czarist thing that had to be used, but not long. And if kulaks kept trying to run things or run away it made everything harder.

In the darkness as Helmut left down the street the dogs were howling louder. A bit beyond official information; perhaps. He shouted a few things to Muttachi, in Highgerman so that Escha, undoubtedly leaning forward in the nearest shadow, could not understand, and went to his room. After a long wait he got up, relit the candle, and slipped across the *groutestov* into the hall. The lock was not in the staples; he listened and there was only silence. Every Russian snored. Didn't they? He realized suddenly that he had never slept in the same room with one Russian; not even in the cells. Perhaps the snoring was a folk-tale? Had any Friesen ever – he was in the kitchen. Back of the stove, third brick from the bottom, there was the key; seventh tile, left under the kitchen shelf: the keyhole filled loosely with dirt. He dug it free and the lock turned but he could not lift the tile with the key and since the cell his nails were gone. He reached for a knife from the cupboard and the cutlery clattered. He listened, not breathing. Only far in the village a dog howled. He pried at the tile, up it came and there was the bag. Fat and light; no gold; good. Kneeling he counted the rubles back into the bag. Almost six hundred, in small bills: very good. Plenty for Muttachi too, but that was clearly hopeless. He could go all the way to Canada via Turkey on this; much better alone than all together, the whole family. If they could only get out, there was nothing problematic for him. If he couldn't get over a border alone past some half-sleeping guard he deserved to be – sack string taut, a shadow shifted.

Where candlelight blackened the corner; the silence had been too complete anyway. And the dull knife so – he shuddered and dropped the sack, replaced the tile, locked it and shoved the key in his pocket. Without looking around he lifted the candle and said, straightening slowly,

"How much do you want?"

There was a hiss; when Jakob turned Escha's face was hunched in thought. "Half," lips twisting.

Which was fairer than he expected, so he could argue the more easily. "No. You have some from – some already. You said it."

"You in feather beds and three years just straw for me!" The same silly equality hounding, as if there was no difference between them. He almost smiled as he said,

"We did the same work."

"Weekdays maybe yeah, but late Sundays I had to load bundles and sleep in the field to start threshing when the sun come up. You've never –"

"Any Russian would have worked you every Sunday in the year, all Sunday, not just a few hours after sundown at threshing."

"Half," eyes green in each other's eyes. Nose to nose, exactly the same height. "Or, we lay it together. Stick around. They won't pin you again. Fix something with Serebro, you got brains. Food, building with just us. We can do what we want, Jascha."

"Just get that – that bitch out and stop sneaking after me!"

"She just comes after noon." He was grinning; the ends of his reddish beard twitched. "Half."

"All right. Hundred, then."

"There's more than two."

"Hundred fifty. That's ha – that's all."

"Uhh," Escha hesitated, and he added quickly,

"It stays right there. If you bust that open they'll see and milk you every last kopeck."

"You got the key –"

"And I'll keep it. You'll get yours."

Escha said after him, as he turned, "She likes you."

"Shut up."

"Pfffft," Escha laughed, spouting his catechism, "It's the new age, we're free. So let your *schwengel* nose around – nobody's watching!"

Just you, he almost said aloud, but caught himself. "I'm not like you; I can't afford it," he muttered, but he knew the sarcasm was lost. If it had only

make me pure make me pure make me

"*Noasch*, I already paid her a whole month. You can –"

"God almighty!" He screamed at his tormentor, at himself, at the unavoidable picture of her emerging into the misty sunlight, pronged in full and overpowering completeness, touchable for the reaching, "Damn you stupid pigs, stop wallowing in my father's loft! Lick your –" he knew no Russian word so he screamed the worst Lowgerman he could dredge up, "– in the ditch where you belong!"

"Oh shut," Escha said, suddenly quiet. "It's easy. Just do what you want. What are you yelling for?"

In the morning Commissar Serebro strode in for inventory. Short, backbone as if set in angle iron, the high forehead and even the mustache announced Lenin's picture. His eye was too quick for his men to pocket either a rag or a wrinkled potato; every bit was recorded on the endless paper and returned to its place. The clerk, Abram Willms, had sat with Jakob on one bench in school, and he seemed now to know even less about Russian spelling than he had then. But Serebro was patient, called out each item, and Abram wrote page after page. Muttachi sat watching them carry in chests and bedding, her wheel still. Suddenly she reached over and said a few words of Russian she knew – "Mine, not Jakob Friesen, mine" – and pulled a thick embroidered tablecloth out of Serebro's hands. The commissar looked at her a moment, nodded, and took up the next piece. After a time her lap was piled high. Finally Willms glanced at her and said in Lowgerman,

"Na, is that really yours?"

The old woman burst into a torrent which, since she could not hear herself, was deafening. To Jakob's astonishment, Serebro did not even look up. But when she said "Mine," as they wrote down the clock, the commissar's lips shifted just enough to indicate he was thinking of smiling. Perhaps next week.

"No, old one," he said. In Lowgerman.

She sat motionless then, and soundless, the linens piled in her lap, till they left near noon. At the door Serebro said to Escha, who had watched all in silence with Jakob, "You have enough straw. Be at the office tomorrow and we'll assign seven cows for you to feed. Who wrecked the horse stalls?"

Escha's big face leaped red. "Somebody – they –"

"We have no lying! You did. In this nice weather get your firewood from the orchard. Leave the stalls for winter."

"Why that's crazy!" Jakob exclaimed. "Those trees took twelve years, in spring the fruit –"

Serebro's look stopped him, the edge of it like that – he was suddenly sweating. "Everything kulak comes down. Not one kulak tree, not one kulak shed, not one kulak wheat stalk. Everything goes. Burn them to keep warm or burn them to see the fire jump. Every building like this is a kulak monument, built with the blood of the poor, the workers; when people see it they either hate or get greedy. It comes down."

But the explanation was too long. "So waste it like in '20 and everybody starves like in '21." In his gathering rage Jakob shifted to Lowgerman: "You misbegotten Mennonite communist!"

For a moment fire flickered in the commissar's gray eyes; Escha stared, face slack in fear, but when Serebro spoke it was in Lowgerman also, precise and clipped in a Molotschna accent.

"Yes, misbegotten. The younger son of a younger son living in the worker shacks at the end of the village while cousins lived fat," he flicked his hand at the room, "and could afford *Zentralschul* and Kroeger clocks. But I was born again, right – you know all about 'born again' don't you? – in November 1917. The world is through with kulak bigmouths."

The Lowgerman blotted over whatever was left of his awareness; he blurted out, "Just party bigmouths now, sure! Just change one for the other!" But Serebro said nothing, his face seeming again almost on the verge of a smile. "What's your Mennonite name, you, from what village?"

Serebro said nothing. The glance darkened so that Jakob could not tell whether it showed only pity or also contempt, and suddenly sweat burst on his body again. Serebro said nothing; his look turned slowly to Escha, standing motionless with his mouth slightly open. The commissar said in his precise Russian,

"You think, Jascha Jakobovitch, like every Mennonite pip-squeek. You know nothing of the world, of the Party, the plans. Russia must industrialize or die. Our workers must pour steel, build dams for Russia; not rake straw so one man can travel first class. Big farms, collective farms with tractors and machines must produce food for factory workers, builders. Russia farms like England four hundred years ago. We must make the jump in ten years. And we will." He said it like a simple fact. "You are brash, but educated and young. Join us. We are making a new age, a new world in the Soviet Union."

"What will you do with him, with my – father?"

Serebro's eyes tightened. "A thinker like you, I thought that such a little run to Moscow . . ." his voice drifted away.

"Well?"

"Don't be stupid."

"What will you –"

"He owes the state grain."

"Because you kept raising quota."

"Yes. We don't need kulaks. But we need you."

"I'm his – son."

"Yes," the commissar's eyes became pinpoints. "And you paid for it six weeks in the hole. I know, and you know, he could have come, any time. But he, he ran for it. Wake up! You are free of him now – free of everything. As free as Escha. He does what *he* wants." Serebro's look moved from one face to the other. "You are very alike, big, your faces – you could almost – strange." Again his lips shifted nearly to a smile. "Well, you are free, remember. To stay here."

The droshky wheeled at the gate and down the street. Escha said, "Some of them say he's real big, going up. Was he a Mennonite once, yeah? He could –"

"Shut up." He could feel the moisture down to his socks. "Go get the barn ready."

"Not much. You shovel it; I get the cows."

After noon that day the Mennonite villagers began to appear with requisition orders. Most of these, too, had worked for the Friesens at some time or other; they sidled into the great room, almost bolting when they saw the tiny old woman at her turning wheel with the chests, as they had been left, thrown open all around her. But she would not lift her head; the wheel creaked and after a time they clutched their paper the more tightly and advanced. The days went, one by one. The cavernous barn held seven cows, eight with Whitey, but that was no work for the two. Sometimes at night when Jakob thought Escha asleep he had the pack made up; sometimes even the tile unlocked. But he did not move out the door. If he tried for Moscow they would probably be found the more easily; they might have permission to leave without having been traced

and if he showed up – better alone south to Odessa or Sewa-
stopol, or perhaps even Berdjansk; or Rostow; try buying
onto a ship for Turkey? Perhaps they were already being
shipped back; Helmut could fish out no word. No one probably knew anything. He did not know anything. He did nothing. The whole village did nothing. Despite the day-long
sunshine there was no fall plowing, no visiting; only the dogs
howled every night as if they were mad. At times, when he
awoke from sleep or just before he fell into it on the blank
sheets he could nearly have cried to long, to do; know;
remembering how it once was, so straight-forward and all his
world so solid sure, and all – the people. And he did not want
to leave either. His feet had healed and he was strong again
with eating vegetables dying in the garden or canned meat
from the cellar – no one ever showed a requisition for those –
or the hams Escha must have lifted from some isolated smoke
house, and he lay about reading an old *Friedenstimme* over
and over or in the Bible, a little, prone on the lying bench. In
the evening when he heard the spinning wheel he still prayed,
as he always had. Sometimes in daylight too; for Muttachi;
for his sisters with whom he had slid down the straw stacks,
whom he had teased and tossed about two or three at a time;
for his mother and her inevitable coughing sickness that
came in the autumn damp – the things he had always, auto-
matically prayed for

o		*god help*		*be with*	*bless*
take	*care*		*of*	*help bless take care*	

but he did nothing. He did not really know what he would
wish God might do for them, with them. Oh, he did want
them to get out of Russia so they would no longer be hounded,
so his mother and sisters would not have to cry as they had so
often in these nine months, as they had when they took him,
so no one would be in prison – yes, he thought all these warm
natural thoughts and though sometimes tears pushed to the

rims of his eyes when he lay remembering, he somehow felt motionless too, a sack hung empty by a string in a wandering wind and the life before his taking as meaningless as the wind that never again blew to stir it. It was, yes, it was like the cell, except that here, strangely, he slowly came to believe there was less. Rather than the agony of cramp and hunger and wet to keep thinking and planning against at every instant of awakeness, here was comfort, looseness, such un-necessity that he could simply float in any position and seemingly it made no difference about anything. So when he prayed that God should care for them all, as one prayed, he could not at times imagine what God might do that would care for him better than just hanging as he was, spinning in effortless unthinking comfort like the wheel Muttachi kept turning to spin wool she had already spun a dozen or perhaps three thousand times. Necessity was nowhere. Gone. He lay, staring at the clock. The day he drew up the weights he had neglected to jar the bronze pendulum and the hands still read nine minutes after eleven the day a Russian from the village in the hills took it. Every day brazen Mennonites and Russians came; he opened the door in the morning, stood aside, they came in and carried out. Escha usually looked at their order and then they would pass him again. Jakob never looked at their faces but after a time he became aware that they had an amazing variety of heels: an entire range from wrapping rags to angled kulak boots. Escha stood behind him, close as his shadow, watching with him as they passed. Only in the mornings however; in the afternoon Escha was never there. And every noon when his shadow vanished Jakob knew there was one thing, and also another, squatting on the rim of his mind, the folds and variegations of whose blackness he must above all ignore. That was all that was left, to think, to brace against. And he wedged against these, these last two remnants of do not, in final, desperate refusal.

But it was inevitable; as he also knew. The last week in

November, how should he know which day, he heard the singing from the barn and went, finally. The familiar aisle opened under the black beam; Escha leaned against the manger, arms beating steadily, chanting. The eight cows shifted their placid heads to him, away from the girl in the aisle.

She was moving slowly, languidly, her arms hanging down and her heavy skirts brushing her kneeboots – where did she steal those? – fluid on Escha's effortless bass, so deep her boot-tips skated on it with scarcely a touch to the floor. She moved wider gently, her hands rising gently, till the beat moved to fingers lightly glanced over palm and she was in the sunlight's cross at the aisles and wheeled, skirts a-wheel above her thighs, her black eyes lifted and she saw Jakob. She began coming, to him. The rim of her skirts flickered, slowly, her hips swaying, her neck thrust out of the embroidered blouse like a stalk ending in brief red, tan and swinging black like the hips, but opposite and lapsed in beat. She came endlessly on toward him as the bass rolled and rolled and skipped the second sway like a caught heartbeat and rolled till her coming ebbed, swaying, lips parted like blood, and imperceptibly she withdrew, her eyes all fire, and he dragged after. Heavy, plodding but the rhythm nudging him as she drew away, moving sideways and he turned, she curling in circle, hips and head a little quicker now, her black eyes swaying him in their steel, rigid, unbendable. Her hands came up again, her arms, and steadily the rhythm soaked down through his shoulders, chest, waist, hips, thighs, feet as her hands moved up her arms alternately, again and again, pushing the white sleeves higher on the round warm arms. Abrupt behind him on the beat came the finger snap, sharp as bone breaking, and his feet were in syncopation, circling her slowly but faster, body buoyed inevitably by the beat, by the fantastic lifting bass springing under his boot-soles and through each muscle like light, by the swinging gyre of her eyes and arms and hips. Her foot motion sank into her body as she circled quicker and quicker; her arms rose toward his cheek, her breasts thrusting out with each flung arm, thrusting the blouse aside deeper and deeper, and the weight of her was on his arm, the pivot of her body crooked in his hand and arm bend, hanging ripe, her head falling away in a fall of black hair, suddenly crowned by the domes of her violent breasts, her lips swollen in red, terrible beauty. That moment she was totally moving him like a great tree in the wind, her ribs and waist a giant mount rearing under him, lifting him to flame, growing immense beyond possibility – and he could not. He dropped before the ride.

At the instant his arm dropped the run of bass broke behind him in a great cry and Escha with a gallop caught up their motion; her deep voice gathered the beat. They circled to her core. Faster and faster they weaved, Escha outside, he inside, nearer, farther, nearer again, her hips and breasts now spiralling beside them, now above, her voice and hands sounding, and they were sinking lower always more quickly with her looming high and then Escha's arm crooked his and whirled him

> *kick one leg   the other   boots crack the floor*
> *flash glory out and in   boots thud through me*
> *through the thud   glory to god in the high one and*
> *another he pulls   circle her chant and flinging*
> *hips   glory to god and peace on earth   flinging*
> *hips and rise up higher   spring short crisp to*
> *beat   goodwill   steel arm gone I thud   he*
> *leaps high   goodwill to   soaring boots and legs*
> *thrust out and crash   toward men   my arm*
> *flung out on earth her great hard carrying breast   her*
> *hand down hard spinning me spinning glory on earth my*
> *clutch   reel over complete and uncoil free quick short*
> *steps leap   leap   fly   forever at my stretch-*
> *ing toes and fingers in the highest*

and he jarred. Burst.

A bulging eye, flatness, another bulging eye pushed protuberant out of the dark. Ogling. A murky flatness finally slipped over, lifted. Old Whitey blinking at him across the manger. She would place herself wide-legged before the trough on a hot day and slurp away, tanking until she was clubbed away about to burst. He thrust himself up and hunched about, head drumming. The sound was laughter; the girl's round face watched him with open panting mouth, her body tilted against the ruined horse cribs. And Escha sprawled on his elbows in the straw, chest heaving, laughing; looking. The girl's voice repeated, deep between breaths, her hand on her right breast,

"Wonderful, wonderful."

Bulging eyes unblinking on him. They had seen him, pulled him, sweated him on, seen

*always do what you want what you want not like he knew
me or even read me like the Cossack a mare's foaling time
in her belly's sag like he was inside feeling with not a
thought needed   feeling me*

him. Madness ground in his head's agony and he was on his feet, not looking at them still chuckling, moving, each step coiling him tighter, not daring to lift his face until with everything he was or had ever been he struck down smash at the other's smiling looking face. But his last steps were warning; Escha shifted and he did not hit him flush; still the drive of glancing knuckles was enough to stretch him slack the breadth of the aisle like a mirror image flat without defense and Jakob was on it. Kneeing, kicking, his fingers thrust down, thumbs gouging at eyes. Hands spurted up, clawing. He chopped his teeth together on a finger, jerked and felt bone crumple, heard shrieks as they rolled in the aisle, one animal slamming, crashing, tearing, and a curtain of ice soaked them. Once and again.

They fell apart and the girl loomed above them at the

trough, bucket hoisted in her great arms, slopping over, gluing her blouse tight. As they stared she dashed the water full in their faces.

He scrambled up, slipping on grit. Out, out around the corner, compost heap, threshing floor, back orchard, stumbling over twigs to a far corner, out and down to the black dry earth, the crushed leaves. The autumn sun warmed slowly into his empty shudders.

It was the coolness that follows the sunken sun which woke him. Bare branches; evening clouds pulling a gray blanket over the flaming sky. After a time he dragged his body to its feet, catching at a branch for balance. It snapped in his hand, but that was long past matter. He did not think of going into the house. In the barn he stood among the debris of the horse stalls and listened. Straw creaked, there was a pause and the girl laughed short like a cry. He had never heard such a sound and it was quickly over, but he felt split open. He heard it until he noticed the long row of moist cow eyes staring at him across the aisle, the splintered cribs. He could not run that; he turned back, through the orchard and into the house by the back door. There was blood and earth upon his face and he washed carefully at the basin. The cold water burned. The spinning wheel stopped when he crossed the *groutestov*, but Muttachi made no sound and he did not know if she looked up.

The ceiling, the bare space on the wall. But for his face he could have fallen asleep again. Long after dark came Helmut's tap on the window; it went on and on, like a hen pecking, and finally stopped to leave only the dogs' yowl far in the village. A thought came, or went. Without thought he had been known, completely, as he himself either could not or had refused to know. Which did not matter. Thought had been his redemption; he had been taught to think: in the home, in the church, in the school he had been taught to think on his sins: this is not right and this is wrong and this is everlasting wrong. He had been taught man is not a carefree brute; he is a thinking creation made in the image by the hand of the holy terrible God who has said once and for all in a voice dry and hard as the rock of his mountain, "Thou shalt not." He had been taught his sins. But now, like then on the studfarm, he had played with himself; alright, wanted himself to be played with, and he was beyond control. He was twitching and shuddering beyond control and though from one strangely unaffected part of him he stood back looking at himself, pathetic, and recognized with terrible clarity the horror he was working upon himself, he knew he would do it again. What had to be done now had to be done where only the impossible eye of God could see. No other.

And there remained, still, the last thing he could avoid thinking.

He did not leave the *ackstov* till noon the next day. Then he went out, ate some canned cherries and what was left of the smoked ham and went into the barn. He walked around behind the staring cows, opened their stanchions and kicked them out he did not care where. The girl called in the loft,

"Escha?"

He took the stall shovel, clotted and heavy, and silently found his place. The barn stood empty. At last the housedoor scraped and the other came, knuckles to his eyes, stretching, and striding up the aisle whistling. Strange; to sing so well yet whistle slightly off-key

> *blessed savior make   blessed savior make me hiieyah*
> *there hiieyahhh   pffft   like paper in fire get*
> *outta there there into the stall   get outta there slide in*
> *there where you belong   whoa now easy and tight*
> *you slippery devil   like fire blessed savior o my blessed*
> *savior make me*

and he climbed the ladder. The girl sat erect into the sunlight coming through the doors, the smell as the first time, and said,

"Oh." He stared down into her moist red mouth. She smiled a little, her dark mane swinging easily back and forth. In a lunge he kicked her red boots aside and fell on her softness and her sudden ringing laugh gurgled, snapped.

He was finished and empty. Completely. He was aware of nothing; nothing remained. After a time he knew her looking at him, the sunlight still strangely afire on the long rafters reaching for shadow at the hood of the roof. She said, in her deep peasant flatness,

"So, so you had to. Now."

She came on her side against him and lifted his face against her breasts. Her languid hand moved; he felt himself easing to warmth, slipping into darkness; unknown and bottomless; undreamable.

Two blows in his ribs, a hand clawing his shoulder up and he was awake. And the rooster voice,

"Get your pants on, you damned killer."

"Huh?" He sat up; the man hunched in the hollow beside him on the empty blanket, soldiers with guns levelled behind. "Killer."

"Yeah killer! Hup!"

Others came running, thickening the silent crowd he clambered down into, jerking his fingers off the rungs away from the boots. The crowd opened to Serebro in the horse stall and the rooster booted him again; he walked forward and looked. What a body. Strength to tear the rope on the one pillar left standing. But no head was enough for a spike on a torn plank. Perhaps turned over, threshing around. Never wait, never think; do it. Dead center. He looked up into the ring of familiar, silent, Mennonite faces.

"I thought you were smart," the commissar said. "At least enough to keep your cows from running around, announcing things on the street."

They pushed him out, hands trussed behind him with the

same rope. A huddle of long dresses on the front porch, and a cry. Muttachi. Serebro gestured and the rooster yelled, "Stuff your gap, Mennonite mama! Your fine grandson's a killer! He'll get it, that's what."

Several women's voices were beginning the wail and she could not have heard him, even if she had understood Russian. Her high keen, not very different from her usual sing-song, followed them as they turned down the long street spidery in fall trees.

Helmut was running beside the soldiers, neck stretched, hissing in Highgerman, "Jakob, Jakob, I wanted to tell you – last night – knocking. They have your father – your mother and sisters are out, Germany, the 25th, but your father – they're shipping him –"

The rooster's whip lashed down. "Get outta here, your pig language – get!"

A little screech and then there was only the sluff of the crowd following. Women and children stood staring at their gates; the sun was clouded over and it was near cold. The hills lay folded up like blankets. Escha had been too violent. Never bother to think anything through or wait; just threw his body around like an animal. It was good to teach children their sins and watch them close, make sure they kept their conscience poking their actions and thoughts away from each little twitch, kept their hands where they belonged. Ha! and that wasn't in your lap! But that wasn't enough either, somehow. Alone, you felt your backbone from the top right down to the bottom tip. Alone; yeah, completely alone for what little time was left. No more unthinkable black shadows waiting, watching, knowing more than he did himself and leering for a slip. That was better than good. He felt

blessed alone out the 25th and shipping him blessed alone

clean, strong, swinging his long legs along in the center of the communists and trailing Mennonites down the hard road to the church now converted to soviet offices.

Serebro strode up and said, low in his Molotschna voice, "There's nothing clear. Just deny and I'll handle it."

Serebro was openly smiling. His face curled up like a mustached, shining happy angel. Jakob wheeled completely and with every spurt of violence in his long legs kicked him where he'd never forget it, again and once again. The commissar sank to the ground screaming, and Jakob was laughing so hard, laughing so dry and hard, he did not stop when down into his face the first gun barrel smashed.

THREE

My Life: That's As It Was (2)

AFTER YOUTH instruction was through in July my *velobta* and I went for one day together with Abrams to Winnipeg to the Exhibition. We rode on one of those big wheels with seats, and that's hard to make clear to little Johann and Friedl too. They want to know, how can there be a wheel as high as two churches and then their father has to tell them again, "Just listen to Urgrossmuttchi. She lived once in Canada and has seen something – just listen, there's more than that." And they do. We rode and just as it was on top and coming down with a swing he got sick and when we got off the man in the seat in front of us was mad because he had gotten dirty, right on his clean suit he said. He yelled and jumped around and hit my *velobta* on the nose and then his friends pulled him back. Johann was big but he wouldn't lift a hand, so he was sick and bloody too. Next day I went on the train to Swift Current to help our family settle. It took three days sitting with hot burning cinders flying in the windows, but sometimes a fresh breath too, and there wasn't anyone at the station that I knew though I had written a letter. I asked the agent where the Mennonites lived by Swift Current.

"Mennonites? Oh, there lots around, Old Colony and other kinds, maybe new too. They're all new to me." He looked from under his dark eye-shade. "Mennonite girlie, all alone?"

I didn't ask him anything more. A man loading barbed wire into a boxwagon told me Mennonites were every day at Cox's store. There they said they were all gone that day already, but tomorrow was Saturday and some would come for mail at the post office. The post office woman said that too and said I should stay at the hotel for night. I had never stayed at a hotel. I took my parents' mail, with my letter there too, and went on the porch. There were no grain fields. I remember the sun was going down and the wagon tracks just went out between a few houses and into the prairie.

After a while some dust started far out and finally three men galloped up, jerked sharp, and tied their horses in front of the post office. They looked at me as they clunked past so close I had to smell them. My father had said it usually rained every spring in Saskatchewan but either that year it hadn't or these were caught inside. The horses were just head, ribs and tail. One saddle had a long gun tied on it. The men came out and the one with the smallest feet stopped right by my toes with his cured smell. He was laughing and swearing at the other two. I think it was swearing but maybe it was French, or Russian. Finally a wagon came rattling closer and the other two pulled him to the horses. In the street, he was the shortest one, he screamed and sawed so hard on the reins that the horse had to slobber and nearly fall backwards off its hind legs. They galloped away, whooping. There were people in the wagon but I couldn't look anywhere. The man went past and came back out and I could tell he was standing by the door, looking, and then all of a sudden I got mad and jerked my head up to tell him a few small things when he spoke. In Lowgerman! Their name was Buhlers and they came from by Gretna, Manitoba. I'd never met them but of course I went to them for night and the next afternoon he drove me in his buggy the thirty-two miles through the Old Colony Reserve south to our homestead. That was a welcome.

Our family was living in a tent with the things piled up all around and working on a sod house. The chinooks had blown away every bit of snow early and the ninety acres of wheat they had seeded looked gray as old dogs shedding. But there was a spring just a quarter mile away with nice water and the land was strange, not flat like Manitoba but strange, humpy and cracked with deep ravines and stones everywhere like lice in mattress straw and not one tree. The creek from the spring ran east. In a ravine six miles from the homestead there was a bush, poplar, saskatoon, willow. My brothers got sticks there to start the fire and for the rest the smaller ones piled together cattle and buffalo cakes, hard as wood and as gray too. Every day towards evening the range cattle went by to the creek to drink, hundreds with little calves running and bawling for their mothers. It was nice to see, but we had to fence because of them and that cost the most money.

When the saskatoons and then choke cherries got ripe my sisters went to the ravine and picked but I worked on the house. My father had measured where it would be and my brothers, thirteen and fifteen and sixteen, plowed strips of one foot, stuck them off with a spade into two-foot sods and piled them on the stoneboat and dragged them close with a team. Then they mixed mud in a round flat hole they had dug. I tramped it out with them, mixing with our feet and pouring in water nice and cold we carried with a yoke from the spring. My father piled the sods straight and stuck them together with mud. I handed him the sods. When my brothers weren't carrying mud they handed sods too.

When we were all so dirty and sweated piling dirt walls straight my brothers, and sisters too, teased me I didn't look anything like a bride. I knew that better than some so I hit as many as I could with my hands stuck full of manury mud and they ran around yelling and laughing in the hot sun. That helped me a lot; who do you think had to wash clothes too. We made window openings with packing cases and laid sods on peeled poplar poles from the ravine for a roof and bought a few eight-inch boards for ceiling so my five oldest brothers could sleep on top of a kind of second floor. The cellar was under the kitchen where we used the rest of the boards on the floor and when we moved in my sister and I smeared it from inside and outside all over with mud. When my father drove to Swift Current for flour I got my brother Gerhard to come to near the Old Colony Reserve where there was a white hill. We filled three sacks half full and next day mixed it with water and painted the whole house outside. Then it looked quite nice.

The white house mixed everybody up. One Sunday at the end of August, after I waited three weeks, a buggy came and I thought sure this will be it. But it drove past on the road south. Toward evening it came back again but this time it turned in and, really, it was Johann K. Friesen. They'd driven all day in the sun looking for us because in Swift Current they said we had a new sod house, all black. Then everybody laughed at me so hard I went behind the house. The sun going down and somewhere a coyote howled; the Cypress Hills lay on the prairie like blue dust, far away.

We stayed two weeks as engaged, visited all the relatives that were there and in September my parents drove us to Swift Current to the train. My father had blessed us at home. When the train came in with steam and cinders sishing everywhere he said to my *velobta*,

"Remember just this, the first two nights a good whaling, then all the life a smooth sailing."

"Na but pa!" my mother said.

"That's from me," my father said. "And an old father always said to each son in our village in Russia, not my father who didn't have so many, but almost more than enough, but an old neighbor there eleven times he said it. 'You make sure every winter she's barefoot, flat-footed and bare, and then she'll always be warm when it most matters.'"

They two were laughing but my mother just said, "At the end at least you could say something a little earnest."

My *velobta* said, "Maybe the marrying is enough earnest," and my father looked at him quick. He had been so quiet all the time, big and quiet, and they had hardly talked together, but now my father really burst out laughing and clapped him on the shoulder, both laughing.

On September 21, 1903 we were married in the *groutestov* by Kornelius Friesen in Schoenbach, Manitoba. Elder Wiebe the Older had the wedding text, Mark 10:6-9. About fifty families were at the table for the meal. Johann's older brother and his wife had moved out of Friesens' *sommastov* and we had that. When he came in I was standing in the middle of the room. They'd even lit a lamp though it still was long till winter, and he stood with his face in the shadow and the light was in my eyes so there was only the shape of him, standing there. All at once he said, "Well we wanted us, and we've got us, what do we want now?"

Somebody in the kitchen dropped dishes with a crash, I snorted so loud. On the side of his face where the lamp shone was a little scar, a white shiny vee cut by a horse's hoof once when it kicked past him. I had never seen it before, though we had kissed twice. This time light burst and rolled over like it was falling right off someplace into somewhere big, gigantic. Huh, that was a whaling all right.

We lived seven months in the *sommastov* and then the next son wanted to marry so we rented an old house where the barn was broken off and in April, 1904 moved close to Winkler. My man did woodwork for a Dietrich Martens for fourteen cents the hour. In fall he went back to Schoenbach to run the threshing machine for his father. In the summer sometimes he was gone all week too, working at building here and there, and I often went to our neighbors, old Bernhard Wienses, for night when it looked like thunderstorms. The clouds came up so heavy, boiling and terrible black. One night when I was there, just as we were going to sleep a lightning hit in their chimney and smashed everything. Some bricks fell on the bed where I was lying with our little Johann.

It was a little later, November, 1906 when we already had two nice children, Johann and Esther, that God sent me great temptation and doubt. My nerves were very bad; I could not be alone. The devil stood right beside my bed with red horns and said, "Do it, do it!" though he never said what. Twice the elders had to come to pray. Then I learned to know our Lord Jesus. Through many prayers and sleepless nights and God's grace I found forgiveness of all my sins and came to the true quiet faith. I was teaching our little Johann the night-prayer I had learned as a child, but I had to learn to pray it again then, like a grown-up who knows has to pray to God:

> Tired am I, go to rest,
> Close my eyes, hands on my breast.
> Father, may your eye divine
> Watch above this bed of mine.
> Where I did some harm today,
> See it not dear God, I pray;
> For your grace and Christ's red blood
> Makes all of my evil good.

Then I knew what my father said each one has to take and know for himself: it all comes from God, strength and sickness, want and plenty.

We thought we should go to Saskatchewan to my family. The CPR was laying track south from Swift Current but the winter that year was too hard to work and we had to drive the thirty miles by sleigh. Before we could we had to stay almost a week at Buhlers because of a blizzard. That was the year there was so much snow the cattle froze and the ranchers that were left quit and moved to the States. In spring the wolves were fat as pigs and the whole country stank. In the poplar coulee where we cut firewood and picked saskatoons cattle rotted hanging in the trees.

My man worked on the track that summer and I was with my parents. Thundering didn't matter to me any more. I liked to walk outside when it came, chasing in chickens maybe, and in the heavy heat like a wall suddenly the heaven would split open and CRASH! If you were looking right at it where it split you'd be blind when it crashed, as if you shouldn't have seen anything so beautiful, or holy. And then the cool rain came like the blessing from Jesus. The crops were so good and they were building elevators on the railroad just two miles away that my man got interested in staying. There were enough Mennonites for a school too, many our relatives on my mother's side and a few on my man's. My father always said he had no relatives in Canada at all; that was why he had married my mother who easily had twice too many, and now that the children were marrying too a decent man had to be careful that he didn't get completely discouraged and resign from visiting forever. They built a school and my man bought three lots in the new town, Southampton Roads they called it from something on a boxcar but after a few years it was just Roads, then he went back to Winkler, Manitoba, sold our house there and that winter he built a store in Roads. Farmers had to come from all the way to the border, twenty miles south, to buy. We lived there almost ten years. Crops were bad sometimes and the businesses in town got less but my man took the Ford agency and we got a car too. I even learned to drive and stay between the fenceposts.

In July, 1918 we sold everything to a Jew and with our seven children moved back to Manitoba where there was a better Mennonite school. We wanted to be farmers again and rented a farm near Altona. That winter we bought a cow and four horses and some machinery. Everything was expensive when they stopped the war; wheat was $2.50 a bushel. In 1920 we bought a farm from Mennonites by Hague, Saskatchewan, for $9,000.00. It had some buildings but only three rooms in the house so we built bigger. We got too much rain in July. The oldest Indians couldn't remember such rain, the oldtimers said, and the water went across our yard as if it thought it was a river and didn't get off the land till Indian summer. Our wheat stood to the ear in water. Before Christmas my man drove south in the wagon and tried to collect some of what people owed us by Roads to pay taxes, but there we lost almost $3,000.00 because some wouldn't pay or had moved or were widows. It was hard then. In Manitoba too, where the Sommerfelder *Waisenamt* had loaned money to farmers, it went bankrupt and widows and orphans lost what little they had. Wheat went down to a few cents and the farmers had to leave the land. In 1926 we had paid off over half our farm and prices got better but then we left and went to Manitoba to share-farm one summer near Friedensruh.

We had ten children, the oldest boy twenty-one and almost old enough to marry. We thought we should move to South America.

All my married brothers and three sisters with their families had moved to Mexico in 1922-23, but my parents with my youngest brother Heinrich Friesen had stayed on the land at Roads. Now my two other married sisters and the rest of my mother's relatives in Saskatchewan wanted to leave too, to Paraguay and my father said, well, if that's the way, then that's the way. In November, 1926 the first Mennonites moved to South America, but we were still making ready and my parents came from Saskatchewan and were making ready too. They had quite a few boxes packed and nailed shut but he got a stroke and couldn't. My father was sixty-six but once he said yes he would have started again if the stroke hadn't paralysed his left arm and shoulder. Heinrich said then he'd stay if that was the way it should be. It was a clear sign, and I thought maybe it was for us too but my man said nothing. It was hard with our Esther too, but just the other way. She was twenty and Dennis Willms, the oldest son of the second son of Gerhard J. Willms, Winkler, wanted her. None of the Willms would go to Paraguay, not they, so we would have to leave our Esther. We told her she was still young and could wait for someone else.

"I don't care," Esther said, "I don't want any South America."

"Since when do we have such a big mouth," my man said.

"Since now, since all this about that wilderness. What do we want with it, that 'green hell' like they say!"

"There are reasons enough."

"So many went to Mexico, Dennis says they're lots easier already with the schools. They don't want to lose all such good farmers, Dennis says."

"Your Dennis says lots," my man said.

But she was old enough; they married in October, 1926. Her man was trying to sell Chevrolets and when we drove away April 16, 1927 she was already gone over five months with her first.

We had our auction in March and we wanted to say good-bye to our relatives and friends and then it came hardest of all. Saturday, as my man came from Altona, he had a headache. On Sunday we wanted to visit three places but in the morning already at his sister, Johann Kaehlers of Blumengart, it was so bad that we had to go back where we stayed. Then at morning he just had to stay in bed, where he was flat for five days, sometimes with fever to 105 and his face swollen with blisters. We had to cut all his hair off because of the blisters. We had sold everything and had to pack more and now he had to lie still, and the train was leaving for New York where the ship was standing ready for South America. So it was I and the children and my mother, and Heinrich helped too. By God's grace my man became a little better and we could get everything on the train on April 15. Heinrich took us to Altona and we sat on the train overnight where Esther and her Dennis came for a little while and at morning we left. To start my mother drove along with us the few miles to Gretna. We never met again on this earth; nor my father. Only half his face could smile the last time we saw him. But we have the everlasting hope of the halls of heaven where parting and tears will not be.

On Holy Eve, Easter, we were in New York. They took us right from the train to the ship because the ship was waiting. What a mix-up getting on with all our things and such buildings leaning over us and getting our cabins so we could lay our children down. Our youngest, Abram, was a year exactly on Easter. As the ship wanted to move we went on the deck. Lights shone up out of sight like in a bowl and there in the dirty water a man was swimming. They had such strong lights on him you could see his black hair and long nose and soon a small boat came to him, but he wouldn't get in so one of the men in the boat pointed a gun and then he did. They were policemen and they brought him to our ship. He was some kind of terrible man, maybe even a killer they said, and wanted to swim back to New York to stay. I would have let him.

Leaning on the rail my sick feeling came up stronger than ever and now I could go to bed, and I did. And that's where I was the whole time almost to Buenos Aires. Once I lay down I just stayed lying; I couldn't get up, even for church. We stopped at Rio de Janeiro and everybody walked to see it but I couldn't get to the deck. By Porto Alegre they could help me to a long chair on deck for a little. The sun was warm and shone on the buildings sticking up like fence pickets, only so big, and I had more courage then. For our older girls, Maria and Tina and Anna, only twelve, the trip was very little happiness too; they couldn't even sing in the choir on the ship with all the small ones and me in bed. Neta was seven and seasick the whole way, in bed with me. But my man was well and we would feel God was with us, and He sends all, strength and sickness, want and plenty.

We saw the nice lights of Montevideo spread along over the water but the ship did not stop and next morning we were by Buenos Aires. A little boat came beside our big one and we saw our things carried into it. We had come 10,000 miles and that was the boat that would take us to Puerto Casado another thousand miles up the river, the agent said, into Paraguay. He would go back to New York for another group.

From the top the boat didn't look like it would get around the breakwater, leave alone get us over 300 people with everything into it, but it was a freight ship with the inside just one low opening where they had put bunks, one above the other, down both sides and a double row in the middle. My man got in a top one and it was so low he banged his head getting out, and he didn't have any padding there either. But with all the things piled around we lived there over 300 grown-ups and children, and slept there and on deck. The boat went so slow you could not tell looking at the shore. The food was all different from the big ship, cooked beef and soup with green things floating and noodles and galletas, which are like little buns but a little harder than a rock. The children could not eat them. Some men crunched two together to crumbs on the table boards and then scooped them up. The brown Paraguay sailors with thick black eyebrows laughed. They ate galletas whenever they wanted, sprinkling them over with sugar like candy and gnawing with their sideteeth. It was beginning winter and the weather cool and nice. At morning white mist lay rolled flat as wool all over the wide brown river. The sailor spoke only Guarani or Spanish so nobody knows what day we crossed the border.

FOUR

Black Vulture

"MOSTLY IN THE evening I sit here," the elderly man said. "Look after the satellites. See – there's one."

The young man stared past the branches into the immense starred sky. "Where?" he asked finally.

"Look at that big star, there, just steady a little, then you'll see out of the corner of your eye one moving while the big one stays still. See?"

"Yes," John said. Then he did see, one of the innumerable stars obviously separating steadily from another and he laughed, very happy the old man could show him this. "Oh, yes!"

"Almost every night you can see them go over."

"I've never seen that in the north. You're right in the modern world."

The other chuckled. "Do you sit and look? Maybe the Americans don't want to shoot them over their half of the world yet. But they will soon enough. The Russians and they."

A violent rainstorm, the first in nearly two months, the night before had dropped brown puddles the length of the village street and now the frogs filled the evening with their rattling and groaning. After a time the elderly man spoke again, "Well yes. That's the way it is. We're far on the edge here, watching, what we can see of it, go past."

"Listen there," John said suddenly, "that, that terrific noise. That can't be a frog, huh, not that."

"It's half the size of a foot when it blows itself up. We call it 'lumberwagon' –"

"That's really a frog?"

"A choir, of the big ones, yes. A few things here the dear Lord exaggerated for fun, I think, living here is so hard otherwise in the sand and cactus. When we first were here and in our tents after a rain we heard that and it sounded just like to you, so terrible deep and loud we thought our only calf had fallen into the only village well. I went looking, even!"

"But it was the frogs?"

"Yes, the frogs. They're happy right after rain, and it's a good night sound."

"Where are they otherwise?"

"Who knows. Maybe when it's too dry they rest where they can dig into the mud. Right now, after rain, in Zentrale they'll sit under the lampposts where bugs or ants swarm, sit and flick out their tongues all night, catching bugs or ants."

"Filling up."

"Filling up. Their sack bellies." There was a momentary silence, then the older man went on, "Such a sound is very nice, at night. We call it 'lumberwagon' because it sounds like a wagon with loose boards going down a rocky road. Of course that's nothing to our children, such a name. In Number Eleven an Enns once found a stone as big as his fingernail. That's the very biggest."

"No stones at all?"

"That one should be in a museum."

"Boy, that must be nice farming. The stones we picked at Rabbit Creek, Saskatchewan!"

"Yes. But look at the roads. We can never have beton here with just the sand. And then the north wind, wait till you feel that stiff with sand."

"Yeah. I guess there's always something wrong. With every country, if it's not one thing it's another." With the sound of those his words in his ear, John grimaced and shut up. Heaven help him not to sound condescending; stupid, inane, all right since that probably could never be quite avoided; anything but condescending. He had vowed to himself. He tilted back, eyes to the moving point of satellite; the frogs lumbered and shrilled in his ear.

"Yes, yes John," the elderly man said suddenly. "If your father and mother were here now and not you we'd have more to talk. Na?" he laughed a little.

"What would you talk with them?"

"Oh, there's so much. They were in Moscow too, there'd be so much, to remember. Don't they ever talk about that to you?"

"They used to, I remember when I was little. But not very much, now. They don't seem to remember as well as you, here."

"They live in Canada but here what else have we to remember? Or talk about? The one big thing."

"Then," John said slowly, tension draining for he meant every word now and could let sincerity speak naturally in his tone, "would you tell me? About Moscow?"

"Na, young ones –" the strong voice stopped a moment. "Here the youth hear it all over, 'In Russia we –' well. Especially the 25th of November. Just a little while ago on the street in Zentrale I heard a boy, maybe sixteen, say to his friend, 'But in Russia *we* did it *this* way!' He knew all about Russia, and irony. At sixteen. Here they hear too much about Russia. Especially on the 25th of November."

"What's then?" John asked.

"Here we have it every year. Didn't they tell you?"

"I don't know. I can't remember."

The elderly man's face was lost in shadow under the tree.

The moonlight showed only his splayed feet in blue cloth sandals on the sandy ground.

John said, "If you want, I would like very much to listen."

That's as it is. When you're young you live every day like it was complete and tomorrow the world will just possibly be new, different, maybe all exciting new and different. There is always a big chance the best things are waiting to happen to you tomorrow; today and the stupid things you did is just going by. By the time you see that tomorrow may be quite a bit like today, and that the day after that will be mostly the same, that perhaps the finest passed you yesterday, you're not young any more and haven't been for as long as you can clearly remember. And then it's still a few years till you know that before you were even born a lot of things about your life were already decided. Not everything, but a lot. And maybe the only thing new in it will be the stupid things you'll be doing or thinking. Well yes.

That's the way it seems to me, now. If I try to add it up, I guess I started knowing some of this the night in November in Moscow, 1929. It was a long time then since I'd thought of myself as young. Youth is good, and it's sad one has so little of it in proportion to the rest of one's living. But I certainly wasn't thinking that then. I could do any man's work, and had for years. I thought. Twenty-two I was and thought grown up, short and about as heavy as now but, you know, muscle everywhere then. If the Army had ever smelled me out I'd have been in before you could blow your nose between your fingers. It was my birth year – 1907 – that was being drafted and don't think I wasn't tempted: one hundred and twenty rubles a month just to hone my shooting. So I thought then, knownothing boy. I was the final bump that decided Pa to make the hopeless trip to Moscow to try and get out of Russia. We had a fair farm, almost a full *hof* as they were measured out then and I would have got it because my older brothers had been pretty well settled on their own in other colonies – that is, before, but the oldest had been in Moscow since summer trying to get passports for his family and the one just older than I, David, in 1927 had gone with his bride to settle in the Amur River district in far eastern Russia, north of China. The government there wanted to open the land and they got four hundred rubles to move with very cheap freight for farm machinery and cattle on the Trans-Siberian Railroad. The government divided the land and let them settle without paying. Maybe a thousand Mennonites went; they hoped the Moscow government wouldn't be able to collectivize the land that far away for a long time to come. Such a silly dream! For our David too, such a dreamer such a wonderful dreamer who even when they were in China already, over the border with their whole skin and not a communist in two hundred miles to touch them he still keeps right on dreaming and leaves all that he – but that's not this story. That's a different one; altogether. There's no connection, with our David.

Well yes. In the Molotschna, Ukraine – half the world from China – who had a chance to dream, at least about them leaving us in peace? I dreamed, but not about that; nor Pa. We left our farm like it was, hardly trying to sell anything because Pa was sure if the village soviet heard they'd stop him going. On his own that is, because he'd have gone; to wherever they whipped him.

So we did like the others: told no one, packed what we could, sneaked away one night. A railway porter smuggled us tickets – he got enough for it – and late in November we had been in Cliasma, one of the summer suburbs of Moscow, over a month and no nearer passports when I saw this – this thing. Actually, I'm not sure when I first, or if I really saw it. At least I can't remember it as if I had so I can't say "this and this and so and so" is exactly like it was. You know how it – well, perhaps you don't yet, such a Canada boy! – but when you keep thinking so long of one thing, after a while you can't be certain whether you actually saw it like that, then, right from the start, or whether that little time so long ago has foreshortened in your mind, the understanding you got from later when most of it had happened shifting to earlier in time as you remember it, your remembrance sort of organizing itself in a more logical way as you keep thinking over the years. That as you think over the years this central – thing – gets more and more meanings, like a sponge soaking all your memories into it and leaving nothing, just it. Oh, of some of the facts I'm still sure, but – this thing was like something you don't want to think about but is always in the back of your head. Black. Or like when you stare straight ahead and on the farthest edge of your seeing you know there's some thing, but when you turn to look directly, there's nothing. And when you look ahead again, there's still the smudge. Do you understand?

Well yes, sometimes I don't either.

When I came in that night – two days before the 25th of November – I went to my cousin's room where I slept. It was across the hall from my parents and we had had it too; my three sisters slept there before Pa's cousin – oh, call him – Balzer – got thrown out of his place and the GPU would have dragged him off with his whole family – you couldn't just stay on the street and most landlords were hopeless by then – if we hadn't found room someplace. Balzer wasn't old, but his big face hung foldy.

"Where've you been so late? Your father's been here ten times, I'll go across –"

"I'm going right over, don't worry. Whew," I gave my snowy sheepskin to Balzer's wife. Her I could stand; she kept busy and quiet till you wanted to talk. The two smaller children were asleep in a corner and she got the boy to hold my coat open by the heater.

"Where you been so late?" Balzer asked, "Your father –"

"He knows," I sat down and leaned against the wall. The

boy was staring at me over the coat-collar. One of his sisters was dead but he was well again; only his eyes now were too big.

"Did you get all the names?" The room was so tight you could spit across it but Balzer whispered anyway.

"Say, how many times did they warn, keep quiet! Did you –"

"Oh, we just talked about it in the family." My glare finally got through to him. "The kids are okay – they'll never say a word, to anybody. Not one word. Don't worry, I made sure enough of that."

It was true; the small two didn't matter and the boy by then knew top from bottom better than his pa, but to be so stupid as to make him know so he'd have to be quiet – well – I hunched around. "We think enough. Not so close, let it dry slower."

"How many?"

"Here," Balzer's wife said to the boy, "the box is close enough. Sit here and hold it."

"How many?" Balzer asked again.

"Maybe seven hundred."

"Seven hundred!"

"Uh-huh."

"There's way more than just seven hundred! In Cliasma alone there's at least two thousand and if you add Mamontowka and Puschino there's over five. You've got to have names, the more the better, thousands of names. Just with a seven –"

"Only family names, heads of families, they don't need anything else. And we couldn't get into Mamontowka."

"Why not Mamontowka, there's even more there than here. And there's more families than that, here too. Wouldn't some of them sign? Did that Jakob Friesen here? I knew it, it's just li –"

"He signed. Right on top the first page."

"— him not to. It might get him in deep but if it works he'd be at the head of the line with his fat money-sack open in his hand dropping rubles so he won't get his shiny boots dirty!"

His wife passed me some cold smoked ham and a toasted bun; the aroma of roast-barley *pribs* came from the pot on the heater. "Say, I have to tell Pa, and Mama'll have food."

"Just eat," she said. "It's all out of one pot."

Balzer was pacing two steps back and forth, then stopping at the door listening. "Walls so thin, just a board and paper; if you look at them they lean. You can hear that Friesen snore two rooms away and across the hall. If those ever come and they even look at this —"

"Ernst," his wife said.

He looked at her. "Oh I know. If Epps hadn't taken us in, what would we have done? I don't know — or, I guess I do. But two months sitting here, just sitting while our child dies and our money and our food's gone and just sit and stare at these stupid paper walls. Sometimes you wish it was just over, no matter what, let everything go to the devil and go where they. . . ." His whine stopped. He was doing something in the air with his arms, then he beat them down, as if forcing them, down against his big body. "These summer houses will be rather cold in January. Perhaps we could get a little better house, closer in, it wouldn't cost so much to ride into Moscow either."

One word would prick his quiet. I watched her hands; her fingers weaving a needle between darning strands on a sock. "It's maybe not far enough. Driediger said we couldn't go into Mamontowka; GPU started cleaning it up today."

"Mamontowka! Then there's only Puschino and then us!"

"Yep. No need to worry about January."

His wife said, "Maybe the letters with the signatures —"

"Sure, the letters, that will push it," Balzer said. "The Comrade said it would work. With Germany accepting us and thousands of people petitioning for passports and everyone in the world knowing about it, they can't keep us. They'll have to let us out. That's why more names –"

"Like the poor nuts in Perlowka and now Mamontowka, out straight to Siberia." The ham was stringy, like it was scraped off the bone.

"But the letters will sure be –"

"They're nothing without Germany. World opinion, okay, but where'll we go, heh? If Germany doesn't take us till that slow Canada or some country decides they want us as immigrants, we won't be here when or if they ever do. And Germany hasn't made a peep, yet."

"But the Comrade said!" Balzer paced again, nearly stepping on the boy by the stove on my sheepskin. The boy had heard it all so often. Balzer's wife was looking up from her sock. I said,

"Strelnikov is good. He wants to help, but he can't be sure. The petitions will maybe help, some, if they get to the right people. Anyway it's something to do – try anyway."

"How does that work?" she asked. "One part of the government wants you to go, another part might want to let you, and the GPU keeps shipping people to Siberia?"

"I don't know either," I said. "Driediger thinks it's because there's maybe no connection between different bureaus and parts of the government. Each part leaves the other alone, does its job as it wants. And a sure thing nobody asks the GPU its business, probably not even Stalin. They just stay out of the way and send it a note when they want someone cleaned up. It keeps order as it wants."

"And everyone terrified." By the heater she seemed almost to shiver. It was hard to see in the gloom but her hands kept mending.

Balzer laughed, "And that's such a thing! I never thought of that. How'll they get the letters to the right people? Anybody walks in there stretching out his hand with them and he's finished. They know he's a leader and he'll get it from a to z. That's something: cat and mouse!"

The *pribs* was raw and hot in my throat. "It's real good," I said to her.

"Orenburg barley."

"How'll they deliver them?" Balzer said again.

"The best crop in eight years since the starvation, wasn't it," I said. "I don't know."

"Didn't you talk about it, plan it? What's the use of risking a lot of signatures, our names written there plain as paper for any snooper to see, and running all over Moscow and . . ." His arms were moving again.

"Don't worry, somebody'll do it. Who knows how."

"Running all over Moscow, who knows how, with our names. . . ."

His wife said, "You Franz, let others do the rest. You do enough."

She was that kind. She'd sit there sewing and hardly even look up and then say something that made you wonder how could you be that far behind again.

I stretched my feet towards the heater and blocked Balzer. I felt content. "You have to do something."

"Just a big adventure," Balzer muttered.

"Yep," I said. "Everybody's scared now, some so scared they can't even go alone to the – well – or have singing parties in the woods like before. Who wants to just sit?"

"Those singing parties," she smiled a little. "You'd make yourselves obvious just by singing so well. Even you don't feel like singing now."

"Me? I sure do. I haven't had hold of a guitar for weeks. Maybe we should have one tonight, heh Balzer?"

He stood in his long hanging face. "Oh don't try to put it on, you young lunk. If the GPU ever stops you and sees your birth certificate with '1907' all over it, you'll find something else than jokes coming out of your throat."

"So it's five years in the Army."

"No responsibility, care nothing."

"At a hundred and twenty rubles a month I can *fly* to Canada when I'm through. And Pa could get the others away easier if I'm not standing around."

"You and your godless talk, shooting, joining the Communist Army! That's why I'm getting my family, my children, out of here. When you see your own relatives going red . . ."

Getting his family out! But for her I'd have cleaned his machinery right there, the big leech. He was that kind, latching tight where he could without any extra effort, jaw always unbuttoned and flapping. It was true enough too, at the time he said it. I don't deny that. But sometimes if everyone knows the truth anyways, it's worse than silence to say it. If everyone within hearing distance knows it anyways. The Balzers were strangers to me before; they were from – Pa had maybe three hundred cousins, but the two weeks I'd slept in the same little room with him were enough to work out a speech that wouldn't have left him much. A man alive learns more than some of him wants sleeping in one little room with a family. Nothing that's said, just looks, hearing in the dark; no words at all. Oh, I had a speech, but he never left and she was always there; and the poor kids.

She said, in her calm way, "There are your parents."

"Why do you think I'm here now." It was unnecessary and far too loud. It was good the door scraped across the hall.

Balzer unbolted the door; a wagonload of bolts wouldn't have helped the silly thing. Pa's voice said, "Is Franz there? I thought I hea –" when a terrific bang sounded on the outside door.

Everyone turned to stone. We'd all known it would happen sometime; I'd heard often how it happened, but just at that moment when I was so mad and all right out of the blue that terrific banging, my heart jolted. You know, just Whuh!

Well I don't know who moved first. Probably the landlord

running from his room at the far end of the hall as the banging kept up and heads poked out everywhere. The shout sounded as if some big Russian had stuck his head right into our room: "Open up! Open!"

No word, everyone staring at each other. Not even Balzer. Finally the landlord whispered, "Back in your rooms, everyone, in your rooms, very quiet. I let them in, Epp you live here with your family –"

"Franz?" Pa's voice said.

"Yes."

Pa said, "Mr. Listov, you know about his certificate; if they find him . . ."

"Yes yes." The Balzers weren't registered at that house and Listov was in for that, but good. Yet he was the calmest of all. "Just Franz and Balzers stay in this room. And keep quiet, everything. Epp, your family here, Friesens, everyone next, there, and us on this side. Shut all the doors. Yes! yes!" he raised his voice against the hammering, "I'm coming!"

No need to tell Balzer, shut the door; bolts clicked like shots. As I blew out the candle I saw the boy's saucer eyes and his mother bending over the children. A person twenty-two who believes himself decent and a man in every way except for certain things he has not yet done, sometimes thinks strange and silly things. Flight brings so many things with it you have no way of knowing or thinking about, before. It starts when the pressure is unbearable: "We can't live like this, we have to get away," and you think that will be what's hard. And it is, but while you are getting "away" and when you are finally there, if you make it, you start to see that just the getting there itself is, in a way, probably the least of what happened to you. Just the "getting away" itself. You are still human while that is going on, and "away" is not so simple; even when everything clicks getting there is never so smooth and simple. In that room, that was not the usual Mennonite way, living in a two- by three-meter room with a family, a woman only ten years older than I and fine looking as they are sometimes despite the work outside and children. Sometimes at night when Driediger and the others hadn't sent me around much with messages, I could not sleep and would lie awake far into the night, hearing them asleep, thinking the strange and silly things of a young man sleepless. What they were, how can I say – I don't have to tell you – I was an action person, *Zentralschul* only a few years because I had to, but wrestling, throwing sacks on wagons at the village mill, riding wild as long as we had a horse, holding things in my hands – and I was an innocent too, about more than I could tell you to this very day. When the sun shone in the window I could not look at her children sometimes; what I had thought, whatever it was, seemed so unthinkable then. But that feeling I remember; and seeing her as I blew out the candle, crouched over the stirring children, holding a pillow ready in her hands.

Outside was the trampling, the swearing of the loudmouth who'd hammered, wanting to hear why the landlord hadn't opened quicker. "But it is late, comrade," Listov had just the right turn of respect in his tone. You had to be careful; everyone was very equal in 1929. "It is after ten and we retire early. So we save wood – haha – less fire you know." How Pa found such a landlord he never explained; he just said he'd prayed all the way to Moscow.

There could be nothing but keep quiet and listen. Pa's papers had been examined three times, but who could know what these were after. The landlord would get it for Balzers – probably not too serious – and sure they wouldn't do anything to Balzer because he was as poor as a Russian and had nothing even before the revolution. He was just sitting there on faith waiting for a miracle to float them to Canada; just wait and suddenly, just like that, they'd let him out and he'd go, without a ruble or lifting a finger. Friesen, with all his Karatow rubles, that was a little different again.

And so was I. If I was drafted, Pa wouldn't leave if they

chased him, which wasn't likely. He was like that: he wouldn't leave one child behind. God had given them to him and he would not leave one in the godless country Russia had become. It didn't matter I could take care of myself, or that by staying near me he and Mama and the girls would stew in the borscht too. About some things he was so stiff and unthinking like a gatepost. Like during the anarchy after the revolution. I can still see as clear as yesterday when the Makhno bandits came. I was maybe ten, eleven, and David two years older, hiding in a hole in the hedge and watching them gallop onto the yard followed by a wagon full of them too. Before they could even yell he came out and said Mama had food ready. One of them was wounded; David and I sneaked up while they were in the house and I nearly filled my pants when his bloody head in rags glared at us over the wagon-rim. And Pa came out and fed him like he was a baby. As if that wasn't enough – they didn't take very much from our place, there wasn't anything – but when they came out to ride away he had to follow them with his Bible and read them a few verses about killing and preach to them – you know, really lay out the biblical chapter to them – about what they had done in Eichenfeld two days before. Maybe you've read of that; the anarchists killed 178 people there in one day and night, every man and most of the women and children in the whole village. One of those brutes wheeled his horse and had his saber out and I could already see Pa's head rolling like they said they'd done to Doerksen a few weeks before a little down the street and David was out and running toward them, hollering and crying, and I after when my mother stepped in front of Pa with Marie in her arms. Marie was four weeks old then and Mama just said, "Chop me and his child down first."

I saw it myself. All of a sudden the captain was laughing, bending double on his horse and laughing. The other, sword high, held a second but in another they'd all three been stretched out slit when the captain yelled, still laughing, "Let him alone! He should preach again!"

Those were my parents. Unbelievable to me too, today.

I sat in that room in Moscow listening to the GPU work over my father. These had come a long way from anarchy; any strand of chivalry they maybe had, once, training had long ago stomped out of them. There was nothing wrong with Pa's papers; his citizenship hadn't been taken yet, so he could still travel or live anywhere he wanted to, but they were questioning him hard about our village and who was there from it and why they'd come to Moscow now for winter from the warm Ukraine. Throwing in easy questions, like always, and then suddenly a bad one. From his answers Pa didn't understand what they were doing. Twice Listov, who seemed to be leaning against our door, perhaps half-hiding it in the dark hall, answered before Pa could, and then quickly the loudmouth asked,

"You got any more children here?"

That was it. I stepped over and reached to pull back the bolts but Balzer touched my arm. Pa was saying,

". . . married son on Krylow street. He has two small children —"

That was him; exactly. Even there he would have gone on, giving all kinds of information that could entangle him, or somebody, but the agent interrupted,

"Never mind. We'll find him. I mean this house, with you."

Pa said nothing. He was a little man, short like me but slight. I could just see that big brute leaning forward and unbuttoning his revolver and I jerked away from Balzer, my hand scrabbling for the catches. But that big fool grabbed me!

"Don't Franz, don't! If you touch them they'll kill us all —"

Like I said, Balzer was big. But I hadn't thrown seventy-kilo sacks around Hiebert's mill for six years just for fun. In one heave I'd broken half his grip and got my hand up to break his arm when his wife hissed behind us, "Franz, you can't! Noise! Listen, the landlord –"

Listov, just outside the door, must have heard us and was talking loud, really loud, "There's one son, Comrade, one son unmarried who sometimes comes here. But he's not here now, not now. He never sleeps in the room with them. Never. I wouldn't allow it; there isn't enough room, never."

"That right, old man?"

Pa coughed, like someone had taken a hand from his throat. He said quietly, "He hasn't been in our room all day."

"What's his name?"

"Franz. Franz Epp."

"Okay," the animal laughed. "We'll meet him soon enough. We meet everybody, one way or another. Landlord, who else?"

"Jakob Friesen and family, these two rooms down the hall, only young daughters . . ." The sound of them tramped further.

I had to get out. If they found me here now and searched me, I'd never even get into the Army. That was suddenly clear like a fist in the gut. But when I moved to the door Balzer whispered,

"Listen! There's one standing out there, his feet, listen."

He was right too, for once. I edged to the window and opened the sheet a crack. Our house was set back but the one beside was built to the street. The moon was white on the fresh snow and, as I looked, everything hung motionless as a picture. I thought they must have walked to surprise us and my hand was moving for the window-catch when something shifted. Capped, black shadow, a figure passed the corner of the other house. And then I saw the squarish patch on the snow by the officer's gleaming boots; that could not be any building's shadow. Just beyond the house-corner, the GPU's long black limousine. Enough of our people knew what that "Black Raven," as we called it then though if we'd known what we do now and these years here we'd have called it something else, enough knew what it looked like inside, but nobody had come back to tell.

I don't know how long I watched. He'd disappear and before I could count to fifty, slowly, he'd show again. Not a chance.

Then noise rose in the hall. They'd been with the Friesens a lot longer than with Pa, then suddenly out of the talking the loud voice broke, "Who lives here yet, Comrade Landlord, this side?" That was nobody but us.

Listov's voice came closer. "I and my wife in the back room, and three children here."

"That's all?"

"Yes."

"Okay. Come on, you."

The sounds were crying and pleading, begging like children. Friesen's voice, "Comrades, listen please! Don't take me, please. I've told you everything, everything. Please, I beg you!" Sobs, shuffling steps, coats brushing in the hall. "Listen, I – I have some money – gold, Czarist rubles that you might like to see. You know, gold . . ."

Friesen had taken everything the revolution and anarchy and hunger could bring; to keep gold through all that took as much brains and guts and deceit as miracle; they said he had got together eight farms and a mill in Karatow, but six weeks hiding in Moscow, waiting any minute for these – well yes.

"Now that is something." The voice sounded as if the face was smiling. "Isn't that something, for a man who wasn't, according to his own affirmed word, a Mennonite never swears of course, a kulak. To still have some slavery rubles! Eh, Comrade Brodnik, wouldn't you say that's something?"

"Indeed." That one spoke near the door for the first time; a thin voice as if he was reading legal papers. "We are asking you for a routine interview."

Mrs. Friesen's voice rose and the children were crying and there was such a confusion in the hall now that suddenly the loudmouth yelled, "Shut up!" with a string of curses that even the children choked. The second said, in his almost comforting, dreadful voice,

"Mrs., this is merely a routine interview. Quite routine."

On the black and white street she was still reaching after them, begging, but they dragged Friesen between them, collapsing now, out of sight and then, as the line of their children – there were five or six girls and their oldest, the only son, had been lost to the GPU before they left Gnadenfeld – stood all the way up the porch steps waiting and Mrs. Friesen fell in the snow, the long shadow of the limousine pulling over her and gone.

I let the sheet drop. "Better get her in, she's . . ." but Balzer's wife had already left her staring children, all wide awake, and vanished. Balzer stood at the door, face hanging open. With happiness.

"They believed Listov! Just like that! One a night must be enough – they believed him – 'and my three children here' – just like that. Ohh God, my God how marvelous are Thy ways, how He answers prayer!"

Many had been, were taken like that; I knew that. Driediger kept lists as he could and I saw him bending over them, longer every day, but I had never experienced, in my night thinking never thought, of this, like this. So I wasn't used to what I was beginning to feel that night. I could have split Balzer's head open and torn it off, piece by bloody piece. But Pa was there, the light shining from behind him in the hall, and he said as quietly as he always spoke,

"Ernst, I think Mrs. Friesen was praying too."

My three sisters stared at me like at a miracle when I got across into our room, past the loud children and women. "Pa," I said, "I have to go tonight yet."

"You have to?"

"Yes."

After a minute of silence he said, "Well yes. Have you had something to eat?"

The room was so warm from them in there all day and it came over me like a storm, just for a minute, never to go anywhere, ever. I wanted to fall down in front of my father and hug his knees and cry. With my three silly sisters standing there, gawking! It was the funniest feeling; to me then. It went like it came: quick.

"Yes. In the other room." I got into my sheepskin and went out. The women's voices murmured down the hall. Balzer's wife came out of their room and stopped when she saw me buttoning up. She put her hand up to my shoulder and I ducked my head and turned, though she did not touch me and hadn't spoken. Perhaps she would not have.

Listov was still standing in the doorway, face into the cold. "Thank you," I said to him.

"Like beasts, like unfeeling beasts." His eyes glinted with tears, voice so deep you could feel the floor shiver. "Ohh – what has become of Russia."

"You must try and get out too," my father said behind me.

"I would. This is no longer Russia. But I have no money."

"Like us. After one hundred fifty years."

"Yes. But I have no relatives, no foreign government will even maybe help us out on credit. I am a Russian, not a Mennonite."

"Yes," my father said as if he too were weeping. I went down to the street and he called quietly, "Knock on the window."

I gestured back and cut across to the shadow side. The train stop wasn't far; the letters in my breast pockets hung heavier with each jolt towards the city. Strelnikov's advice had seemed so good: write identical letters to three government bureaus, explain clearly and politely why you want to leave, and that if they will not see their way clear to allowing it, tell them there is nothing left for your people to do but come to Red Square, all the thousands of you with your women and children, and starve to death before the eyes of all the world. The government would have to act, and if the movement were massive enough they would not be able to hide it, as the GPU now easily hid night visits and examinations, the forced returns and exiles. Driediger had been so sure it would work, especially with seven hundred family signatures to three bureaus. The soviets simply couldn't have so many poor running from their proclaimed paradise.

But to deliver them; that was the hook. No one could know who did it; or how. When I found that the package I picked as we all left at once actually contained the letters, my head spun with excitement. I knew Moscow; I could pass for a Russian even with the GPU, if they didn't ask for too many papers. I had out-talked one of them once, right on the corner of Red Square where I was waiting with a message. All the officials we young men had hounded, the plans we'd made, the conferences we'd arranged, all had honed me for this. At last.

But in narrow streets peering out at every corner before crossing in the white moon, things become a little different. At least I began to know they were becoming so for me. Nothing moved; the buildings leaned like cliffs in the mist and the only sound was the squeak of my footsteps echoing against stone, down opening shafts of streets. I was no stumble-bum. At home our neighbors had a black and tan watchdog called Jonok, and they never lost so much as a hen during the four years he walked their yard before a Makhnovsky sabred him. When I was twelve I could get within five steps of him downwind before he knew I was there. But here, even when I walked as carefully as I knew, the sound seemed loud enough to wake any watchman four blocks away dozing in his fur cap. I had never thought, much, of watchmen before, either near or far away.

I don't know if anyone else ever thinks such things; they just float into your head and there they are, unasked, exposing suddenly yourself. I stood behind a corner of Red Square looking through the grey light at the clustered onion-domes of St. Basil's, and beyond. I wondered what it would be like to be a bird; just swing over the wall and between the dark buildings and through the barred and shuttered windows and drop one letter right on Stalin's desk. Exactly where he'd see it when he walked into the long room rumor said he worked in every day. Well, I was only twenty-two. Or I could do it too if I was invisible, doors opening at a touch, a flame, a hand guiding me through corridors and halls and rooms, leading precise as eternal revelation to the three exact spots. Such silly things. Anyways, I don't know what I expected on Red Square. Up to this point I don't think I had really thought of how I would deliver the letters. I had come into Moscow and to Red Square because the Kremlin was there. The Kremlin as such wasn't mentioned on the three letters, but I must have expected that when I was facing that giant wall behind which, somewhere, sat the men with our lives hanging on their nod, somehow an idea, a means, a notion at least, something would enter my head.

But nothing did. After a time to do something I walked along opposite the wall in the shadow of buildings, to the river corner where the tall watchtower sticks into the sky. Did you see the Kremlin picture in *Die Post* last winter? The tower is there, exactly, I could show you the spot. I walked, and then back. Only one gate; I could not make out so much as a shadow of the four guards behind their four different grates. I did not pray. That I know, though not exactly why. Perhaps I had been praying the usual for myself and family when the GPU was in the hall and that was now impossible – that long unknowing face and its blank happiness – youth waking up has such precise, violent ideals they can forgive almost nothing. But finally I understood; committed to do a job, no one to ask for advice, no whiff of how it could be done. I had been a child to imagine I could.

In the heart of Moscow not a sound or motion. Every communist rigid; silent. Waiting.

I don't know how long I stood stiffening in the cold; finally understanding what I had done, what must happen, in despair. Then suddenly a sound up the street. They were coming. There was no place; only a doorway here, a narrow shadow; I pulled back and peered out. The muffled noise slowly, heavily broke into the rhythm of feet and round the corner came a black mass. A whole army for me? Soldiers, yes, because it was marching, speared guns erect at shoulders, marching to me but then past me along the Kremlin wall. I don't know how many soldiers there were – maybe twenty, or hundreds upon hundreds – for when they were opposite me I forgot myself. It was what followed, partly surrounded by them and following. Figures bent forward with great burdens upon their backs, fumbling through the snow, lurch-bent, the sound of them an inhuman undertone to the crunching march of the soldiers. I could not see a face in all that unending company. Only the soldiers in their bearskins and overcoats defining the long bloated line of shapes broached to stagger along, gun-prodded, with not even the human sound of a curse. And after it at last, silent as drawn by something unearthly, came the Black Vulture.

I was hidden in a doorway, the black of it my shelter, but then I was out in the street and I think I fell, screaming, a GPU hand on my shoulder, long roaring happy faces, saucer eyes staring in tears, but there was no one at all on the silent street. Only myself and a foot winding-rag lying on the snow. I was sprawled on the street hammering at the trampled snow in the moonlight with the wall of the Kremlin above me. Maybe screaming too; I don't know.

Then I was in narrow streets again in front of a low lighted window in a wooden house leaning against a granite hulk. A sub-post office. I went in, jogged the girl sleeping in her chair beside the stove and said I wanted to send three registered letters.

"Well, where are they?" she asked finally.

"What?"

"The letters. I have to see them to register."

"Oh." I dug them out, and she wrote as if every night of her duty someone awakened her to send a registered letter to party president Kalinin. I was getting out my rubles when she said suddenly,

"I can't send them this way."

I hadn't really believed it myself. "Oh?"

"There's no name and address of sender on them."

Of course, Driediger – but anyone's name I wrote was as good as in Siberia. Balzer. It must have been some time before she asked,

"Can you write?"

"Yes . . ."

"Well write your name and address, here."

The letters lay in front of me. I couldn't move; I had been moving I don't know how and I could not dare let my mind wander toward a name. I thought of running. If I tried to run she'd be after me before I got round the corner. Or rip open . . .

"Aren't you sending them?"

"Yes – no – there's a group – of . . ."

"Then write down the group. That's the rules. You have to have name and address of sender. Post office rules."

So I wrote on the back of each letter: "Sender: Group of Mennonites, Cliasma Suburb, Moscow." She took it and my rubles and I was on the street. I don't know what she looked like. She may have been one of those party women: well trained and rather stupid; maybe muscular too. But I've always thought she was an angel.

I was nearly home, pulling myself – just a few more steps, a few more – along under the fir trees that make Cliasma so lovely. There was not a sound, I know that, but suddenly I wheeled (who can say why?) and saw a long black shadow slide behind the corner I had just passed. I ran then, not caring about my noise or motion, just to get to that window behind which I knew my father had been lying, waiting for me, praying all the terrible night.

The frogs along the street were all momentarily still. The elderly man stood, his forehead glinting silver under the giant Paraguayan moon.

"I think Mama has some water hot. Would you like a cup of Nescafé?"

"That little boy – that – was that my brother, Samuel?" John could ask finally.

"That Mrs. Friesen died in Zentrale here, maybe ten years ago."

"Was it Sam?"

"My good young Reimer. A daughter is still here, married with the Kanadier in Simons Colony," the voice added quietly, suddenly gruff.

"Okay. That's – I'm sorry." Mrs. Epp was moving in the kitchen. "But just a detail, at the beginning you said the twenty-fi . . ."

He was staring up into the silent darkness of the parisa tree. "It wasn't anything human," he said. "Just a thing; not even, the shadow of a thing. Soaking it up, following us. Ever since."

FIVE

Over the Red Line

WHEN MR. ADOLF confirmed Liesel's apprehension that the party now would have to be postponed one day, perhaps more, depending on how their group leadership decided – after all, they were the entire steerage and had every right to do exactly as they pleased – Liesel decided then and there that she would not allow a silly old funeral to spoil everything, again. She absolutely refused to wait.

Besides, she knew from her father – he would not speak with her about committee or *schultenbot* sessions, "When you're older you'll understand quite enough without starting already," but at times a hint of his problems seemed to escape him when he and her mother talked, thinking her asleep – that some had agreed to the party only very reluctantly in the first place; now there would be every reason for some old grackle like Stiffer Kliewer to start flapping again until all agreed to gladly forget it forever. "It is of course now clear," he would say and say, "that it was not to be. That it *should* not be. Even if we forget – and who can? – what has just happened, let us remember what we have been through, *and* what is still before us. Yes, some could be happy, some, but as I said before, when this matter first was laid before us, for how many would the happiness – oh, some would be happy! – not mean only a greater sorrow because of those, especially all those beloved little ones, who are not here, whom their loved ones will not see, or hold, again?" And now there'd be easily enough water to carry the day. Of course. Well, Ohm Heinrich was no "little one"; if he had lived eighty-three years already, as far as she was concerned he could as easily have lived one day more and since he hadn't, who could help that? It was precisely in keeping with the spoil-sport ways of old people that as soon as Mr. Adolf made the announcement that there would be a party for everyone, even steerage, at ship expense, a truly grand party like they had never had and Liesel at her boldest could not quite imagine – though she never betrayed *that* – and all the marvelous plans had been revealed about fancy hats and paper sashes and parades and multicolored balloons and even some bonbons – it was unbelievable what they had in store-rooms – someone would promptly die and make them cele-brate another funeral.

Not that Liesel minded funerals. She had found there could be enjoyment there; and, sometimes, in church services. Everyone sat quiet, long-faced and sober, and children were shushed or gone out with; everyone in their dark heavy clothing, voices groaning in harmony, and when she looked at her father's thin face, his tenor lifting easily and falling, eyes like the others as if looking away beyond all earth's oceans and hills:

> On this sad earth I am a pilgrim,
> And my journey, o my journey
> Is not long.

then she would feel just impossibly, almost too beautifully, sad and even before the end of the first verse she would remember that there were only three more and that they were not long and she would be even sadder. But then often Brother Hoppity Hiebert preached. He was the only preacher who danced about behind the table or whatever makeshift pulpit they had managed. His hands and the changes on his face – but when she was close enough to see his feet it was best by far. At the very least he made the announcements, and his announcements about funerals were also unsurpassed. She always watched him then, entranced: will he manage just choking a little; will he be forced to look down and everyone waiting, waiting; or will he suddenly burst right out into tears? Brother Hoppity was always making funeral announcements in German – they stopped with Russian the minute they were over the border – and he had actually cried only once, at the very beginning of the epidemics when six children died in one night. She remembered exactly where it had been: a long hallway so narrow they had to shout to be heard and she had been squeezed against her father almost under Brother Hoppity's feet, a perfect view; but she could not remember if that had been the first or second refugee station, and after the third she lost count. And, most unfortunate of all, it had happened before she was really prepared to watch him closely; announcements till then were long – just dreadful announcements that deadened your legs under you – she had had no anticipation of anything and so missed savoring altogether what would happen until it was past. Women did it forever, all the time, but a grown man, the preacher, during announcements! After that she always maneuvered to sit with her father at the front, if he allowed her, but Brother Hoppity had not quite reached that level again. Yet. She decided she would not ever again have smiled at him if he had done it for Ohm Heinrich.

The door had clicked softly behind her and Liesel listened, on tiptoe. But no tired voice called; she would have been embarrassed with herself if it had. She peeked around the corner. No one was visible in the long passageway, and she stepped out. The floor was like steel and she walked as nearly as she could like the ladies on First Class promenade. The gleaming bulkhead reflected her skirt neither long nor short, just a hopeless kind of intermediate. Hoist it – she had no pins and folds worked out from under the belt – she tied the black shawl in triangle low and tight around her hips and that gave a not impossible draped, trailing effect behind, but there was still a waist in her dress and what should she do with the thick woolen knot a bulge in front of her? Besides, when she so much as took a breath it slid down. And her dilapidated clogs. If she could only somehow get hold, just for the evening – but she jerked away from such unworthiness – they were marvelous on their unbelievable heels, the deck tilting gently. She had tried tying on blocks to get the height effect, but they looked so silly and forever twisted aside. And all the tall gentlemen to offer their arms, to support them, too. She once made the mistake of saying to Hans that perhaps he – he was such an absolute absolute throughandthrough mudhead – she would never in all her life give him another chance to laugh like that, not if he lived twelve times as long as Ohm Heinrich. That would be about like Methuselah, and she laughed to a ring down the passageway. His long, dirty beard wrapped around his knees because he was always cold and shriveled mouth open with one blotched yellow stump of tooth, open and mewling for just one little sop of anything, oh anything! and she would drop in one crumb tiny as a louse and dance away laughing, so shriveled they'd have to look three times before they even saw him in the coffin. Funerals were fine too, certainly. Heavy songs and long solemn processions winding along moaning, heads bowed; they were, and this one especially where there could not possibly be "dust to dust" – how would they manage that? She should have asked her father; a hole in the floor – the water would come up and into the ship for Ohm Heinrich – she laughed again. Before her first funeral, when she was little, she had thought they just tossed them into the air and God took them sweetly up to the harps of heaven. But no one was keeping her from a party. She could almost see the mirror of herself as she walked, carefully, and she was opposite the counter. The purser behind it was looking at a paper on his desk; he arose immediately when he saw her standing there. He wore his pure white uniform.

"Good evening, Miss Driediger." He had a beautiful voice.

"Good evening, Mr. Adolf."

He was smiling at her, the short thick bar of his mustache lifting at the corners, and so she serenely lifted her glance to the map behind him. The two lower continents leaned heavily at his shoulders.

"You are more beautiful than ever this evening."

"Thank you." She had practised before the mirror and she knew she could answer that now without the slightest hint of blush.

"And your laughter also – it was you?"

"It could have been." She shifted the black shawl slightly on her shoulders. "When shall we be over the line?"

He moved and she could see the tall flag-pin "S.S. Hindenburg," which he re-positioned every morning nearer the red line that stretched across the giant map from one bulkhead to the other. There was too much sea. Except for the line, it would have seemed the flag stood still and the heavy continents were working in upon it, lapping in on the breast of the huge sea. "Captain von Paul said we should cross at nine forty-five. That would be exactly one hour and seven min –" his glance dropped from the clock to her and she looked away, lip-corners and eyebrow lifting. A clean point; he acknowledged with a bow, "Nine forty-five," and a low laugh.

She walked down the corridor; when he was there she would not go up this companionway, not in her shoes. She tapped the handrail, smiling. She could tell time before she went to school, to know when her father would return each night from Leningrad University. Off an aisle a child cried. She looked at the section numbers; undoubtedly one of the three little Friesens left, whose father might be in Siberia by now, they said, if he had survived the Lubjanka by God's grace. Two Friesens had been in the first six when Brother Hoppity cried, and an older one later. Nearer, all about were scolding voices, murmurs, complaints, shushes. Except for Hans, the absolute mudhead, acting stupid to her, there was rarely scolding in their cabin. They were the only ones that had a cabin to themselves. They had no little kids. Long ago, waiting for her father every day, she had wished they had one at least, and her mother said she wished so too but God had not given them any more. It was as well He had not; she would have been totally cabin-bound, babysitting continually like droopy Trienchi Friesen hoisting around Greta or Susie or both, enough to hump your back forever. Or they probably would have died, or something, in Moscow or Germany.

She swung round the corner on the corner-grip, the points of her mother's shawl flying behind her, tilted back an instant – only one figure too far down the corridor to have appreci-ated, but they wouldn't anyway – and walked demurely up past C Deck and B, the area reserved for cabin and tourist class. She did not hesitate; no steward could question her, she knew. At each level she left the beastly motors a little further behind. On A Deck she avoided the President Lounge. The chandeliers were so beautiful she had very nearly cried when her father showed her the first evening where he had arranged, with special permission, for them to have church. It was the only place large enough and could hold all the men for *schul-tenbot* too. But now they had ruined it completely; it was absolutely maddening, always the most beautiful things. She could not begin to look through the glass after night before last, immediately after evening church too when she had had almost one and a half hours to watch the single crystal drops of the chandeliers sway to the roll of the ship, always moving, always a hair beyond touch and sound of each other in the moving intersected color streaks of light. In her late evening walk she had passed by, just one more glimpse, and seen – it must have been almost all – the men leaning forward, waving their arms, their words leaping out when a door swung aside somewhere, ". . . what down there in that god-forsaken . . . starve than live there . . . green hell where no beast . . . down there just Spanish bandits and heathen . . . wild brutes that chew . . . what cheesehead ever said Paraguay . . . down there . . . ," her father sitting in their center, motionless as stone under the crystal till some quieted them. But for them, some of the biggest yellers with their trachoma and empty pockets and no relatives to help, her father certainly would not be on this ship. That was thanks, like her mother wailed on his shoulder at night. Who didn't wail on his shoulder? It was absolutely stupid that he was to be yelled at by – by such farmers.

The tang of the sea met her on Promenade Deck. Two stewards said good evening and passed in the warm darkness near the rail. Her height was so frustrating, she must either bend double or crane to see the length of the ship. Fortunately no one was about now and she could stoop in comfort below the rail, over the second bar. The distance was nothing but far below and curving into the darkness ship's lights gleamed and broke to pieces and gleamed again on the curling waves. It was beautiful. As beautiful as the hoarfrost outside Moscow where every fir stood a white frozen bearskin. She gazed, enchanted.

Abruptly there was a tap on her behind and she banged up her head, hard.

"Tut tut, time for bed!" The squat figure was already past and she heard the chuckle. That fatass Mr. Herman, what was he doing here anyway with his flat hat. Mr. Adolf, so slim, looked smart with it but that *schundt* was a sheared-off greasy lump. She spit after him twice, knuckling her head.

Then she heard distant singing and tucked up her skirt and ran, silently, her long legs leaping ahead in shadow as she rounded the empty ballroom.

The funeral was nearly a disappointment. More dark and gloomy than ever, against the sky poked their bulky shawls and fur caps – they had no others so they'd wear them in the green hell too? – they were clustered at the rail and she had to shin up a life-boat support. Once on the taut canvas cover and the edge rope in her hand, she could see marvelously over the prow, though they should have had at least two lights. They were all a blot; black humpy landmasses eddying on the pale deck down the white shafts of the ship. A face lightened back to the night sky; her father, tall and gaunt as one of the pillars and his hands would be behind his back. Like a spasm she thought he saw her and she pulled back, carefully, but when she dared look again his face was turned, perhaps to Franz Epp beside him, but obviously unaware. It was too dark for her to be certain, even of Franz there always shorter and under her father, but she had seen him look at Franz often enough when he came for a message to know what the glance would be like. Once she had asked him and he had smiled off-handedly, "Oh, he's a good young one, he does well and is interested, in things." And added, after a minute, "Those Epps are a real family. His older brother's wife has trachoma and that's why they're on here. Where one has to go, they go all. That's not like some." That was sure, not like some like that *dummayoan* Hans who was interested in exactly nothing except potatoes and a warm blanket. If he died at five hundred there'd be nothing to read at his funeral but born, ate, and dead; not even the usual repetition of what she had heard so often, only rather more now because of the eighty-three years, eight months and eighteen days. If it had not been for the fading excitement of what would occur finally – there was no coffin, of that she was by now certain – she would have fallen asleep. Once she jerked awake as she tilted forward and the dreadful embarrassment of falling among them all set her stiff and alert almost the length of Heinrich Heinrichs' usual judgment-throne sermon. Though what young person would be there? Only Franz, if any and what was the point of warning him – perhaps Joseph Hiebert, Brother Hoppity's son, come for something different than just church – though there had been enough funerals too. But hardly ever any happy singing. She craned but could distinguish no one. Wherever he came to a service he was always warned. He was so tall and handsome like one of – but he would never be there. He hardly came ever to church, and was breaking his father's heart. Since a nephew happened to be a preacher, Brother Hoppity had not been asked. He was there a little apart before the shadow of them all, slight, arms down, oddly motionless. When he preached he danced – well, hopped at least. . . .

It happened before she was quite aware. In a silence after the usual boom of the Stiffer Kliewer "Amen!" Captain von Paul was there, gesturing, and suddenly something out of the shadow moved. Slowly, slowly, a wrinkle moving over the blot and – whee – it was twitched away down into darkness. Liesel stared, and after an endless silence heard a faint splash; there was a surge against the rail, then women screamed. There had been moaning quietly throughout, as always, but now abruptly they screamed. The sharp clear cry pierced Liesel: she felt it pass through her like a shaft; pass through endlessly on and on. After she had no conception how long she knew herself stretched on the canvas, the erect mass of the smokestack above her against the breaking overcast. She sat up. There was her headache now and the motors thrust relentlessly on. Two white sailors were lifting the rail back into place. She sprang up; the party!

She had slipped through the barrier into First Class so often there was nothing left for her in that. In the ladies room mirror large blinking eyes stared back at her out of a pale veed face. At least she was not short and thick like Trienchi and Susch and all the others. They could chant all they wanted:

> "*Liesel, Liesel,*
> *Dried'ger's spriesel,*
> *Uppity and thin as a measle,*"

it made no sense anyway. Though it did not of course have to; tone was enough. And praises be for black hair – no muddy

white – her hair! To even breathe of cutting it tight to her ears –
if only she had had to take the louse cure! – so she could wear
one of those hay-cock hats, if she – found? one, was of course
inconceivable, but if only she could at least twirl it up high and
sleek like Mrs. Factory Enns used to do she would look even
taller and those stupid braids – but her father said "No" in that
voice he rarely used. And it was impossible in that washroom
with snot-nosed kids running forever; and stinking up everything and there was too little time now.

The door sighed and a lady came in; Liesel almost gasped.
Her body was a long thin gold cylinder and something almost
like gold feathers flounced out from her hips showing a hand-
width of glittering leg above the knees. Liesel stared until she
noticed her stare was rigidly returned; she retreated out of
sight. One of her own stockings had snagged somewhere, she
discovered. She tucked the edges in; when she walked erect it
would not show. There was a flicker in the door-slit: she
leaned forward and saw in the mirror a long hand gesturing
with a silver tube tipped red. Violent red. Was that what happened to their lips? She had often marveled how – the crack
was so narrow –

"Come out and look, I won't bite you, you little spy. I can
see your feet," the woman said.

Her feet protruded under the door. Liesel backed against
cold porcelain, face hot: that mockery was Russian! Huh! She
flushed the toilet, settled her shawl firmly on her shoulders
and stepped out past the woman baring her teeth at the mirror
as if she did not exist. Out into the hall toward the laughter.

She had been rather shaken by those legs, she realized, but
now she again felt almost exactly in the suspended sensitivity
that was perfection in First Class. After crossing the barrier
Liesel suspended thinking on what she had heard so often: the
badness that a Mennonite child must never see or hear or
think about to keep its eternal soul clean. Once she had been
deeply concerned about her eternal soul, especially as the

older she grew and the more she heard things repeated about it, the mistier it became. She was still perfectly concerned. It seemed to her that when she was half as old as she was now her soul had been clear to her as some village pup barking or wagging its tail. Anyway, she rather disliked dogs. During the interminable weeks of cramped waiting and then abrupt, furious one or two day life-and-death activity of the past eight months she had finally decided that her soul, since it was so important despite its elusiveness – perhaps because of that – must be prepared at certain times to take care of itself. Especially in stress and opportunity. By now she was certain it could. Besides, how simply looking could be so much worse than lying about snoring forever and forever like that mudhead Hans – he would not even get up when the incredible lights of Madeira swam by, though she hit him long enough to wake him – she could not conceive.

She did know she wanted to look. They sat about the salon at tables, laughing, smoke drifting up, their white fingers flickering between cards, rings clinking against little columns of coin. This was all usual enough, though more crowded; and the bangled lights laid strange chromatic shadows of continents everywhere. She had never been there so late. Faces seemed pointed, and pushing. Here a couple leaned profile to cut profile, in the center they whirled and swayed, skirts belling, long black arms with cuffs blank white as chalk lifting, circling to the lolling music, ebony shoes glinting like knives. Looking in this entrance, slipping around this clump of laughter and shingled heads, staring through the glass, feeling the swing and tug of the music that drifted her from there to here, for Liesel something seemed faintly terrifying. She realized there was not a woman whose lips were natural; perhaps even the rest of their faces – yet they were all so tall and fine, so elegant, their movements so free, dignified, and the men's dark faces with a black slash of mustache bending to the white-skinned women with long fragile necks, laughing, touching, and laughing completely. Such laughing; like a grace. She had never heard such happiness or imagined there could be so many people together laughing in the whole world. They did not ever stop laughing. She could not understand what she thought perhaps Spanish or English or even French, but the German was as refined as somewhere she remembered her father and his friends in Leningrad before they had dragged back on the train third class to that stupid old village and just talked Lowgerman and German that would here sound like – like – she could think of nothing but the heavy feltboots some men still wore, so stinking when they schluffed by. And all they ever did was talk and talk and talk about the terrible communists and the GPU and having no money and what they would ever do in the green hell with heathen and wash their old rags again and cry and sing long heavy songs and celebrate funerals. Wailing.

But to move like that, sweet with silk shifting across your body, bending like grass to a breath, regal as hoarfrost. . . .

There was changed sound. Through the glass wall she saw a woman dressed as the gold Russian, but in beige. She was alone in the center of the floor and the strange music seemed to be jerking her like a doll on strings, her limbs flying in every impossible direction and feet flipping sideways so far she must surely split. On the mirror floor it was unbelievable that she could remain pointed on her thin legs, twisting so violently, so fast. Then a man was against her and they were jerking and thrusting together, heads, legs, the split of his coat, arms, flicking like an unsyncopated humped monster; a writhed fiend. Liesel noticed her own knees twitching, twitching to the music. She shrieked a little; ran. Ran.

Coolness came to her, and the fresh salt air. She ducked through another barrier, dropped along a narrow stair; there was only the overcast above her broken almost completely to bright stars; around some bulks and suddenly the rail there turned on itself. Finally she understood that the endless flick-ering points of silver ahead she was staring at was the ocean far below; that she was on the very bow of the ship; that everyone was behind her and she faced only sky and sea. There was no space for even an instant's regret at missing this anticipation. She put her chin on the rail – it was round steel here but no chill came to her – she was in sky and sea, suspended, passing forward into silver. The faint sounds and rhythms of the ship soaked through her and she felt the world lifting, turning under her, she alone the motionless solid rock where light and darkness slit. A feeling like distant thunder inevitably roaring nearer rolled in her to an echo of the fiend's rhythm she had fled and suddenly a sharp clear cry, everything within her surged as though tiny seeds spilling out of herself, pouring over the world. She floated free.

She lay on the ship's point, her chest on the lowest rail, her head where the bow curved under endlessly to white froth plowing. She pulled herself away and stood up; adjusted her shawl. The bridge and riggings of the ship piled gigantically in lights and black blocks above her. Very nice. She touched a coil as high as herself and her finger came away black; she spit on it and rubbed her leg. Black dresses were good for something; she had always known that. A woolly fuzz, and the spot intact; perhaps not. She moistened it again and rubbed hard on a hard surface. Almost gone in the faint light. For a time she stood looking at the narrow stairs, but she did not want to try a door – perhaps they were locked – and finally she trudged up and bent through the barrier. Laughter and music again; she moved languidly.

She heard something moan and she stopped. Behind an air funnel. Gradually in an angle of bulkheads she made out a shape erect, two shapes, staggering a bit as if glued off-balance together. She stood in the shadow and eventually could distin-guish the white uniform and the arm reaching down, hoisting the skirt which darted gold stray light in all directions, higher and higher so that dark bands of stocking tops and garters emerged on white thighs. She wondered in idle distaste why, if they wanted to do that, they did it so awkwardly, the man standing between the woman's legs which she now seemingly was trying to twine up around his hips, and slipping, making that silly sound. Her shiny stockings were probably too slippery. Finally the man got sensible and laid the woman – or perhaps they collapsed – the woman was flat on the deck and she could jerk the garter rigging and stockings up over her white knees. Their heads, dark bumps in the darkness, still seemed welded together and the man knelt over her, a white arm between her arching legs, the other fumbling into his trousers. Leisel suddenly felt the funnel at her back and she turned without thought, back to the light. Cold and ugliness dropped away like blots.

Warmth, laughter welled from a companionway, and drew her gently. On the landings huge murals faced her; fecund green trees spiraling over yellow beaches with men holding white flags at men with feathers and brown like wood; great blotches of color that straggled everywhere pawing out from the very wall. But she felt only aloof now; perfectly aloof. Down she walked, step by step, the shouting and steamy warmth always louder, and then through thickening smoke a huge room yawned where she had never been. She worked between gowns and suits, and another double railing confronted her. She stared, transfixed.

The ship opened without end down into the sea. Under fierce light its greenishness licked sometimes to the very edge of green tile, sometimes retreated. And even stranger was what came rolling towards her in the water, a shimmer of figures suspended from ankles, feet, contorting, swelling with the bulge of the sea. They broke at her feet and she raised her glance. There they were complete. On a throne in the center, holding erect a tri-pronged fork, his long robe shimmering from green to blue to purple when his white arms gestured, sat a king with a jagged golden crown above his face black as Cossack leather with menials bending and kneeling and running before him. At a gesture one leaped up, seized someone in the crowd that surged around one side of the sea, those farthest trying to advance and the nearest frantic to retreat, and dragged him, straining and laughing and perhaps half-willing, before the throne.

"Aha-aha!" the roar rang above the noise. "Confess, confess, you are guilty, guilty, you are guilty!"

"O most awful lord, I confess," came the tiny reply. "I am – guilty."

"Attendants! The penalty and initiation!" and the culprit was hurled, running, through a curtain of water heaved aloft and spilled by other menials, and welcomed by the cries and shouts of a multitude whose dripping heads and clothes testified their cleansing.

On and on went the judgment. All to the right of the sea were guilty and they came, some laughing, others protesting, some in tears, still others confessing and dashing by before the judgment water was ready to fall. Liesel was being pulled nearer by the shifting crowd but not even the rail sliding through her hands gave her any sense of personal motion; she simply looked. The attendants pulled forward two large dark women above her who for a moment faced each other; all they needed was a red line, the shorter one high and the tall one across her middle, to look precisely like the two lower continents down there on Mr. Adolf's map working their fronts out at each other. She burst into laughter.

At that instant, like a new world opening, the double rails swung into space and she fell.

Not headfirst, but completely, erect, from the people about her. In the long instant before she touched the sea deep below its retreating rim her mouth fell open, soundless, then her toes touched and she screamed, and the cold water knifed up her at one stroke. Bitterness exploded in her mouth, her throat; her feet struck and her knees bent, collapsed, but she buoyed, her face felt air and the gaping faces above and then the green brine stomped her "Uhhhhhhhh" into her lungs as her body collapsed, jerking, twisting, spinning.

White ebbed into the darkness above her, rocking, rocking, like mud dropped to black water. Agonies flamed through her, and voices gurgled. ". . . immigrants in steerage . . . skin and bone . . . that gate . . . without . . . poor . . . dreadful condition . . . dreadfully careless . . . dreadful . . ." Mr. Adolf's face was there in the angel whiteness and her arms, lying above her, started up to him, and his face clamped down to her – air – kneeling over her – black over – white arms – her legs pulling up, curling – screams poured out of retching, her self disintegrating in arched convulsed terror.

Then she was sitting. Her hands slapping only the deck because she had been left alone. Her father's pale face crouched down to her; she did not care who was looking but clutched at him. His long arms came round her like a cradle.

"She'll be good as new, just a little rest," Mr. Adolf's voice said.

A woman said, "She wouldn't be alive without this young man –"

"Thank you," her father's voice rumbled against her ear. "Now I must take her back."

"Here's a blanket."

"I'll come by immediately in the morning, Mr. Driediger," another voice said. "If you need anything at all, during the night . . ."

"Yes, thank you." She was being lifted; she kept her face against the coat rough. "No, thank you, I can carry her."

"Pardon me," a heavy woman said, "that shawl – it's so soft, beautiful, black – hand-made no doubt – I'd give you –"

"No," her father said. "It's always been – we have little left."

They were going up endlessly and then the sea-air clean as a gasp in her nostrils. She shifted her head. The beams of the Promenade Deck moved between them and the lifting sea. Mr. Adolf was swinging a gate aside for them; a blanketed blot. She shuddered, hunching down tighter. She murmured in Russian, which she knew the other could not understand,

"Pappa, are we over yet?"

"We crossed, yes."

Mr. Adolf said goodnight; when he was gone for certain she could look out. She realized finally that her eyes were adjusted; that there was nothing there at all. Even the sea was nothing more than a faintness, as if her power of seeing sank into a muddish green that stank of brine still.

"It isn't any different, from here it's just . . ."

"It's just a man-made line. Were you at the funeral too?"

"Not – not right from the start . . ."

"I would think this would do, now."

"Yes."

They were almost to their cabin, the motors throbbing, when Brother Hoppity Hiebert appeared from nowhere as he invariably did and her blanket and wetness had to be explained. He limped about in his agitation, touching her lightly here and there and laughing with glee when she finally smiled. But when they were alone by their door and her father placed her on her feet, she groaned a little. "O pappa, now everyone will know!"

"So you understand?" His hands to the keyhole. "And next time, at least leave the shawl."

She stared, suddenly aware of his tone.

He did not go in to switch on the light. "We can't lose everything beautiful at once," he said. He stood at the open door; standing aside, waiting.

SIX

My Life: That's As It Was (3)

WE DID NOT STOP in Asuncion and when we got to Puerto Casado it was May 18, 1927. It was nothing like now, with mills and the big hotel and stores. There were some long sheds and palm trees and many many tents gray everywhere, and there we saw again familiar faces; my man's brother and one of my sisters' man and others, all at the dock to get their relatives. But the faces were so burned, so brown and all so hollow and thin. We were the fifth and largest group to get there; the first 270 had been there already since before Christmas and New Year. They had been greeted by the President of Paraguay when they stopped by Asuncion but they hadn't moved to our land which was about 150 miles west, into the Chaco bush.

About, they said, because nobody had seen it yet, except the delegation for a few days in 1921. A group had tried to get there in February but they didn't have enough food and there was no water so they had to come back and they weren't exactly sure where our thirty *leguas* were. There was lots of land and it looked all about the same, full of cactus trees and brush and empty. The Corporacion Paraguaya had sold us the land for five dollars the acre and later we heard they bought it from the Casado Company for $1.25. In 1942 we bought another big piece for fifteen cents, but in 1927 the Corporacion didn't have a surveyor there yet. There were almost 2000 Mennonites now in Puerto Casado not making a move, doing nothing. There wasn't work for many in the Company mill, they said, so everybody was just eating up what they had left after the long trip. Some who had worked hard in Canada just sat, waiting, as if the heat was already too much. Who had ever seen so many Mennonites sitting with their hands empty? It was almost winter then.

Three months later, in August, 1927, the Corporacion got surveyors on the land. A few families had then already tried to move west to Pozo Azul and even Hoffnungsfeld, as they called it, to make gardens at least, but most of the 2000 were still by the river and over 100 had died. The day we docked was the funeral of Waldmut Harder, once our neighbor by Hague, Saskatchewan. At first only children had died, but not any longer. By Casado alone they said Elder Wiebe the Older preached 140 funeral sermons in eight months but I don't think it was that many. Sometimes there were several buried together, sometimes three or four because it was very hot and funerals were always the same day unless the death was in the evening. When the doctor from the Casado Company came in September he said it was typhus, so contagious all who were sick should be in one place separate and no one should go to the funerals.

But how can you bury your children like that? In September before we got to the Chaco we buried our third. Neta, nine, and Benjamin, five, were earlier. Neta was always sickly and Benjamin was so quiet, just sitting and singing a little, as if he was never for this world. Now it was Johann, our first Johann and then our biggest who worked so hard always, such an obedient son. He had big bones like most Friesens but was shrunken together and dry with his mouth bitten from the sickness; we had to buy long boards for him from the Company. My man cut all day on the board head-stone; "Johann J. Friesen, deceased son of Johann K. and Frieda Friesen born

Aug. 1 1904 died Se. 10 1927 his age brought to 23 y. 1 m. 9 days."
As we carried him we sang what was sung there at Puerto
Casado so often:

> *Come now and dig my grave,*
> *For I am weary the wandering;*
> *From earth would take my leave,*
> *For I am weary the groaning.*
> *For I am called by the holy peace*
> *Of angels, whose rest can never cease.*

We packed what we had unpacked again into boxes because the road after the short railroad was just army trail. We
had to make food ready for one or maybe two weeks. We
roasted *twieback*, brought beef from the Company and
smoked it, and potatoes and noodles too. September 13 father
and Isaak, fourteen, took down our tents and rolled them up
and we stayed for night with his brother Jakob K. Friesen. On
September 14 early we went to the Company train. Our things
were all on and we rode that day to the end of it, seventy-six
kilometers west, the train was only built that far then. It
stopped often to load wood, mostly red quebracho. That was
the first we ever saw wood so hard it sank like iron and made
the axe bounce, shivering when you chopped. As the sun went
down we came to the end where our second son, Kornelius,
sixteen, was with our oxen and wagons that had hauled freight
into the Chaco several times. We told him how Johann had
died, that he had sent him a greeting at the last. Kornelius did
not say anything; then after a little he showed us where we
could set the tent for the night.

The night was cool; it even rained a little and we could
almost all sleep. At morning Kornelius rode to find our oxen
on our one horse and we started before noon. One ox looked
good but the other was thin as if the next warblefly would
carry him to green pastures. There weren't any of those, there.
Bernhard Fehrs' sons, Heinz and Aaron, drove two other

wagons but we had to leave some of our things there. We had a bench on one side under the canvas for the children to sit and the rest was stuffed with bedding and clothes. On the back we had a *etiskauste* with food and cups. The other wagons had freight, and also twelve chickens that cackled as we walked, the oxen moving just so fast you didn't quite stand still, though you could think about it between steps.

We had never seen such land before; by the river it too often rained but here, and perhaps from the many Mennonites with their wagons on the trail too, it was just dust and heat between the low bush. After a few hours the thin ox lay down and no hitting helped. Kornelius had hauled freight with our Johann and he said there were maybe some other oxen of the Mennonites there so he rode off on the horse with a sling-rope and in an hour he came back with a big one, blue-grey with horns nearly four feet across. He had to swing his head sideways to get between the bottle trees. We had cooked butter soup and noodles so we ate and hitched on again. The blue ox was wild, but he was strong and after enough beating he pulled, just you had to stay away from his horns. Our father was all tired from one afternoon of it, but he could pull. For supper we had tea, smoked beef and honey on roasted *twieback*.

We found soon the best wood was palosanto. It did not smoke and burned smelling sharp and sweet, like a great church Kornelius said he and Johann had looked in at the door in Rio de Janeiro. Isaak said maybe they made that smell there because the people were so dirty and Marie said it would have helped at Casado, but our father said it was something about how Catholics thought they should pray. Marie and Tina cleaned up and Anna and I washed the dust off the others and rubbed a little fat where they had scratched bites. Then we laid ourselves down with God. The littlest slept under the wagon and the moon was clear, bigger than I had ever thought it could be from this world. It was so quiet your blood made whispers.

For three days it was hard. Along the railroad still nearer the river there were palm trees and tall grass with water holes, but here was more and more low bush full of spines and prickers and the grass was bitter. We had never known that in Canada: when you chew there it is sweet, not pulling your mouth together like poison. The oxen wandered far each night to find some sweet. There was just a little water in the deeper wagon tracks from the last rain for the oxen to drink. After the second day we had to drink that too so the girls walked ahead and dipped some out before the oxen got it all.

On the fourth day at evening we got to the Paraguayan soldier camp. Here was good grass and water. The soldiers looked like boys, so small and brown and none had guns, only an officer had a short gun for one hand, and they stood around with bush knives almost as long as they hanging down. Before the sun was gone they came walking past by three or four, barefoot in the sand and not feeling the cactus everywhere. They looked at us and Marie and Tina, even Anna who was just twelve and thin, and laughed, speaking in their Guarani. Kornelius said they liked Mennonite girls, their white skin and light hair, but the officers were very strict and had shot two soldiers by Pozo Azul for bothering a girl. They were friendly and helped us too, getting wood and holding oxen. They looked like thin little boys that should have their hair cut and noses wiped, not broad like our boys, but when you saw their black eyes you saw they had everything a man had and you didn't have to understand a word to know what they would do if you let them go for what they wanted. Just like everywhere in the world.

The next water was the well at Pozo Azul and it took two days, the worst of all. It was spring, our first spring in the Chaco and we weren't used to anything. Where the road was chopped through the bush there was no wind and the heat lay like a wall fallen over on you, and in the open campos with the dry bitter-grass it was worse because the north-wind poured straight like out of a heater stuffed with jackpine, only salted with sand. We had to stop for three hours over noon but couldn't give the oxen any water and in the evening the stupid blue one was so fierce he knocked over my man and the pail too with the little water for him. Sundown made no difference because the wind still came from the north till almost morning. Neta and Benjamin would not have gotten through that, and now I wondered about Anna and Greta. But Abram, so little then, only a year, was good. The second day we met Mennonites coming back for freight. They said there was some good water at Pozo Azul, and a big enough graveyard. Mrs. Heinrich S. Abrams and her baby had died the day they left and a few families all had typhus. At evening when we got there my man went to visit some sick and dying too. Mennonites lived at Pozo Azul till the villages were measured out in the colony, finished maybe a year later. Nearly fifty stayed in the graveyard.

Along the road after that there were more camps, a few wells, and it was easier. On the ninth day, September 23, at evening we came to Campo Grande, where we were going. The sun was down and we saw a light burning; it was Preacher Samuel Dyck and we camped by them for night. I made yeast yet so I could bake in the morning because they had built a little brick stove already.

Campo Grande was a bigger Campo about in the middle of what would be Simons Colony, once they got it surveyed. It had a laguna at one end they said never dried up; it hadn't rained since August and there was still some water for all the families camping there, waiting for their villages. We set our tents at the north end near the bush and two days later it rained for ten minutes like a bucket so we started a garden. It was nearly easier pulling the plow ourselves than to make those oxen go straight, but we got some planted: beans, cucumbers, marrows and watermelons, peanuts and three kinds of kaffir. The seed we had brought along from the States and when it rains it grows faster than in Saskatchewan.

We were at Campo Grande a year. In a way there'd be so much to say about such a year, and in another way nothing. Some talk about it too much. We wanted to get on our land, that was all.

We started to know the Chaco with its little food – potatoes never grew nor wheat, and sometimes there was just flour freighted in with not even enough for salt – and sicknesses and mosquitoes and polverins by the water and how to build a house, waiting, and all the *schultenbots* to lot out where the villages, not surveyed yet, went and men chopping out lines for the surveyors so they would move just a little. And waiting. The ground was sand and clay, not a pebble for 600 kilometers west to the mountains, they said. After Saskatchewan I never thought I'd be lonely for a stone. Waiting. In September, 1928, after two years moving and tents, we came to Schoenbach, our village. Of course there was nothing, only pegs in the bittergrass. The first thing was for the families, there were eighteen with four Reimers and six Wiebes, to dig a well, and that almost didn't happen. Only after the twenty-third hole they found sweet water under the paratodo tree by the bush. After the sorrow the well digging cost, it was one of the best in the colony. We made clay bricks in forms from crates, for a house. The children tramped water and clay together and Isaak filled the forms while Father and Kornelius hand-sawed boards for the door and window frames. One board took most of a day. At least we didn't need ovens to bake the brick. Tina, sixteen, dipped the bricks in water and Kornelius and Father laid them out and Isaak and the others mixed mud and soon the house with two rooms was finished. The roof we made of galvanized sheets which we had brought from Canada. Instead of saskatoons, the children picked algarrobo pods, inside sweet as candy.

We had a cow already too, bought from the Casado Company. She was a usual Paraguay cow, just a beast. If you could get hold without a hoof in the face it was like jerking on the tire of the Ford we once had at Roads. Her calf had to start her or you couldn't get a drop and if something happened to the calf, they said cows just ran around bawling with pain till they dried up. Many years later some got Holsteins from Canada and soon they had to be started with their calf too, nobody knows why. Maybe it is something in the air. This one we tied her head against a tree, tied a tight rope on her foot and then I pulled it tight around a post so she stood on three legs, all stretched out. Then if she kicked she whammed over on the ground. After a while she didn't kick any more when we did that and Marie got the calf on her and then could milk. Marie said for two quarts it wasn't worth the work; we'd get further just to chop her up and eat her. But the children needed milk.

In October, 1928, just in spring at the start of the big heat, our oldest Kornelius drove to haul freight from the railroad. Schoenbach was closest to it then and we earned a little that way, hauling. Nearly three weeks later a Paraguayan rode on our yard with a telegram all the way from Casado that said our Kornelius was lying very sick with typhus by the river and wanted his father. But our father could not move from a strained back and rupture he got when they were digging for Klaus Wiebe in one of the well holes that slid shut with sand. They never got him out, it was so dangerous; they had to put a gravestone there beside the street and leave it. That was a hard time.

Greta, just eight, was sick with fever, and Abram too. It was planting time and the oxen were gone and after Isaak, fifteen, got them back from the railroad he could hardly do any plowing, they were just too hard for him. Our neighbors were good to us then, as much as they could and more, helping us. There was no doctor in the Chaco but we still had a little Watkins medicine left from Canada. Then the last, and this one we called Johann again, was born November 1, 1928. It was almost too much, and who likes to remember such times? Some too much. There is strength that comes when you pray. When Johann was eleven days another telegram came from Casado saying that it looked like his death with Kornelius. Our father could walk a little then and he and Marie drove back to the railroad with the Company truck that had brought the telegram. The day after they were away our cow dropped dead when she drank water at evening; the vultures were all that even got to taste her. So much of everything comes at once sometimes, just when you think that the most maybe is over. Terrible bunchy, like my father said. But I had been strong since the sea and we had hope. It all does come from God. Strength and sickness, want and plenty.

And blessed be God, for our first Christmas in Schoenbach, our home in the Chaco, we were all together. Our father and the two children came home from Casado December 22. Because of the rain they had to hitch six yoke of oxen to drag one wagon and then the next through mudholes and Kornelius was tired and swollen all over, big he couldn't button his shirt or wear shoes. After a few days it went down and on Christmas Eve it rained three inches and was cooler. Chaco lightning makes what happened in Canada before a rainstorm look like playing with matches. Because of the nice big rain we could not go to *hauptcheuik* for the service. Everyone in the village came to our yard and the children said their Bible verses and Christmas wishes.

We ate watermelon for dinner and sat where there was a little shade. The children had learned a song in school, just as we had thirty-five years before in Canada, and our parents too in Russia, so we sang it together:

Gently falleth the snow;
Still and white rests the sea;
Woods glisten under the moon;
Joy to thee! Christchild comes soon!

My man said it might fit better to sing, "Gently falleth the sweat," and everyone laughed, but for some women I could see a different word could have fit even better. Maybe for me too. But the last line was the best.

When they were all gone and the children sleeping Kornelius told us about his sickness and how he had been tempted very hard in Casado about his soul's salvation. He had promised the dear Lord that when he became well he wanted to preach the gospel in the Chaco. So go the ways, and he has done it, too. After Christmas we had to plow and seed again what Isaak had done; the ants had cut it all to nothing.

In 1930 some Mennonites still left in Russia ran from the communists and made a colony west of ours. There were about 1500 Russlander, mostly different from us but some we heard were even perhaps distant relatives; they spoke Lowgerman and it was better that there were more people in the Chaco. Theirs they called Fernland Colony and Mennonites in North America helped them very much; they had nothing, some not even clothes. Everything came through Schoenbach and past our well so that helped us too. Almost a hundred of them died in the first year, again mostly from typhus. There was still no doctor. We had schools built in most of the bigger villages already and every Sunday could have church in them. Our *hauptcheuik* was in Blumengart then, where Elder Wiebe the Older lived. We knew better about what would grow so that helped everyone. In 1932 we saw the first airplane; we were picking cotton with some Lengua Indians on our land and they saw it first and ran into the bush to hide. Later our father came from Campo Grande with flour and said it was a plane from Bolivia and that there was war between Paraguay and Bolivia.

"I said there were more soldiers at Pozo Azul last time," Isaak said. "And there was even a tractor, I think."

"Where will it be, the war?" Kornelius asked our father.

"Franz A. Hiebert from Dorfsheim said he was in the bush looking for cows and they met soldiers they said were making a way from Pozo Azul to Isla Poi. It's going to give war and they have to have a truck road."

"Right through the colony? They'll shoot right here?"

"Maybe. By the Russlander too maybe."

"Why are they fighting for?" Kornelius asked.

"How would soldiers know that," our father said.

"The officers too? That Captain Raul knows some things, boy!" said Isaak.

"They know nothing more than if they'd gone to school and could read. They just pull a trigger or chop around with a machete. That's their work."

"What would anyone cat-scratch himself for over the Chaco?" said our Marie. "Just bugs and sand."

"Nobody talks here like that," our father said.

All of a sudden Isaak, he was only nineteen then, said, "Well at least in Canada there weren't soldiers poking and shooting around, trying if they could hit something."

"You hear!" said my man. "Marie, you can take your water pails to the well. And Anna's too."

In September 1932 there was war at the waterhole of Boqueron, 50 kilometers from our colony. It lasted all month and there was no rain. In the evening we could hear the cannon. Sometimes night and day they hauled wounded with wagons through Schoenbach to the railroad and over 5000 Paraguayans ended that month. They said they never took prisoners or counted Bolivians. Most weren't killed in the battle; they just didn't have water. We had the best well in the colony but they used it only for the wounded wagons, never to haul to the soldiers. An officer with a bare gun stood by it all month; perhaps they had no barrels to haul. Some said the Paraguayans finally won because the Bolivians held the waterhole and the Paraguayans didn't care any more what happened because of thirst so they never stopped charging. It's hard to think of war here, everything so quiet, but then it went on to different places of the Chaco for years, here and there. The Bolivians even bombed Fernland Colony Zentrale once, but they never did Campo Grande. You could never tell when a soldier wouldn't show up out of nowhere. Women had to stay close to the house and Tina and Anna could only go to the well in the day. The soldiers were always hungry, stealing watermelons and kaffir at night, but the Paraguay officers were very strict and the government even paid back some cattle the soldiers butchered and ate.

Those years too we had the second wedding in our family. In July 1933 Bernhard Fehrs' son Heinz married our Marie. They started with a farm in one of the new villages, Brudersheim in the south, but in a year they sold their little bit and moved back to Canada. My brother Heinrich and Esther's man, Dennis Willms, lent them money. During the first year when we had to stay so long at Casado and on the road over 400 people moved back, as they could, but in 1934 just a few went back every year. Our Marie had a strong head. Huh, maybe Heinz needed one.

SEVEN

The Well

ONE EARLY SUMMER as the November sun stood so directly overhead that it cast no shadow, Anna Friesen discovered when she leaned over the rim she could not tell whether she was looking into the well or out of it.

The well was Schoenbach's most valued possession. It stood at the north end of the village, the last of Simons Colony on the crooked trail to the rail-end. When they drew lots for the village in 1928 the settlers did not know they had it; they had no well whatever and to an untrained eye the arid campo gave not the slightest hint about the passing of a stream, leave alone a beautiful one. But wherever Mennonites had lived, whether in Canada or as far back as story and strong memory could depend on Russia, there had always been such village names: Gartental, Blumenau, Rosenfeld, Friedensruh. Each word was a place; it contained no word context for anyone; it was. So Schoenbach. If they were going to live in Paraguay's "green-hell" Chaco, as they were since Anna's parents and the Elder said, then one of thirteen villages would be so named. The village was planned and named while they were still at sea a year before any surveying was done, when actually only five Mennonites, delegates of 1921, had ever seen the Chaco however briefly, and no one the campos on which they were to settle: Schoenbach.

The well being what it was, the village name simply named again their thoughtless faith. (Ten years later visiting German scientists would conjecture, even agree from soil samples and aerial surveys, that the campos actually were ancient stream beds. But what possible practical difference could this make to the two or three Mennonites who would hear about these reports five years after that; fifteen years after the fact why puzzle your head about why, if that were so, what remained of the sweet stream should lie six meters under the sand at the edge of the clearing and not in the middle where digging first began?) A thoughtful man hauling his family through the cactus brush to the campo and raising his tents on his lot-assigned strip of sand and bitter-grass would have cried, or laughed, at such a name. In the privacy of their work some women did cry; most men had no time for either. Wells had to be dug. If the sand did not collapse, at some level they found water in every shaft but when they hauled it up the few gaunt oxen swung their muzzles over it and bellowed. Not even adobe bricks they tramped out with their bare feet held together; it was brine. After the eleventh hole four men went to plead, with despair and no success, for another campo. The others persisted to the very rim of the bush, laboring inside the cribbing that was to prevent another such sand cave-in as had already buried one digger forever at the village center. Near a paratodo tree a moisture one evening became the next morning the sweet well. Everyone gathered bare-headed in the sun and thanked God, drinking. And after the initial adjustment no one in Schoenbach was ever again sick from the water.

Neither the entire village nor the Lengua Indians who soon heard and camped nearby in their wanderings nor the high ox-carts squealing on toward Endstation had ever dipped the well dry. (September 1932 and the Battle of Boqueron could really have proven their well but since they did not have, and very thankfully never wanted to have, or had, the faintest

notion of military strategy, they never understood why that
month did not discover the well's bottom, that is, the stream's
end.) After Schoenbach there was nothing on the railroad trail
except puddles, if that, and though Endstation was only
seventy miles away, by ox-cart that meant undoubtedly six,
perhaps as many as fifteen days, depending. The irony of
Chaco cartage was invariable: in dry weather the road was
loose and dust-choked and oxen could thirst into immobility
between waterholes; if it rained hard enough to plow in the
settlement so that eventually there could be some produce to
sell for the staples that had to be hauled in, the level trail
vanished in bottomless mudholes almost as numberless as
mosquitoes, that demanded three floundering yoke of oxen
on a four-hundred-kilo load to gain two, perhaps four miles
in all the daylight one day provided. The Chaco day too was
almost invariable: twelve hours of light and then at one stride
the darkness. After the moon rose there was light again, but
the oxen must graze; they did so even more deliberately than
they walked.

Before the day's heat but considerably after the cattle
watered and wandered away to forage what they could among
the spined bush, the women and older girls of Schoenbach
went to the well. They did not come like the Lengua women,
one pot balanced on their head and the other in their hand,
staring wherever their eye strayed; their pails hung from a
wooden yoke, the weight of which sat mainly on the back of
the shoulders. As a result, though Lengua women always
walked about like stallions in spring, the women of Schoenbach stooped forward whether they carried water or not.
Which was a becoming posture for a woman, according to
Elder Wiebe the Younger. Humility is required, humility in
keeping with a bowed head and eyes fixed upon the dust from
which all come and to which all must again return when He
comes to judge on His mighty throne. Looking everywhere

with unblinking shamelessness can lead to nothing but – things like the Lengua women who in their savage dances were said to lay their hand on any man they pleased, to lead him to whatever she wanted, out of the firelight. Not that anyone, and certainly not the Elder, had ever seen an Indian dance. But they had heard, and knew. It was what must happen when women stared about and held themselves so erect, so fluidly and powerfully free.

And Anna Friesen knew it very nearly happened to her.

Not that she ever walked like that. (Twenty-five years later a visiting American scientist would conjecture that Lengua and most other Chaco Indian groups were matriarchies, but when this was explained it would merely corroborate what the ministers had read all along from the Bible concerning heathen; by denying the divine order that the husband is the head and authority of the wife, for Adam was created first and then Eve, the Lenguas simply showed themselves to be, as Elder Wiebe the Younger quoted, "given up to uncleanness through the lusts of their own hearts, to dishonor their own bodies between themselves.") Anna never knew how her body walked. No mirror is necessary to re-braid hair and there was no water or even windowpane to reflect her posture. But she knew that once she did not keep her eyes where they belonged and that one seeing was enough. She never thought it through, piece by piece; she never had or would think that way; Marie's complex, reasoned planning, which simmered long and boiled over sometimes when the three sisters were alone, merely made Tina smile but Anna very nearly physically ill. She could not, she did not in the least want to think like that. It was repulsive. It would have been equally repulsive for her to recognize, even for an instant, that she could possibly behave like one of those brown women whose rags, if any, hung shamelessly open wherever they hung and who with one casual shift slid her sleepy child from breast to hip; but there was not anything nearly as precise as that. Only something she might have recognized as a stray whiff of possible, of faintest potential perhaps, if she could have worked out her sensations so articulately. She could not, of course; she did not want to. She knew only that once she did not keep her eyes where they belonged and that suddenly she was terrified at the sound or sight of the Elder in *hauptcheuik* once a month or when he came to preach in Schoenbach, though he had always spoken softly to her as to any girl, and could not read a verse, leave alone sing from the *Kirchenbuch*. Nor so much as think her prayers to herself when she knelt with her sisters, but only mumble sounds that would have horrified even Marie had they all not been too exhausted to listen to each other at the end of each day when they fell upon their grass mattresses. And what had happened happened because of the well.

Everyone knew without any direct mention of the matter that it was particularly proper for the Kanadier women in a village like Schoenbach to keep their eyes and heads down. In mid-1930 the Russlander were settled in Fernland Colony just west of Simons; their freight carts also passed through Schoenbach on the trail to Endstation. These Russlander were Mennonites, of course, and had the same family names; indeed, some were perhaps even relatives, too distant to be precise about but when colony and village and name and great-grandfather's given names agreed, surmise was safe. They spoke the same Lowgerman as the Kanadier, though with a very different accent, with some unheard-of words. And they had emigrated only once for their faith. Not that the Kanadier were proud; Elder Wiebe the Younger preached that pride was the most devilish of the Devil's many weapons. Besides there was no need for pride. It was simply a fact that a child in Simons Colony might know; their fathers left Russia in 1874-80 and emigrated to Canada because the Russian world was becoming impossible for their beliefs, but these Russlander found theirs adjustable enough to stay on until

1929. How they had become modern it was unnecessary to discuss; some, they heard, had attended technical schools and even universities in Petersburg or Kiev, perhaps Moscow. No wonder communists had to take their land away before they would leave.

Elder Wiebe the Older, who remembered very clearly the trek from Russia to Canada now almost sixty years ago and who had led them from Canada to Paraguay in 1928 not because the Canadian Government was taking land away from anyone but because, he affirmed again, it no longer allowed them to run their own schools in the German biblical way they wished, as it had promised them it would allow forever when they moved to Canada in 1874, held his last sermon three weeks after the Kanadier drove to Endstation to help cart the first Russlander to their land. He did not mention Russlander. Without raising his thin old voice but with his great jaw thrust forward as Anna had always seen him, he intoned that the Bible, the Catechism and the *Kirchenbuch*, the plow and the shovel were the faith of their fathers. It was enough for them, and it is enough for their children and children's children, now and for evermore. To have too much is to want more. New ideas, book learning, singing in several voices are unnecessary and dangerous. The desire for knowledge leads to pride and self-deception. To long for change is to fight one's destiny. Fighting one's destiny is rebellion against God. Man's duty is to obey, pray, work, and wait in terror for God's wrath.

So when Russlander men began driving through Schoenbach, as they must on their way to Endstation, cracking their whips above the ambling oxen and sometimes yodeling greetings in Lowgerman, Anna had no problem about where to look. Kornelius and Isaak told stories; when they met the Russlander on the trail, or perhaps camped nearby, they would hear them sing songs probably not even found in a Catholic hymnbook; of millers and soldiers riding to the hunt, and lovers. Those Russlander certainly knew nothing about *tschmaking*, as they called it, in the Chaco – they used breast-straps instead of collars on the few horses they had and almost choked them to death in the mudholes – but they could sing Highgerman and Russian in different voices that sounded like coyotes or wolves under the moon in Canada, and laugh and quarrel far into the night. And crazy to laugh! Hearing this, Anna knew without being told, as did every Kanadier girl, that despite their Mennonite names and talk, these men were too different, too wrong and – obvious – to even think about, leave alone remember where gaunt faces, glimpsed for an instant, broke into smile, their carefree greeting brushed something to an unwonted shiver. They would not get into heaven. When their slow procession stopped at the well it was best to wait on the path far down the road, or better yet, return later as they did for Paraguay officers. And remember, as Anna did, that on Saturday Abraham K. Funk would come and with her sit another long tongue-heavy evening away.

Abraham K. Funk was never much in her thoughts. Why he should be there when the Russlander drove by she did not try to understand; whenever it happened she simply felt later that he should have been. Neither did she explain to herself where he had been so lost that her thoughts had never once found him the day she looked into the well, but she felt a discomfort that morning which she sometimes experienced in early summer, a discomfort that came with Marie's hard jaw set and the Northwind rising with the sun and roaring like a furnace down the village street, grinding at grass roofs, blasting sand through cracks in curled doors and into windows pinned over tight with canvas. Under its shriek they heard the Russlander carts creak by south; they could not be seen for the blanket of sand winding about them. Once in an eddy Anna peered out of the dark house and distinguished a hunched shape high above the eight-foot wheels and the piled sacks before it was again hurled away. But for her dress pasted tight over her body and the crunch of her teeth, it might have been a Canadian blizzard. And she did not want to think of Canada; she had been too young to know.

When the last sounds were by a long time she shouldered her yoke, folded a cloth inside each pail cover and told her mother she would try now. Out the gate she went backwards, lunging back and pausing, the pails banging together before her when she could not hold them, staggering in the moving drifts of the hollowed path and lunging on again. Once the north-wind betrayed her and she fell heavily back, one palm striking down on a cactus spine swept bare by the sand. She scraped it off against a pail, pulled her yoke on again. She fought, reached the fence around Klaus Wiebe's grave marker, but that was no protection. None at all. When she gained the well at last she sank in the shelter of its high box. After a time the pain of her hand burned through her exhaustion and she began to fumble at the thorns. She leaned against the well, picking with a corner of broken fingernail, putting her teeth to her hard hand. It comforted her. She was doing something necessary and need not, for the moment, outface the wind.

That was how Joseph Hiebert found her. His left ox had gone lame overnight and before he reached his village he would be a day behind the others. He did not much care. One trek on this road taught there was no companionship in a storm; each driver must remain with his cart and a minute or a day behind made no difference to the misery. The Schoenbach well emerged briefly and he cupped his hands, bellowing to his span. Before he had his canteen and matté-horn unstrapped the lame ox was already kneeling, sinking to the hot earth, the yoke dragging the other down also. He bent forward against the weight of the wind and coming round the well's corner almost bumped head-on into the girl with the heel of her hand to her mouth.

For Anna what followed was like the whole day, tangled in impossible convolutions of sweat and heat and sand and an unwanting to remember. Bits flashed at her sharp as diamonds unbidden. He was there, long and thin in black lines, and his name too, though he had no face, and his voice suddenly laughed and his hand, barely wider than her own but with a long steel tension, clamped hers so tightly while he pricked at the thorns with a needle he pulled from a pocket case that even when she twitched involuntarily her hand hard on his hard knee moved not the slightest. And the new drink the Paraguayan soldiers, his voice said, had discovered: cold water drained over yerba leaves made terere, and it strained out scum and sand and most puddle-water taste. It felt scratchy, then smooth as cream in her throat as she sucked it up through his metal bambillia; that was really no worse than drinking from his canteen since the pail was impossible in the storm and she was thirsty. Yerba with hot water gave matté, a drink only Kanadier men drank, but yerba and unheated water gave terere, faintly musty and unknown till then, therefore outside regulation. Like the day, the black mustache, the Lowgerman voice slightly off-accented, it was new; strange. And the stories the voice told – perhaps they sat in the well's shelter for hours with the sand blasting by them down the street, removing paratodo tree and cart and oxen and Schoenbach – of the jokes he tried on Kanadier boys like telling them that one edge of the world was just beyond a few yards of brush north off the trail and how some of them always drove on the south after that – did he think she believed the world was round or how could he expect her to laugh at such blasphemy, as she did? – or how he had ridden along Indian trails and found not very far west of Fernland Colony the end of the world nailed shut with boards or how he was teaching four Kanadier boys "Kommt ein Vogel geflogen" in four-part harmony so they could sing something new at the next Simons Colony engagement. There, exactly there she should have said about Abraham K. Funk; she should have thought at least. But she had done neither, neither then nor before that when for some unnecessary reason she looked over the well-rim with Joseph Hiebert at the ripples of his sunken pail drift gently across, away, and after a time the wind lulled an instant and the fierce sunlight showed them strangely side by side, looking together at themselves; and through the endless blue sky.

Once after that she saw him. He came with Isaak on the yard where her father and Kornelius were fixing a cultivator. He left alone a little later. She could just distinguish his length from where she was with her sisters on the back field; she was leaning a moment against the smooth warped handle of the grubbing hoe. From somewhere she heard his father was a Russlander preacher who usually preached from the Bible, but who never read his sermons and leaped around behind the pulpit. One day she heard young Hiebert had heaved his load of cotton bales onto the flatcar at Endstation and then climbed up too. To the men standing about his yoke of oxen, staring up at him, he yelled, "Keep them, butcher them up!" Years later it was heard in the two colonies that he was in Buenos Aires. The streets there were said to be narrower than Chaco roads, but between unbelievable buildings of stone and glass and jammed with millions of people, black, white, brown. It was said someone had seen him eating and drinking at a table with a painted woman.

There came a time when Anna Funk no longer remembered, from one year to the next, how once at the end of the village with Joseph Hiebert she bent down and looked into (or was it out of) the Schoenbach well as if to see to the end of the blue sky. Then she would think, "I last remembered, oh, it must be almost three years. I have almost forgotten." And she would smile a little at her baby of that year, a quietness she knew as joy moving within her.

EIGHT

The Cloister of the Lilies

THE SIXTH DAY pushing east up the Lower Tunguska River from the Yenisei the captain swore they could shoot him but his boat would move not one centimeter further. For two days guards had stood behind him, rifles cocked at his head, but this was the limit; it was worth his life, damn all Transportation Planning, to freeze tight; they could do just as they pleased. In a flat below the next gorge the commandant finally gave in. He had the prisoners break the ice through to the bank, baggage, prisoners, guards were unloaded, and the boat surged back downstream in a gray haze of woodsmoke and curses.

The prisoners dragged their baggage to the trail that led up among the stunted spruce. The ground was low, frozen marsh but the snow soft and after a kilometer even the commandant's profanity, the guards' boots, rifle butts, were useless. They piled their duffel in a ruined building beside the trail and trudged on, leaving two guards and three prisoners to wait there for transport from camp.

The Cossack stared after them, then up at the pale sun. "Only five hours light," he said. "They'll have to move, forty kilometers they said."

Friesen stamped his feet in the snow and heaved again at

his end of a beam. "They'll have to move," he said. "In this cold."

"Get it up," the guard Ur said. He never swore; when his eyebrow twitched any prisoner jumped.

They lurched with the splintered beam into the ruin. Dmitri was trying to blow up a fire in what had once been a fireplace and Palazov sat batting at the smoke with his rifle, cursing. By dusk they had the chimney stump clear enough for the fire to draw.

Friesen touched his frozen fingers into the puddles by the hearthstone, rubbing carefully, working moisture at their burn. Once frozen almost any cold froze them again. Dmitri fed splinters into the fire. "This was a place," Friesen said. "One thousand two hundred kilometers from a town. With even colored stone on the floor. Look."

"All of it is smashed, the barns too. All the barns," Dmitri said.

"The second floor too. Up there there's little rooms along both sides where the roof fell in, small almost like a solitary in camp. You know, or the Lubjanka, hunn."

"With such nice walls," Dmitri said. "A fireplace of stone and such nice –"

"It was a jail," said Ur. He was taking apart his rifle; they had never seen him without it.

The prisoners said nothing. For an instant they had almost forgotten the guards.

Palazov spit on the hearthstone. "You think the czar, shit him, didn't have some out here?" He laughed looking at Friesen. "You fucking kulak."

From the jumble piled high against the collapsed end of the room came the Cossack's big voice. "Here's a picture. On the wall, a whole row . . ."

Even Palazov moved to see. Level with a man's eye on the leaning wall was a design. The Cossack rubbed away grime between cracks and they saw a long row of them burst in sudden pure white on what could once have been a gray wall.

"What the hell is that?" Palazov said.

"A flower, a row of flowers . . ." Dmitri held a burning stick closer.

The Cossack was still rubbing. "Here, here's a big one," he said.

They all stared.

Friesen said finally, "That's white lilies. The stem bends like that and that's the white lily. The big one half cracked is like for a center, you know, here."

"Small balls in hell," Palazov said.

"You know what this place was?" Dmitri said, his gaunt face in the firelight pale as the flowers with excitement. "This place was a cloister, see, there is a vase here, here under the stem, holding the stem, see! The vase and lilies are for Mary the Mother of –"

"A cloister way the sh –" Palazov shouted.

"Yes! Yes! Out far away, in exile, that is what they wanted, far away so no one could find them or bother and they could humble and bow their wills and fast and pray to –"

Ur's rifle knocked him prone against the duffel.

"Hail Mary full of grace," he recited, sing-song. His greasy gunrag whirled like an artist's brush on the mucked wall. "Stalin lies with thee. Blessed be the fruit of thy womb." He tilted back, roaring, hand and rifle barrel stroking the splayed outline of a woman's flanks, the white lily sprouting at their spread. "Mother of bastards, we absolutely adore thee."

Palazov grabbed the torch from Dmitri and took a step closer. His breath caught. Hesitantly his hand rose, touched the vase.

Granular snow stung in the wind as the cold tightened. Outside Friesen could no longer see the spruce beyond the clearing. But inside, when they lay it was bearable, almost warm. Warmth enough to stir the lice in the bundles. They had pulled in enough beams and the guards could think of nothing more for them to do. The guards flanked the fireplace, one sitting and one dozing.

"Maybe it'll be a big blizzard," Friesen said to the Cossack, "and we can lie still, sleep."

"Food."

"Well . . ."

"If they don't come, we won't get ration tomorrow."

The guards of course had a food box, but that meant nothing for the prisoners.

"At least it wouldn't be chopping; only sleep."

"You have to make it up on rest days, so where are you ahead?" The Cossack had been in eight years. There was nothing about guards and commandants and camps that he did not know, and he had no hope of surviving his twenty-year sentence.

"I never got more than five rest days a year yet," Friesen said. "At Totjma you know we worked one hundred and sixteen days once. I'll take a blizzard."

"Not without ration. You can never make it up on the slop."

"I'll take a blizzard, here."

The ceiling was too high in the great ruined room, but fortunately there were no windows. They had piled over the holes in the ceiling and propped boards against the door opening. The firelight sprayed sparks when Dmitri nudged a rafter in further.

"Another day," he said softly. He was arranging a bed by Friesen's feet. "One thousand three hundred seventeen."

"You count them?"

"Do you not?"

"No," Friesen said. That was not exactly true and he added, "Only the anniversary. November 23, 1929, that's when they took me."

"I cannot think of that," Dmitri said; he was laying himself down in the slow, careful way of prisoners.

"Think of the lilies," Friesen said.

"A day ends, maybe, but no year."

"'Of the field. They toil not, neither do they spin, yet your heavenly Father car. . . .'"

"Will we get ration tomorrow?"

"Not if it keeps up."

Dmitri scratched. The ruin groaned under the storm. Take therefore no thought for the morrow. For the morrow shall take thought. For the morrow of itself. Sufficient, sufficient. . . .

Friesen was asleep, entirely in the dead sleep of prisoners, and then he was awake, entirely, motionless but ready to leap, his eyes opening into the room past the rim of his coat in the barest firelight. There had been a shout. A shot? No guard sat by the fire. Really? He was moving when the doorhole jerked, figures thrusting out of the storm, Ur's puzzled voice, ". . . sleepy, missing like that . . . ," panting like four beasts, an immense shape, Ur swiping a tall half down with a thud of his rifle. "I didn't even nick you?"

"No," a man's voice gasped.

"Friesen," Ur said, "plug the hole. Dmitri."

Friesen crawled, shivering, to the door. A very near thing, that move. The light flared momentarily. Ur was searching the first; a second shape huddled between the door and the fireplace, heaving coughs. The coughs formed white puffs in the murky light.

Ur muttered, searching, "You didn't expect a fire, or a gun, poking around here, eh? Ugh!" The man went sprawling. "Some kind of shithead, running away without one piece of bread."

"We do not come, from your camp," the man said where he lay.

"What do you know, my camp. Up you, here, to the light," Ur said. "You'll put me inside, no more watchtowers for me."

"We do not come from your camp," the man said hopelessly.

Ur exclaimed suddenly, "Huh! Palazov, here's a woman!"

Palazov jerked erect. "Wha?"

"A woman, here's a godda –" but the cough tore across his exclamation.

Ur and Palazov stood looking at the mound, sunk down beside the fire.

"You sure?" Palazov asked.

"Well you stupid –"

Palazov laughed aloud. "It's been so fucking long!"

"And that you forget!" They roared together, standing against the firelight.

"She's sick," the man said.

They both turned a little. They stood with their right hands in their pockets, rifles slanted in the crooks of their arms.

"Maybe he wants a deal," Ur said.

"What?" Palazov muttered.

"A deal. There's a chance. The storm and we tired like we are, maybe we fall asleep."

"Yeah?" Palazov said slowly.

"Neither of us has, of course, seen these traitors to the proletariat, these rightless sonsabitches. How could we, listen to that outside. Tired like we are."

The man said nothing.

"Up, come on," Ur suddenly kicked the Cossack and Friesen. "Pile some of that junk around here, right here. Cozy little wall, a nest by the fire."

"Move!" said Palazov.

They piled up boxes carefully before the woman, avoiding the rags on which they had lain. As Friesen set another box carefully in place under his eyes the woman coughed again, the entire indistinguishable mound of her shaking, coughs bursting white as from a fissure, terribly. Consider the – consider – Friesen wheeled.

"She's sick, maybe almost . . ." then he stopped. Ur's face glinted in the firelight.

"You say something, Friesen."

"No."

"I thought I heard something."

"Yeah," Palazov answered. "I thought I heard something."

"Me too," said Ur in his flat voice.

The wall they had built could not fall over. Friesen had a bundle and was pressing it firmly against the box the Cossack held in place, concentrating that the wall they had built would not fall over.

"No," he said again.

"Prisoners sometimes try to escape, stupid as it is," Ur said. "A guard sometimes has to rush his shot and the prisoner gets accidentally hit in a very painful place."

"Yeah," said Palazov. "It happens, when they run. Often between the legs."

Ur's gunbarrel stabbed Friesen in the kidneys. "Holy holy Friesen, saying verses, groaning hymns in the work gang, praying with hands folded like Christ, maybe a little for yourself with a gun at your ass, eh? Maybe you wouldn't need no gun, who knows if you ever get another chance. There's always ten more years waiting if accidentally you survive the first, eh?" The barrel was excruciating; Friesen had to brace himself rigid against it not to knock over the wall.

"Shit, Ur," Palazov was breathing heavily, "waste it on that shit. Let's go!"

Dmitri pushed the burning logs together now and then. The building was warmer than prison barracks ever were; almost dry; and they could stretch out completely on the bundles. The only sound was the storm whistling, the rustle and grunt of the guards.

A louse scrabbled in Friesen's armpit and he clamped his arm but it did no good. He lay staring at the darkness, longing in despair for sleep. At first the fugitive had been shivering, but now even that bare motion was gone, lying where he was thrown so near they would touch if either moved a hand. Came a time Friesen thought everything that could had happened; and then he was wrong; again. He was stretching on the rack again, beyond endurance. Finally he could not contain himself; he had to, and turned, groaning a little as if in sleep. Palazov did not move.

"Why run?" he whispered. "Barracks at least are barracks."

Ur was snoring now. Palazov sat propped against the wall before the fire, stroking his rifle. Suddenly, without a motion, the man's whisper came,

"I did not want to. But she is sick."

"Then . . ."

"I did not want to." Friesen could barely distinguish words, his good ear at the man's shoulder. "But she cannot last a month as God is good and she wants to see the children at last."

"That's where they'll watch."

"But she must see them, the children. There is the possibility we could see them, even a minute or two as God is good."

The woman coughed again and Palazov started. He kicked Dmitri. For some time the fire flared gigantic shapes across the ceiling.

"How long had you left?" Friesen whispered.

"We had both three years labor, then five free exile."

"They say alone is sometimes better, if there's any chance." He added, "And you wouldn't get another ten labor."

"But she has perhaps a month. As God is good."

"What did they say you did?"

"They said we, and others, burned the GPU office in our village." Friesen caught his breath almost in laughter; he had not heard that one before. "The area superintendent was coming and they had to burn it, their records were so bad, we heard."

Friesen said again, "She should have tried alone."

"Sometimes she needs help. A man can do things."

"Yeah. Lie still, listen."

He said that not able to see anything of the man; his voice came from the flickering darkness, a sound straight and thin as if it originated in no body to give it feeling or texture. A thin sound that began and ceased in the rigid darkness. Friesen longed suddenly, violently, to see the man; if he would so much as stir! and then his own whisper rose in his memory and he was glad, glad for the nothing. Just as the voice came, "He cannot be a hero."

"Yeah, but to just . . ." Friesen stopped.

"How long of your ten have you done?"

"Three; almost."

"What you said to him there, it was very foolish. You know that. You cannot fight like that. They have everything to fight like that."

Friesen said nothing.

"There is one thing only, if you still care about anything. Survive."

"Hunn?"

"Survive."

Friesen said, "My wife and three daughters are in Paraguay. I have two letters."

"Paraguay? What is Paraguay?"

"South America, in the middle of –"

"South America," the voice breathed. For an instant it held almost a wisp of motion, a hint, but only for an instant.

Friesen's face hurt; he was nearly smiling in the darkness. "It's not cold there, only terrible hot. They never need thick clothes. They don't have much but there's no police. Not a single one." He was almost talking aloud.

After a silence the man whispered, "You had perhaps a son?"

"Ah-h." Then he could manage, "No, no, I have – no son."

The other was silent; finally perhaps sleeping, as it seemed to Friesen. He should not have thought of his wife and daughters, even for the one jolt of happiness and then it would not have worked round – the voice had pushed, had permitted nothing else. He should have thought of stretching out in some warmth and no more hungry than usual yet and not too many lice and the great lilies he could manage to wipe a little cleaner perhaps and see again, surely once before they went. The woman coughed then and he remembered again the white in the darkness of her coughing; Ur was standing. He stood black against the firelight, then made a sound, bent down. When he finally got up from behind the wall, Palazov lay down. Dmitri groaned, unmoving. The Cossack slept soundlessly; he never stirred. When he lay down he was motionless, asleep like the very dead.

The man's voice was in his ear, "You see, she will be dead in a month as God is good and she wants to see them. Once, even for a minute. There is the possibility two can make it. If only a minute."

"These won't make a deal."

"We know."

They were silent.

"Otherwise the possibility is not at all."

"'Possibility'? What else can you expect, anywhere? And anybody shoots you at last they'll get promoted."

"It has been seven years."

Friesen hissed, "How can you stand it, lying here, only lying!"

The toneless voice went on, "How close could I get to him?"

"Ur – he's quickest. Maybe a meter, or one and a half."

"And if I could, if it were possible for me, if I did, what

would the authorities do?" Friesen said nothing. "Now we are only fugitives, and they have us, they know it. There is the possibility, as God is good. But I try something foolish . . ."

Friesen almost said, "Ur's a devil, he'll never . . ." but he had done. He should have done much sooner. The stillness lengthened. Friesen was suddenly overpoweringly glad the man had avoided him, had talked right past, away from him. He could not remember such great, clean relief. And outside the storm shrieked assurance for at least tomorrow, assurance no prisoner ever had from one day to the next, the longing for which beyond even hunger and cruelty sometimes forced him near what he knew could only be madness. Now sleep come, come quickly, yes, come, oh yes –

"If your wife was here," the thin voice drove on, "in four or five years you could think all I have thought, in the camps. There is only this: if you want anything, survive. There is nothing else. There is nothing else. If you have nothing left you want, jump up and be done, quickly.

"You think you could not stand it. Your wife, it would be, it is worse for you than for her, you in your manliness. After three years, and alone, you still can think like a great man: 'I could never let them do that to my wife.' But she and I, we are no longer like that. We are nothing at all now except there is one thing she wants, I want for her. To them she is a hole. She cannot care about that; there is only one thing she wants. So I, the great man, I can think, 'I cannot endure it. To see her tortured down to her very life, I cannot endure it'? She has to take it, and I take it. For her I take it, I lie still. There is only one thing we both want and the rest is nothing, as God is good."

It had gone on and on, straight and inflectionless. Like his voice the man's form lay totally devoid of human motion. As if stretched out and nailed down on its back.

"You . . . at least show . . ."

"What?"

"Her, at least."

"We have been in labor exile seven years together."

Into the long void suddenly Friesen was talking, talking, ". . . leave Gnadenfeld because I was classified kulak and all the other children would have been lost too, I had to. At least for the girls and my wife. There was only Moscow left and some of our people had got passports, got out to Germany and even Canada our neighbors – once they had our Jakob, would they ever let him out, once they had him? How could I know they would? You know, who ever heard of such a thing from the GPU hunn? To let a young man, twenty and strong, big and strong, out once they had him? And then caught me in Moscow too and Jakob hadn't come to Moscow and neighbors wrote he did something to a party man, at home in our village where he was free already and could have . . . but I had to leave, you know for Moscow. Who ever heard of the GP . . ."

Friesen's words vanished into darkness, as they had risen. They ran like a desert stream, visible an instant and gone.

"He was in jail?"

Friesen started. "Hunn?"

"Your son, he was in jail, arrested by –"

"They came to our farm, and I was away so they took him then."

"And when you came back you took your other children and went to Moscow, to leave?"

"But I left plenty of money for him, over six hundred rubles, if by some miracle . . . you know . . . but he never came. To Moscow."

There was silence.

"We arranged to send him food in prison. Every two days. Who ever heard of the GPU letting. . . ."

Friesen's words sank away. The woman coughed half-suppressed, dreadfully, behind the wall. After a long time the fugitive's voice came, as motionlessly mechanical as it had always been.

"A man could endure ten years. I knew one. Perhaps even

get out. If he was set enough in his mind and body and learns carefully, and watches, always. There is the possibility. But he cannot afford thinking what you keep thinking; then it is impossible. You must survive. That is all. Survive as God is good."

"You keep saying that," Friesen whispered.

"Yes."

"Then why did all this happen? To us?"

"To live, it is the most necessary possibility."

Friesen was never sure to what question the man gave this answer. Whenever he thought about what they had whispered in that nameless ruin, he and the faceless immobile man whose name and place he never knew, before whose immobile accepted suffering his own had finally broken between his teeth, sometimes he thought the man meant that to live was the essential; sometimes that to live a good God was the essential; sometimes that to live, to survive and to suffer was the essential; sometimes that any one of them could be the most essential. Any one a possibility. And sometimes the possibility was all of these things essential at the same time, any one impossible without any one other, and after one spasm of thought it did not mean any of them at all. Whatever the man had said had been some kind of stupidity, some punch-deadened prisoner's immovable madness that sometimes, just as thought touched it, seemed for an instant to blaze with a kind of holy wisdom that was; that could be known, but never said. If he remembered it correctly; later he could never be quite sure about that either. Oh, some things remained sharp as chiseled stone, but so much vanished, even that once learned rote as a child and known in perfect thoughtlessness. In the gray immobility of years there was only your muscles, your gut throbbing now, never so much as a smile or a scrap of paper to shore remembrance of the day past. Leave alone the impossible waving lily fields of Mennonite childhood. And whenever he thought about that place, fumbled out each image and each word, as he could remember, it had to end there because after the man said that, Friesen, as if falling through an opened door, fell into sleep.

He was awake and shivering. He had never heard Ur curse before and he was shivering beyond any cold as he awoke. The doorhole gaped and there was almost light outside. After a time Friesen understood Ur was cursing himself.

"Holy!" Palazov was sitting up, his astonishment choking obscenity. "It was that second time, Ur," he said finally. "You had to fall asleep."

Ur kicked aside what was left of the door covering and plunged out. Palazov stared after him.

"And I was saving up big for morning," he said.

The storm had wiped up every track and laid drifts over the trail. It was two days before sleighs broke through from the camp barracks. They were very weak by then and Dmitri had to be dragged to the sleigh. After about twenty kilometers, when Friesen collapsed to the pure white snow for the third time, the guards let him ride too. The Cossack walked every step. When Friesen left Lower Tunguska Camp in spring four and a half years later, their gang was marched out by a different road to a labor camp on the Lena River. Further east.

NINE

Drink Ye All of It

THE LOUSE WAS tight against the skin, blunt feelers motionless. A moment before it had been scrabbling terribly, lurching whenever one of its six flailing legs found purchase against a hair or in some, invisible even to his eyes, fold of scalp. He edged the candle nearer, concentrating. But that was worse; he did not know if he would have been able to see the fuzz on its body, perhaps even on its legs and head, because they never stopped; more light always seemed to push them to frenzy. But then it happened. It lurched once more, rooted, and stopped. He could almost, almost – absolutely inert, its pin head rigid from its body and clearly tight against the skin in the shadow of a hair – finally. He moved his head a centimeter. Suddenly its head reddened transparent, blooming rose and fading as quickly. Again and again, a glow in the hair shadow. When the pulsation dulled – a fantastic bellows – he saw the body. Long and full, tightly segmented like a tiny corded bale nipped in at the tail, scab brown against white hair, whiter skin.

"David!" The light jerked. "The blanket, it's

clutched tight	*gasps muffled unmovable tighter and*
tighter to prayers	*groaning sleighs in the fantastic*
it's inhuman cold	*enough to split the rigid dead in*

the cemetery behind the domed church   worming
along   the bottom of the sky split with
light   they will hear they will hear they will see they
will   a child's cry will poke through any snow-piled
wall   o my lovely quiet quiet and warm under the
blankets tight so so so you must still to the river   a
little more still to the river   o my lovely you must
so   tight   tight and still when the blankets come
away   no terror or sound to wake anyone
again   or rocking lull ever to stillness either

smoking!"

He jerked, hand leaping over the blanket. For an instant it
burned.

"What were you thinking, the candle so close? You could
have set –"

"It wasn't, not really, smoking; more steam," he fingered
the blanket, his heart slowing. "Mostly steam."

"And so tight! Can't I even go out a minute when I have to
and leave you alone a minute? You should know – anyone
knows enough now – about tight hold –"

"Yes," he said. "Yes. Just a minute, not so tight. There was a
louse, I –"

"Louse!" One arm clawed for the baby, the candle thrust at
him, hot with wax. "I cleaned them all out, every single rag,
this morning, every morning! Where was it, na?"

He raised the candle. The pore patterns, the exact roots of
the hair; the louse was gone. Without his intense myopia he
could not have distinguished the faint discoloration where it
had paused. A head so small it found a hair's shade.

"Na?" Erna said at his ear. Because of his eyes, when he was
there she always let him look.

"It's hidden itself, well," he shifted the blanket; a flicker; it
was under the baby's ear. "Here."

"Just kill it, quick."

In the dark crowded room she was too close for him to look at it again. A prick of grit and moisture. Both rubbed away against his

> *quick little rub-out it's never been never been never been a*
> *spot of blood it can't be seen against my dirt black trousers*

leg. A tiny cry drifted through the steady noise; Erna was saying,

"... blanket, can you hear, will you fold the blanket against the wall?"

He did that, and Erna sat on the ledge, too wide for a bench and too narrow for a bed, though they were happy enough now to have eight feet of such space and it sometimes warm. He pushed a bundle against her to lean; the candlelight gouged her cheek gaunt with exhaustion; he snubbed it out with the flame, she fumbling at the buttons on her dress. He stood slack above her, eyes on the indistinguishable wall, smelling the vagaries of the packed room, quite and mercifully blank. Her hand touched behind his thigh and he sat beside her.

"I didn't want to nag, *Liebche*," she murmured.

"I know."

"It's just so – uggh – here. And after waiting so long the piston wrong yet too."

"The driver himself went, now."

"Now at least he'll know the size. How long yet?"

He could hear the baby at her breast. Its face flickered in faint blotches, her skin white and gray and gone. Always inevitably longer than you could allow yourself to fear, than you dared fear. Probably this piston was the only size they had in Nen-chiang and the driver would have to go all the way to Tsit-sihar, or Harbin itself; dear God.

"Are you listening? David?"

"Yes."

"It was six days for the helper, when he goes himself

three in the morning and forty below do you know what
we're doing you idiot   running away   skipping
out lawbreakers understand   criminals   they
see us and we're shot not a question asked or needed
traders don't travel fifty sleighs piled up with seven kids
and slabs of frozen beef and bundled women see   that
cow you cut her loose   and that sewing machine
off   it's your skin understand   the horses you
trade there if you don't kill them pulling all
this   think   they can three hours belly-
deep   we're lawbreakers and over the river we're
nothing if we're rightless here soon less than nothing there
do you know a word Chinese toem schinda noch
immol   cut loose that cow you   get your skin

it should be quicker, na?"

"Yes." But he left his tone unguarded.

"David, listen. I can't feed the baby on this linseed and barley – I just don't have enough milk. I just tried feeding him before and now . . . David, are you listening? David!"

He put his long arm about her shoulder, fingers gentle on her mouth. He could hear the baby now, crying its thin cry, feel it nudging against her slack breast. A louse moved on his belly.

"I just don't have enough; I never had much. And at two months."

"They don't have cows here," he said. "You know that. We thank God there was even this shed half underground stinking and lousy as it is."

"O we thank God, yes."

"Well."

"But the other food?"

"*Schatz*, we pooled it all, right away. Everything. You know that. The committee had –"

"That committee. Yes, the committee, you looked, sure,

where they showed, but some here, some there, under the rags, skirts maybe," she paused. The child's tiny body fit his hand, his arm cradling it against her, her to him. "Maybe not even only some. And only two of you committee here now, the others who knows where ahead. We *have* to get more for the baby. David."

"No," he said. "How could we look, that way? Now. Tomorrow I'll try that next village again. There's the one blanket yet, to trade. Bernhard tried today, but maybe I can find some food, somewhere, or anything –"

"Would they take my sweater?"

"You can't."

"We have to have milk!"

"There is none."

"Na, Greta Suderman . . ."

He said nothing.

"It still hurts her."

"It's eleven days!"

"She – gets rid of it. She – should tie herself up, tight, but she can't stand that, anything tight, now. She just screams. And the babies keep crying."

Their baby was crying. Directly into his face bent at her shoulder. A rattly sound, almost metallic, but it still butted her.

"David." She must have said it several times.

"What?"

"Will you?"

"How – it's not – I can't ask her."

"Just ask her to

once concede necessity once concede   still no concep-
tion of ways to be lacerated   infinite ways   never
ending multifoliate ways

come here."

"Or hold the baby," she said after a moment.

"She won't."

"Just ask."

"How can I ask, even that. Everybody –"

"'Everybody'!" she tugged loose from him. "Since when does 'everybody' make you do anything?" In his silence she plunged on, "And whose fault, David, just tell me whose fault was –"

"Not yet," he said heavily and pushed up, away from her. She was truly desperate, now; he had not quite realized that. "Not everybody, yet." He fumbled his glasses out of his inside pocket and the smeared dark leaped to precise lines, black and flame-yellow. He threaded between the duffel piled down the center of the room, past each family grouped on its share of the hollow warm-air ledge that circled the base of the room and was heated by the one fire in it. A truly fantastic "hotel" on a nowhere road with not one hint of the "oriental splendor" you read of in books and dreamt of like a child; a nothing *schlarafenland* except perhaps for the tiny woman squatted, bound, motionless as a trussed doll all day by the fire. Birchwoods everywhere and one little fire; if this hovel were not half underground even the impassive owner would be stiff beside that minute flame. He struck a roof post and stopped; it was a great deal better than a ruined bus on an empty road, dear God.

Little Bernhard Rogalski and his sister crouched face to face on their ledge; with five small stones they played a game known only to themselves. Suddenly Hannili whispered,

"That makes three hams and four loaves of *bulchi*."

"Yeah. I'll go tell the committee," Bernie answered, and slid the five stones under his shirt. In a second they emerged again, and moving.

Hannili said, "And don't forget the Epps."

The stones flew and suddenly Bernie said, "Yeah. There's the milk, just right," and the stones vanished, to her this time. "And fresh buns too."

"Made with butter?" Her face refolded in bliss. "Won't they be so happy!"

David moved from behind the post; his flesh hung limp from his bones, chill and then warm as if fever were alternating him. Then he was already there, the obscurest corner of the short narrow shed; the best that could be done for them. For a moment he could see nothing and his heart moved more freely, but then he deciphered a whitish cloth folding, and refolding in a lap. Greta Suderman, alone. He shivered, clearing his throat and her face lifted, grayish in the black.

"Where's Dan?" he said finally.

She shrugged; he could make out the edges of her solid outline. "Maybe still looking, that bus motor."

"There's not much point looking in there, till we get a piston. The driver's gone for one," he said needlessly. He could not think of anything to say, he who invariably had all the words he had need of.

"As long as it's a machine, that he likes. What does he care for anything but machines."

"He cares . . . about you."

"Sure. And since the river –"

"Well –"

"Don't you think I can say it? Why shouldn't I say it?"

It was like nothing he had ever heard with a married woman; about themselves Mennonite couples never spoke to anyone, especially the women. Perhaps never even to themselves. Did they think it?

"You – it maybe helps, him; it's hard for him, as for you."

"He was always turning around, 'Keep it quiet, can't you keep one kid at least a little quiet?' That's all he said, 'one

crossing that river loosened so much so much we never knew we had to tie   tied

kid' . . ."

"Greta," he said, "you couldn't know, how could you, and

he was afraid. We were all, and God only knows how close – we knew it would be –"

She was standing before him, gray face upturned to his. "Were you? Were you?"

"What?"

"Afraid. Were you?"

"I – we were all afraid, what else –"

"You, you were afraid, you?"

"I was afraid."

"Then why did you do it?"

"Why?" Here too? His mind retreated by instinct. "We all agreed, why."

"What kind of answer is that?"

"It's the ans –"

"My sister and her man live in Number Four, my brother there too, and what chance have they now, or how'll they be now? They'll never get –"

"We talked that all through," he had to cut in, "a hundred times. Dan was there. It was the only way it would work, for us, you know that. We all agreed every man raised his hand, and it's worse than bad but we can't help –"

She said, hard as if she had not heard a word. "Why do you come here for Dan?"

"I – I didn't come for him. We – Erna wondered if you – could you come a minu . . ."

He hung helpless; she was staring up at him, but her face fuzzed in the darkness through his glasses and he could not see her eyes; that was what had made it possible, he realized, to voice even as much as he had.

And perhaps for her also. For sudden as a hawk stooping she seized his right hand and thrust it into her warm, hard bosom. "Who doesn't know what you want, Mr. Committee Chairman! Your little David, your precious little living David," she was almost spitting in his face, pulling it down to hers with the pressure on his hand, he paralysed. "And my

Jonka in that shallow hole being clawed right now out of that shallow hole by Manchurian wolves, wolves like these bloodsuckers here of Chinese, of Mennonites that just want the last bit of whatever it is you –"

"Greta. Greta." His eyes clenched cold and hot he could not endure what he felt from her; he had to raise his other hand against her face, her eyes, and hold it against her also, against his cold paralysed hands her body shuddering like a wound.

"Ah God, ah-h, listen, Greta listen to me! It was accident, it almost happened to three other mothers, it was God's will, you cannot blame yourself and your friends, it is God's will little Jonka is with the Lord now, free from pain – can't you see how some of these – he is free now, happy, and there will be more children for you, this was your first but when in some far land we are free then –"

She had thrust him away and was down in the dark of the ledge again. Behind him the Rogalski children played, oblivious, and the room rustled, whimpered on in its desolate slur. Much later, if they ever got – such a thought – some might remember, perhaps rebuild a tinge of gossip out of this, but now everyone was honed in on himself, his immediate helpless, empty hands. He sat down beside Greta Suderman. She seemed almost singing, under her breath:

". . . men, they say it so easy, words dropping 'there will be more, there will be more where this one comes from.' What do they know about the pain of bringing them into the world, the pain of carrying them and the pain of bringing them into the world. Men invent machines and big ideas and make plans and tear whole villages and countries out by the roots and the women keep quiet and lie down for them and bake bread and carry children and when we hold them too – you shovel them under like a log. What of anything do you know, men . . ."

"Greta, we all have pain. Who is without?"

Her face jerked up. "What hurts you? Your relatives all in Canada and Paraguay, your David still

*say nothing say nothing not a word   to anyone even
Bernhard   over the river now and say nothing   see and do what's under your nose that's right
concentrate don't allow one wide implication to so much
as flicker   anywhere   concentrate   now only
now in a*

blanket."

"Greta, we all —" but she tugged aside at his tone.

"All right," he said, "all right. I'll say it. To you. Say that all
those left in the villages beyond the river, our brothers and
sisters there, those we all sang with 'Now Thank We All Our
God' in church festivals, once, we . . ." his hands were both
on her arm and her breath caught like a gasp but now she
did not move. "We left them in the lurch, back there, on the
other side."

"But . . . what – what was there, else?"

"Nothing."

"And in the village you," she said, "we all agreed . . ."

"I know that: we all agreed. Others fled before in families,
but we did as a village. That's why we're all together; we are
here only as we all are, here. We aren't Sudermans and Epps
and Rogalskis and Martens any more, we are all one family,
and what we do is for all. Otherwise what possible way can we
live with our —" he stopped right there. Say things he had never
yet worked to the end in thought, dear God.

"The Dyck baby is – weak too," she murmured suddenly.

Leaning back he could just make out her profile. "We
haven't asked you, and we won't. You have had more than your
share of pain. We won't ask now if you have extra food. But we
are together now, just as we are together when the bus breaks
down and we all have to get out and stand, and walk, cold in
the snow. If you can share what you have with Dyck's child,
with ours, you'll give more than you can believe."

He stood up and the fingers of his right hand momentarily

brushed her hair as he went, through the room taut with body smells, hunched down and thrust himself up through the door. Daylight was always a shock; except for some calf-gut covered holes the hut made no pretense at windows. And the grizzly cold. Across the yard by the tangle of thorn fence a huddle of Mennonite coats and hats; as if trying to warm the useless bus dragged there five days before by a team of oxen. He turned. The sun had sunk behind the jagged mountains, but its last light bronzed the belly of cloud. He removed his glasses and distance smeared to burnished orange in blue. The page in the Blagoveshchensk Library, so rarely used by the "intellectually starved proletariat" now liberated – ha –

> *Ta-Hsing-An-Ling Shan-mo the Greater Khingan Mountains of China seven hundred miles from the great bend of the Amur River south to the eastern limits of the Gobi Desert the eastern bastion of the Mongolian plateaus mountain system an important divide intercepts the wet southeasterly winds a factor in the contrast between fertile Manchuria and arid Mongolia   great tilted blocks of rock toward fertile Manchuria   impossible to tell under snow or the rocks either from crossing the Lesser Khingans   only the motor wheeze and too much snow and too many people and stuff and everything too much   much too little   black and jagged from here black in the heartless cold   nothing like the thin blue sketch, beckoning from across the river the beautiful mocking blue*

"David? What are you out here, with no coat?"

Bernhard. His friend; sheepskin collar high, eyes blue as mountains.

"Nothing else yet on the road?" he asked, unnecessarily.

"Not since the driver got the cart. You better go in."

"Yeah. Almost time for service."

"Think it will work?"

"Even with just two buns and water – and a deacon – we perhaps should have tried . . ."

"It could, should help most of them. Encourage."

". . . but tonight, it's the best night. I think."

"Should we call *schultenbot* after?" Bernhard asked.

"No. Time enough tomorrow, eh?"

"Yeah. Time enough."

David was suddenly violently cold; the fever indicator had flipped over and stuck. They were walking together to the door and he shivered, thrusting his hands into his pockets; then Bernhard put his bare hand on his shoulder. A big, warm hand; David was for two steps on their village street, smoke like prayer through trees at every chimney and his father striding beside him on the squeaking snow, under the immense solidity of a loved hand, voice high above, "Supper is waiting, Mama will have supper long waiting."

for I have received from the Lord that which also I delivered unto you that the Lord Jesus the same night in which he was betrayed took

"The beginning is hard, most hard, who can doubt that? We see it all over, everywhere in the Soviet Union, not just here, the first always have to work harder and endure more to help the great commune happen, that the revolution broke through capitalism to get, to make real for our children, ah, for them it will be good with no rich or poor. No hungry. No one fighting for more, everyone living for everyone else, working in peace and harmony on the common land, together to the fields in the morning, together eating our bread and living in quiet and singing of our land, with always enough to eat and work, everyone our friends, everyone workers." The friendly face smiled, the lips drawn back on huge gold teeth etched by tobacco. Oh there's no doubt *he* means it, the good of the people, the morals raised and the poor fed and no stealing and everyone equal but why do they have to kick out our religion; how can you be a Mennonite under communists; why can't we teach our young people to pray and study the Bible; why do we have to work for those mud-lazy Russians when some won't lift a finger if they know they'll get fed; look at our kolkhoz doing twenty times more than theirs and getting no more; is that fair? "And how many head of cattle are in this village? And horses? The young people, do they like to go to church? Who is your minister? Why is that decoration with a verse on your wall? How wide is the village street? Who is your other minister? Did you get a good tariff when you moved here from where?" Questions and questions, one asking and smiling and the other never a word, just writing, and three days later the same two whirl up in their droshky and the other one starts, ask, ask. The same questions and the first writes, and who can remember exactly what he said, these new eyes glaring, and what differences they find when they compare what was said three days before? "We don't believe you won't go over, I'm a Mennonite too and know you better than a five-kopeck piece, we know you've got some Chinee stuck in a cellar and you'll up some night, run for it and what will happen to our village then, you think, and you run? They'll herd us into camps and slave us till the hide rots off our bones. We're watching; don't ever doubt it. We'll take turns day and night watching you, every man in our village, if you make one move we'll know and if we can't get ready in time to take off too we'll get a man out fast enough to report you, you hear. You can't leave us." But how could even one village get over, forty or fifty sleighs trying to get past guards that are quadrupled already along the river; work out your own plan, can we help it your leaders don't plan, how can we help that? We have our wives and children, don't we? We can't think for everyone, can we? You think you can watch us every time we go to the backhouse? And if you pressure one of us, maybe he won't hear about plans either, here in his own village, until the last minute when he can't report to you anyway; so? "What a beautiful black stallion, what do you want for him?" "No." "I'll buy him." "I'm not selling." "Not selling? I'll give you twice your price, just ask it." "I'm not selling." "Of course not. He's worth more over the river, eh, in Chinee dollars, not rubles that aren't worth a thing anyway." "I'm not selling." "Of course not, not when you're going over the river and that guide Wong Gordon lying in Harder's cellar, eh, for a good black night. Of course not." "All right, three hundred rubles." "Just three hundred? They won't be worth fifty dollars over the river, why so little?" "Would I sell my best horse if we were going over the river?" "Well, that's true, and only three hundred, well, maybe not tonight anyway." But it had to be done, otherwise everyone in the market at Ura would have known, once that devil of a Chinese smuggler made such an offer, so the black had to go and in the forty below when no guard from Number Four could stand outside or believe anything could happen that same night they took

> *bread and when he had given thanks he brake it and said take eat this is my body which is broken for you this do in remembrance*

"But we'll have to eat when we get over there, *schinda noch immol*, I've got this all packed, solid." "Yes, solid, and your horses can't drag it three kilometers through the snow, we're not going a highway. Off, here." "But eat." "Trade the horses, make sure they live. You, the cow stays. Put her in the barn, somebody from – they can have her. A whole bed in there? Off." "My father made it!" "Off." "I told my brother, that's why they're here. If he can't go along he says he's riding ahead." "What?" "Ahead, to the border guards." "All right. But you have to care for him, over there. They've started, move!" "The Bergen sleigh broke, we have to –" "No, the rest keep moving, the young men, on the horses, here, unload the sleigh, on the snow, what are these trunks, gold?" "But the dishes, our family clock!" "So bust your sleigh and sit there and hatch your dishes God in heaven do you know we're criminals running? Two on this sleigh, these three here and maybe the rest will hold till the river. Move!" "We can't face the cold. The children." "Cover them, keep them under, it's not far. The first are on the bank, now get, move there." "Why didn't you tell me before tonight. I didn't have a thing ready, not even the steer butchered or my wife the buns, we've got nothing because you didn't say a word till one minute – come or you have to stay!" "How could we, the GPU always sitting at your door; drinking tea!" "Could I help that, them drinking tea?" "No. And we couldn't either. Move." "You have to stop, stop, you have to, my father's . . ." "What?" "He must be dead, my father. His heart doesn't . . ." "We can't stop here, there's their village, you can see it in the dawn, that's where they live, over there. Hold him up, we can't stop we're almost at the bank, hold him, the bank's too steep for the horses, the first down but if we don't all get over without breaking down they'll still, move!" "The bank, the sleigh it . . ." "You want to break up and drag that junk under the guns of the GPU and all over the world, dear God

the same manner he took the cup saying this cup is the new
testament in my blood this do as oft ye drink it in remem-
brance

In the elbow of the Amur between Blagoveshchensk and the Jewish Autonomous Oblast where the black spongy silt of irregular floods between Zeya and Bureya Rivers lay deeper than digging and the wheat grew man-high, where the spring rain turned flying-eaved Russian houses and the ground black as tar, the Mennonite boys fishing for sturgeon, puddling in eggs and swimming in the wide Amur with a hundred shifting shoals and phoenix-like islands, the young men swimming their horses over one night and returning another with silk and saccharine and aluminum dishes and stories of freedom and how to get to Harbin, free-state city of the world, where the earth froze and split in giant cracks to break a horse's leg and where in autumn a tall man stretching could barely see over the sunflowers and wheat and corn to the faint blue straggle of the Great Khingans, distant as a whiff of oriental scent, a world that lay afar and tempted, in this elbow of the river between Blagoveshchensk and the Jewish Autonomous Oblast it was done. In the thirties of this century. After the February and October revolutions and the anarchy and the starvation the brotherhood in North America sent relief and pledged their farms and businesses and gave and twenty-five thousand left for Canada and Paraguay and Brazil and the United States with debts in the millions pledged for them. But in the elbow of the Amur each family, at best each village, stood alone. We cannot think of Number Four; can *we* get out? How can we think of what happens to them; can *we* get out? The guards are everywhere the GPU smiling and writing down answers and giving us code names for when we inform on our neighbors and smiling, slipping us privileges or threats with lips curled back on gold tobacco-stained teeth and looking down from their horses, smiling, what can we think about Number Four? Can we cover up well enough they won't suspect we're going, tonight; can we get out. We can't let Franz know because his sister is in Number Four, they'll tell them, it's all out and *kaput*; tell him an hour before we leave; can we get out? Across the elbow of the giant Amur twelve kilometers of field and three of frozen river without being heard

> *in remembrance of me for as often as ye eat this bread and drink this cup ye do show*

A miracle. There it was, a miracle that whole village, almost sixty sleighs creaking past them as dawn leered up at forty below and the breaking of runners and screaming horses down six-meter banks and across the hummucked ice and between islands and standing clustered by the shacks of Ku-Fani in the rising sunlight like spears, singing "Almighty God we praise thee now," the Chinese and children staring at women and men crying, in wonder, and grown women and men crying they suddenly knew for more reasons than they had till that moment recognized possible, looking across the frozen Amur back to the flat lines of the valley they had fled and escaped, its faint clumps of smoke like blue mounds on the rigid air

> *the Lord's death till he come wherefore whosoever shall eat and drink unworthily shall be guilty of the body and blood of the Lord but let a man examine himself and so let him eat of that bread and drink of that cup for he who eats and drinks unworthily eats and drinks damnation to himself*

And bargaining and almost losing the Russian-speaking guide Wong Gordon (You said half horses, now only twenty-one?). And searched by the Chinese police and paying head-tax (Five rubles each, large or small, living or dead; so bury that old man on the island, in the river, and don't pay). And arguing in Russian for visas and buses for the six hundred kilometers to Tsitsihar and the other five hundred by rail to Harbin (We'll have to pool everything we have; some haven't anything, even with the horses sold, those that have must borrow those that haven't). And four days jammed two- and three-deep in groaning buses with gas and vomit and labor groans (Quick, everyone out, everyone, just the women, into the cold it won't be long). And a quick burial by the side of the road (Far over yonder sea of stars there is a better land). And sputtering on the steep turns of the Lesser Khingans till gasp and stop and immobility (There must be a village ahead somewhere, somewhere at least a shed). Carrying each other in the frozen darkness with fear like teeth at their bones the last four kilometers and stumbling into this earthen hole

not discerning the Lord's body   the same night in
which he was betrayed   drinking damnation

He was completely awake, firelight glow somewhere beyond his feet, the darkness a cave over his head. He felt neither cold nor hot. There had been a white hill from which he had drunk as at a cup to complete disintegrating satiation, but his mother had said, "Na but child, cover yourself, running around so naked" and Franz, "Can't you even lift that, thinkling weakling?" and his father looking through the orchard and across the valley, "Over every hilltop is peace." Erna, her teeth on his shoulder, trying to smother her moans driving against him, an exhaustion worming down to his rattly roots while the club ran a distant drumming over the horse a windbroken shaft in the dirty snow, "You godless beast, stop it, it's dead, stop it!" He was completely awake but he half sat up to stir the slopes and shadows of his sleep; they would be clear enough by morning still. He was not aware of a sound; only an unbroken rush in his ear, as if someone nearby were gasping, and the pillar that went through the glow and up into darkness. He lay back and sight at least was gone. His mind lay open, indefensible as being, churning with every one collected thing sharp like a broken tooth yet coated and smeared with every other. He knew no formula prayers except the to him now useless ones of childhood and he was clutching like a sinking man to an endless chain hand over hand that slid out at each touch "O dear God my blessed Lord Jesus dearest God and the Holy Spirit and blessed Savior o Lord Jesus my God, my God" until it lifted him at last at terrifying last to the inevitable. The hills blue under their feet in late afternoon sunlight and his father pointing down the flat distance below them, along the black line of the Molotschna River twisting south to the sea, its villages hedged precisely into order by trees and roads, half a hundred of them the length of the river and its small valley tributaries, hedged in by trees and crowned in blue clumps of smoke in the brilliant winter air: "This valley our fathers saw over a hundred years ago, from here, empty then till in God's time they saw black river-laid earth from here," and moved and built and grew fat and cared nothing. Until the revolution. It had to be it had to be. Erna was turned from him to the earth wall, the baby between her arms and drawn-up knees in the hollow of her belly. His hand wandered the full mound of her hip and thigh, but there was cold now and he hunched closer. Her thighs loosened for his hand without a stir and after a time all particular sensation had merged to her length of comfort against him. He wanted to wake all night, to hold her consciously so that he would never forget that – 'every tree-top moves through you: every breath cease' – but rest at last was slackening his limbs and he knew fully he could never possibly forget. He murmured soundlessly against her hair, "Tomorrow, my *Liebche*, – O God my God – my only *Liebche*, tomorrow," as he sank away to sleep.

On the tomorrow morning two events piled upon them so quickly and without warning that they seemed to David as intent to break his resolve as they broke up the group's invariable breakfast of barley-and-linseed mush and hot water. He had not yet considered how what was necessary could be done, and abruptly there was no thinking time.

The first event was the coincident arrival of two vehicles, one a truck covered with canvas and half filled with Chinese going south and the other a large half-ruined car coming north containing only a driver and Aaron Martens. The first four of the five buses had arrived uneventfully at Nen-chiang but when, after two days arranging other transportation, the last had not arrived, Martens had remained in the old walled city to wait while the rest proceeded to Tsitsihar. After another four days, Martens, fearing the worst, hired the car and came back looking for them. It was immediately clear that if they stacked both car and half-empty truck to the ragged roof they might possibly all get to Nen-chiang by evening; they could move as soon as they could pack! But money. The driver of the ruined bus had been paid in advance and was now somewhere in the towns ahead looking for a piston. The assistant could refund nothing from his own empty pockets, and his violent gestures showed only too clearly that if his employer's passengers escaped, that escape's payment would be taken out of his own hide. The truck driver would allow nothing aboard unless he had money in hand. The driver of the car, in contrast to the singing and snorting of these two, made no sound whatever. He stood with his hands inside his quilted jacket, stared at the gesticulating and shouting (both Chinese and Mennonites seemed maddened almost as much by bits-and-pieces translation as by each other's demands), and every few moments walked around his car clockwise, then counter-clockwise, and impassively kicked each tire.

While Bernhard and Aaron Martens tried negotiating without money, David organized the group; first the loathed mush must be eaten; even if they moved at last, they still needed food. Almost all the children, huge eyes watching him from bony faces, were now hungry enough to eat it. David saw Hannili beside her mother; the little girl bent obediently to her bowl; her throat thickened in rebellion as

dear father somewhere in the world there must be food over mountains or plains or seas

she swallowed. Eating was done and packing underway when Bernhard nudged David's shoulder.

"It'll go," Bernhard said. "The truck driver finally caught on if he takes us he has a chance at least of getting paid; otherwise he has just his half load, right now. He caught on after he felt Suderman's pillow. So we can get to Nen-chiang, if we can get most of it into those two wrecks."

"What happens there for money?"

"Martens thinks we can telegraph to the others to Tsitsihar

for more. There's a refugee home there, they'd lend it, surely, on the German consul's word from Harbin. And maybe we can find the driver of our bus, get some back from him?"

"Huh!"

"Yeah, that's what I told Martens. But at least we get out of this hole. You talked to old Stoneface?"

"I was waiting for you. You get along so nice with him."

Bernhard laughed without humor; they moved together through the now almost happy noise and jumble. Toward the second event.

They looked away from the flat inscrutable face, the few Russian words, and their eyes met in the light from the brazier fire.

"He wants money," Bernhard murmured in Lowgerman.

"He wants money," David responded.

"He will take only money."

"He will take only money."

They were boys together, the stones falling plunk! plink! into the Molotschna River, the mud squashing up between their toes.

"Who has money?"

"Who has money?"

"Do you have money?"

"Do you have money?"

"The whole wide world screams for money."

"My throat is sore."

"Mine too," Bernhard said, and stopped.

David followed his glance. Little Bernie and Hannili stood at Bernhard's knee, looking up from one to the other in huge-eyed incomprehension. Bernhard jerked, muttered in Russian,

"Let him feel that coat again."

It was clear the bearskin coat was attractive; thick, soft and warm. It would be very warm, yes. But a great deal of food had been eaten

barley-and-linseed and melted-snow water

by after all almost fifty people now the morning of the eighth
day and that must be replaced by money and the house so full
no one else had stopped and all the firewood

*trees everywhere birch like hair and we cut every stick that
burned here*

needed to warm the whole building all day and all night: a few
Russian words, gestures, avoided looks said all this eloquently,
most eloquently. David looked past him to the woman sitting
on the wall ledge above the brazier. He had not seen her walk
since they celled there; perhaps she could not. Her trousered
legs with their infant's feet lay before her like folded sticks. She
seemed to do nothing but look at them; though Erna said she
shifted pots on the grate and had looked up at her, once. Perhaps once or twice a year the man lifted her from her spot and
dusted her; an icon with tiny folded feet.

"What?" Bernhard said very loudly in Russian.

The nasal voice sang again and the two men stared at each
other.

"Did you – hear – that?" Bernhard stuttered finally.

"Yes."

"He has to have part money and the coat – or if not part
money then . . ."

David finished, "A girl, the lightest, yellow hair, thirteen or
fourt . . ."

"Yes, yes," the man's face held no expression but his tone
had shifted. "No money, girl, no money." He seemed then to
look up at their silence; slowly he put down the coat at their
feet and began to unbutton his shirt. They watched him in his
ritual.

"Great god."

"It isn't the first time," David said.

Behind them children talked and people staggered with

bundles, but the two men and two children stood before the Chinese, watching him pull first one sleeve of his shirt stiff, then the body, then the other sleeve; put the seams of each into his mouth and his yellowish teeth snap rapidly along them, crackling like a brisk fire. When he had completed every seam he lifted the shirt above the brazier and shook it gently. Broken lice fell like soot. Then he slowly began putting the shirt on again.

"What!" Bernhard jerked.

"Somebody got sold."

"David, you can't –"

He brayed a laugh; two grotesque hands clawed in him, wrung him like a sodden rag. "Don't be stupid, Bern, don't be all stupid."

"Or," the man's arm up one sleeve, perhaps looking up at them again, "good, good, my wife good three four year, little girl, there," his browless eyelid seemed to flicker an instant. He inserted his arm carefully in the other sleeve.

"Listen, Bern, listen," David said rapidly, "I know what, just stay here a minute and I'll take the children to their mother and bring, what I think. Just take it easy, easy. Stay here, so he won't think . . ."

He fumbled for the children's hands and before he was finished was propelling them down the room. Between pushing, heaving people: "*Bengel*, hold what you're holding!" "Take that sack, it's tied." "But it's so heavy, Pa!" "Child, that sweater, where did –" "Lift it!" Hannili was patting his hand, David recognized when they were almost through to the Rogalski space on the ledge.

"Uncle David, Uncle David," Hannili murmured.

"What?" He patted Bernie, nudged him through the confusion and stooped.

She was totally calm. "Will I have to, like the man said, will I –"

"No, of course not," he hugged her tiny body tight so she could not see him. "He wasn't talking about you, about that, at all. Nothing like that. He doesn't know what he's saying in Russian."

"Oh David," Erna greeted him, "feel him, na, just feel him! He's

yes I do I do it must be it has to be yes dear God but how now in this tangle I need time she needs time I need she will understand yes but how now so fast dearest God my God how

like a little drum. Greta is packing, now."

"Yes," he said, his hand dropping from his son to her waist, the other taking off his glasses, kissing her, his face tight to hers.

"David! Everybody –"

He laughed almost. "Since when is it 'everybody', eh. In this dark hole." He turned as she chuckled. "Where's the blanket?"

"But we only have two left."

"Have you tied it in?"

"That bundle," she said, resigned. "I tied it outside, knowing you, but we only have –"

"*Liebche*! We need it for old Stoneface." He was tugging at the

a shirt the extra shirt   perhaps underclothes but she   and how

blanket and she laughed aloud behind him, nudging him with the baby.

"Oh David, it's so *good*, we're leaving this

leaving   shirt and underclothes   leaving

terrible place. Leaving!"

"Yes. Thank God," he added, a flicker coming to him and he plunged toward it, reckless of anything save his reckless faith, "oh, I should have a shirt, a few underclothes. There's some more got over ... I'm to go back ... help them. On the way, you see."

"David?"

"They're over, near Ku-Fani."

"But how –"

"The truck, you know it came from the north. One of them, the people, had the message."

"But if you knew since it came ..."

"It came so ... it was ... just decided who ... a few minutes. And there was no need, my *Liebche*, to worry you ... for you to worry," he patted her knee beside him, fumbling

> *say no evil do it not do you think God's eye is not on his children large and small and his ear hears each word fall*

with the shirt in the bundle. "In a day ... two or three days we'll catch up with you. It'll take a while, that you get out of Nen-chiang."

"Why is it always –"

"You just forget the others. Aaron came back now."

"When someone had to go over the first time to find what was what, it was you, and then when someone had to find a guide, again. Why is it always –"

"You just forget the others, someone has to do it. Just a shirt, for the few days, and some underclothes. Here they are, here."

He kissed her again and went; quickly, before his embrace betrayed him. Facing the landlord again he piled blanket, shirt, underclothes together onto the bearskin coat and thrust them against the landlord's folded legs. "There," he said, standing erect beside Bernhard, "That's enough. That's all. No more. You had two pillows, three blankets, before, three days now." The woman sat there like a stone and his emotion almost broke from him, "That, those – things can keep you warm you –" but he found himself as the landlord's voice began and rose in obvious anger. He turned, pulling Bernhard with him. "That's, that's – let's finish loading and get out."

But the truck was already crammed to the last inch, heads protruding above duffel everywhere under the canvas, breathing clouds into the hard air. Erna and the baby, some others, were standing by the car. David nudged Bernhard.

"Just a minute, there's something."

"What?"

"Over here, a little away." At the corner of the hut where they had stood the night before, David said rapidly, "I'm going back. I told Erna that some more got over, message from one of those in the truck, that I was going back to help them get on the road too. Will you take care of –"

"David," Bernhard was shaking him, hand clenched on his shoulder. "We did what we could! We all signed the paper and left it, like you said, that we were doing it on our own, that no one else in any single village, not one person, knew of it. That it was our work, no one else's fault or crime. We did that, that's all we could do!"

"But it's not enough. You know that."

"But what else . . ."

"You know."

Bernhard stared at him.

"But . . . but, you can't be stubborn like this! They'll keep you and it won't help one of the others a bit. We know that. Don't you? You know that. You're just throwing –"

"No. We strongly suspect that, but we can't know, that. Absolutely. The way we know some other things."

They were both silent. The truck growled into gear, whined to the gap in the thorn fence and stopped. Aaron Martens was waving to them and David pulled Bernhard past the corner of the hut. In the brilliant cold the mountains stood like fangs along the horizon.

"David," Bernhard said, suddenly quiet, "let us draw lots, who shall go."

"No." He removed his glasses and looked into his friend's eyes. Blue eyes he had known and loved as long as he had memory. "No. You have three children, I one. And Erna can take it; I know. I'll send her a letter . . . when I know more. Will you help her then? Care for her, and the boy."

"Yes, David."

"Yes."

And they both knew only life-long trust made their decisions possible, though neither could have said who faced the bigger task. They gripped hands a moment, not able now to look at each other, then David put on his glasses and they walked back across the yard. The truck waited at the gap, the car plumed smoke.

"My sheepskin is better," Bernhard said, "take it. South it won't be so bad."

"Okay." They exchanged coats as they walked. "You tell Aaron; it'll encourage everyone, a few days."

"Yes." It was clear what had to be said, to whom. For the moment. "Goodbye David."

"Goodbye Bern."

"God be with you."

"And with you."

Bernhard walked on alone to the truck. Erna was waiting by the car. David held her a moment and put his face against his son, but he did not kiss either. "If it's more than four days, I'll write you a letter. But it shouldn't. You'll be a few days in Nen-chiang." Then Aaron Martens was there, shaking his hand, talking, and after another touch she was in the car. It whined toward the gap and he walked beside it, stuffed to the ceiling with people and bundles, smiling at Erna, waving. At the fence he stopped; the last he could distinguish was Greta Suderman's face turning in the rear window. He went back to the hovel, face down to the trampled snow but seeing nothing.

It was two days before he accumulated enough rides to reach Ku-Fani. The Chinese villagers were astonished to see him return, especially Wong Gordon who had done his work for the Mennonites and returned three days before from Nen-chiang. His shiny warm face tangled itself even more than usual over his limited Russian: no, no one since they; the border was sealed; patrols rode in threes every half hour; he had watched them just that morning through his binoculars. When he was brought to understand what David intended, he argued until evening in a torrent of Chinese mixed with Russian fragments. Finally, still shaking his head, he sketched a route between the islands; he was adamant David take a horse.

"Otherwise, guard see, no chance, no chance."

"But if I can't get it back . . ."

"Plenty horses, plenty horses. Come back, keep one, okay." And he fed David the best he had in his house. Nothing like hot ham and potatoes; it was such good "Chinee" food David could hardly swallow it.

That night he crossed behind islands, waited for a patrol to pass, and was back in the wide fields. Thanks to Wong Gordon, the matter was as easy as any other time he crossed alone. The horse he rode moved or stood at a touch; the patrols were obviously not watching for a single rider coming back from China. Before midnight he rode into his village. He could not have imagined such a dead quiet. Every animal was gone but otherwise seemingly not a stick had been stirred in fourteen days. He tied the horse in the stable, threw together some loose hay from the other cribs, and went into the house. There was a candle stub in the usual place; he lit that. The lamp on the table had burned out to its wick; the dishes from their last eating stood there, marked still with food. Enough paper too in his corner. It must be as cold inside as out: windows clear as ice. Face the bedroom later; plenty of time, plenty. In the moonlight outside he thought he could see the blue line

> *over every hilltop is peace now every treetop moves*
> *through you: every breath cease   the nestlings hush*
> *in the wood now   only wait   you too will soon*
> *have peace.*

of the mountains far away, beautiful as they had ever been from there. But he knew now that was only his imagination. Or romantic nostalgia.

He turned back to the candle on the table, and sat down. He hooked off his glasses. Someone must have been in here: a louse moved past a crumb on the table, of all things. He took off his mittens, pushed back the sleeve of his sheepskin. He felt nothing. He sat motionless, watching, waiting for the louse to come to his warm flesh.

TEN

My Life: That's As It Was (4)

WHO CAN KNOW why the big men of this world and governments do what they do? Even at the end of the world like Paraguay. The Russlander had come here to get away from wars and it wasn't two years, before they hardly had mud houses built among the bitter-grass, and there were patrols and searches on every road and planning for flight and their Zentrale, just a few houses but some good wells, was being bombed. So it goes. They were more west than we and so more in it. Then the Bolivian soldiers went home in June, 1935 so Paraguay won the war. In the two colonies we had a few more roads going to places that weren't any use and lots of iron and shells and gasoline tins lying around where they had shot. Kornelius and Isaak drove to Boqueron once and came back with a wagonful that Bernhard Fehr, who was a blacksmith, banged into something useful. An old man, Nicholas N. Toews, in Halbstadt in our colony was shot trying to get his daughter away from some soldiers, four girls had been mishandled and two babies born but one died in a week and we had been able to buy our flour a little longer by trading watermelons and peanuts and bread to the soldiers. They left us alone now; for which we thanked God with full hearts, and for the peace. We had church and the schools were our own. We planted orange and grapefruit trees and flowers in our yards and tried to grow enough cotton and kaffir so it would last not only for the ants, *butzas*, grasshoppers, parrots, doves, but also for us and perhaps even our cattle. At least every few years.

After 1933 we slowly got better on our feet (though in Paraguay who except a few big pushers can ever say he's standing?) and one by one the children married: Kornelius, who waited till he was 25, Tina, and then Anna, Isaak, and Greta too in 1937, only 17 but there was nothing to wait for so why hold her up. That left the woman's work to me. We tried to help them start, on land in new villages or on some old farm that became empty, with a horse and plow for each boy (we didn't have oxen any more) and a cow and some things for inside for each girl. It all came so much at once, six married in five years and sometimes the drought that for some we just couldn't do it. Then we helped those a little later. No more died. We had enough to eat and we could live in peace. My man was bitten by a snake in 1939 and couldn't walk for seven months because it took so long to get the serum from Fernland Zentrale where the doctor was.

Outside of that we lived and worked in quiet and peace. Children like Johann and Friedl never ask because they know nothing about such things and what you tell them seems to have been all piled up at once, as you tell it, but older ones not from Paraguay sometimes ask, and if they don't sometimes they say things that show they are thinking it anyway, "What do you do, one year end to the next, living there in that wilderness?" Well, what do you do. There are always the new grandchildren on the way, but mostly you wait for the rain. The time goes and you look back and years have passed you never thought of as years; the only thing you really remember, even the birth years of the children, is how they fit with the rain. When it rains you harness every horse and work the land till it's too dry; then you wait again. If it rains often enough, long enough, you plant cotton that grows so in February you can pick with all your children and perhaps even some Indians three or four times over. Then you have cashcrop, and then you can't count the ribs of your cattle either. So 1936 was bad for rain and too good for grasshoppers, 1940 very good for rain, 1941 maybe the worst we ever had. For a month we fed our cows the inside of bottle trees. That was about the war, too, and some Russlander got very excited and almost lost themselves; their dreams were still too strong about the Ukraine, of black ground and beautiful cool green land; valleys and hills. From them for a few years we heard German soldiers were where once Mennonite farms and villages, my father's too, had stood in Russia. One day two cars like the Chaco had never seen came through Schoenbach from Endstation, going to Zentrale. It was the American consul from Asuncion with some Paraguayan officers. The strongest dreamers then had to leave Fernland; after the war their children came back, but not they. After the war too some Mennonites, displaced persons they called them, who had come along with the retreating German army out of the Ukraine, came from Germany and made a new colony on the big campos south of Simons and Fernland Colonies. They called the new colony Neuheim. They had it very hard, maybe more than anyone because almost every man was gone and those that were had been wounded; there were three whole villages of just women and children trying to set up farms. The North Americans helped them, and we too.

We Kanadier had enough to eat, saw mostly Mennonites from one year to the next except a few Lengua Indians, and then Chulupis too, working for us for their food or just stopping at our good well. Until 1948 when we had forty-six grandchildren, eight from our Esther in Canada and eleven from Anna who was married fourteen years and very regular. Only Abram and Johann were at home, both big and strong boys. My man was sixty-seven, I was sixty-five. Some talk about these things too much, as if that was all their life was. But our little ones like it too, and it won't be long with me.

It hardly seemed worth the claptrap for a woman sixty-five. In 1946, a good year for rain, a dentist came to the colonies for six months and he pulled out all my stumps and teeth. The set he made didn't fit exactly and I bit myself on the tongue. He changed it then but after about two years I had to go to the doctor in Fernland Zentrale because the tongue wouldn't heal. He gave me something to rub, but it helped nothing and I had to go back in three months. Then he cut a little piece off, sent it to Asuncion on the mail plane and in a week they said I had cancer on my tongue. They said I had to go to the cancer clinic in Buenos Aires, Argentina.

We talked long about it. All the children came too from their farms and the spring looked as if it could be worse than 1941 but my man said right from the start there was nothing to talk about. On September 6, 1948 our second last son Abram and Daniel M. Kaehlers' Anna made their marriage in our house in the evening. Next day Johann drove us with the buggy to Endstation where we took the train to Puerto Casado. It was the first time I had been to Casado since 1927 but the ride was so easy behind our horses and the railroad was laid to kilometer 145, not 76 like then. At Casado my man and I went to the graveyard and the next day we got on the river boat to Asuncion. There we had to wait with papers and doctors looked at me, and on October 2 we came to Buenos Aires. I had forgotten how such a place was. There was so much of everything that even without anything else I would have been sick.

At morning we went to the Clinic. They knew about us from Asuncion and we could talk with a German doctor there who told us what they wanted with me. They put me on the operating table and gave me two needles under the tongue. The first one hurt very much but the second was not so bad and when they put four other needles, radium they said, all around the wound on my tongue I couldn't feel anything. The needles were like shingle nails, with a hole in the end where the doctor put a thread and out of my mouth and tied the string around my ear and taped, so if a needle came out I wouldn't swallow it up. They gave me pills to take if the pain got too much and we went back to our hotel. The hospital wanted ninety pesos a day and I couldn't understand anyway what the Spanish nurses said, so my man took care of me. I was supposed to have the needles in my tongue forty-eight hours.

I thought I had stood a few things in my life, but not everything, I found out then. Not pain like that when the freezing went. My man had to dissolve a tablet quickly and give it to me to drink but I couldn't swallow. My tongue was black, and thick so I couldn't close my mouth and when I just moved it to try and swallow I just swallowed blood. My man called the doctor, I think I was screaming a little. He came and said it didn't matter if it bled, but I did not take his pills; the other pain was still a little less than swallowing. Those were forty-eight hours like I had never had.

A month after they took the needles out they said we could go home for a month, but the trip cost so much we thought we should stay the whole time. My tongue actually healed and in late November I was strong again. The doctors said it was all gone and we could go home. On December 16, 1948, we came home in the Chaco; I was happy as a child for Christmas and so was my man Johann. And talk – well, my tongue was healed, wasn't it?

Every month I had to go to the doctor in Zentrale, and soon we knew many Russlanders. They were nice, some just like Kanadier. Finally I went every two months; when they had a doctor in Campo Grande I went there because it was fifty kilometers around less to go by buggy than Zentrale though there wasn't any Russlander visiting. Everything was good until

June, 1951, they found it again under the front of my tongue. We had to go to Buenos Aires; four needles two inches long this time for sixty hours. Then they said again it was gone and two months later we were home. But it was the same all over in 1953; now we knew Buenos Aires, had friends there, and needles four inches long that were supposed to be in ninety-six hours. Maybe they were. I can't remember that trip, though usually I have a clear mind. What I know is it comes from God, strength and sickness, want and plenty. And when we stood on the little ship looking at the piled up Buenos Aires get small behind us I said to my man, "There we're not going back, not again."

And we didn't. It came back the fourth time just a year later and they said it was too far for needles and they would operate in Asuncion. They had a clinic there now. I said to my Johann, what was the use of it, such an old thing, seventy almost seventy-one. We had only a few cattle left and what good was it to live a little more and then go meet my Lord with half of me already cut away.

"What do I do if you're all gone?" he said.

So I was in the hospital in Zentrale three days, then we flew to Asuncion and they operated. Three times, the longest six hours. They took half my tongue, right chin bone, and peeled off skin and lymphs and all kinds of things back off my shoulder and neck to the breast. They took skin from different places and sewed it on. They let my man stay all the time with me in the hospital. When they took off the bandages he said I looked like some old dress I had patched. Maybe too much, I said. The doctor, a professor at the University said I would never have lived but I had such strong nerves and everything. It was a wonder for him too, and I told him in as much Spanish as I had that it all comes from God. He smiled, nodding his head and saying, "Si, si!" but I don't think he believed it. To me he was a nice man, but very rich and smart.

Needles scared it less and less but I guess the knife was too much; the cancer never came back. We went home to Schoenbach; the children built us a small house on the yard of our farm and there we lived, happy and at peace. I healed together slanted but what could that matter to my face anyway. We were long ago used to the heat and the house stood by the grapefruit trees where we could have a garden and take care of the flowers along the village street.

With twelve children different things happen, but it always seemed to me ours were wider apart in being different than most. They were always obedient, yes, but some you could see without looking straight at them that they were thinking about it, obedient or not. With only young Johann left to marry we thought we knew about all that happens then, but with him it came strangest of all.

When I was in the hospital in Zentrale there was a nice Russlander nurse there that helped take care of me; her name was Susie Friesen, and when we came back from Asuncion the second Saturday Johann said he would get medicine for me and rode away at noon and didn't come back till so late in the dark we were just going to call the neighbors together to start looking. He had ridden to Zentrale, seventy kilometers around, when it was there in Campo Grande too, just twenty. Well, it was clear soon enough my medicine wasn't all he wanted in Zentrale; when we wove that together my man laughed and told him he was old enough; there were enough girls waiting in Simons Colony for a hundred boys but if she was a decent Christian, na, he worked and paid for his own pants he could wear them out anywhere he wanted, even on his seat in a saddle. Johann wouldn't tell, but how could Susie Friesen stay secret in Schoenbach? She was the last girl in the family and her mother was a widow and Johann was sometimes such a quiet sheephead about such things I couldn't understand how he ever started visiting when she had no brothers for excuse. That's what happens with a last child; with the others I never had time to think about it.

He was no sheephead about this and one Sunday he drove us to Zentrale for a first visit. They lived in a little house behind the hospital and had always been poor; she had come without husband and with three little girls to Paraguay. And then, as we talked, we found that we were related; that her husband, a man whom the GPU had taken in Moscow and who she had never heard of again – he must be now long dead – had been my right cousin. I remembered the village names, the given names my father said sometimes in Canada so long before, and they all fitted. The old Muttachi who would not go to Moscow had been my father's brother's – the one older by ten minutes – wife; he had been cut down by anarchists already in the Revolution and Mrs. Friesen told how she had met some people from what was once Gnadenfeld, Karatow Colony, among the Neuheimer who had come after the war and they had told her how her son had died under the hands of the GPU. And Muttachi later, old and alone, a burden on the collective farm as the kolkhoz leader had always said. Here they had been for twenty-two years in the Chaco, a few kilometers from us and poor, and we had known nothing. She took me into the bedroom then, and on the wall was a picture. Except for the beard, it was my father.

In the evening we drove home. The horses trotted and my man said, "To think, all those Friesen men, all such strong men, killed so terrible. And the women had to see it and live, and try to live."

I still couldn't say anything; Johann, driving, said, "Well, here's one Friesen left over. That's sure."

"You're a Friesen two times," my man said. "So just be careful." I looked at him; the moon was bright but he wasn't smiling.

That's how it is with the world: who can ever foresee how.

Susie said she would marry only if she could care for her mother, and what could have been better? The children built us our little house and Johann married and moved into our big one with his wife, and Mrs. Friesen in the little room where the girls had slept. Every Sunday Johann drove them to their church in Zentrale. She had had it too hard and only lived five months more; the things we talked together I will never forget, or repeat. I suppose some things in this world only God has to understand.

I had almost thought that a life as long as ours would come to its end slowly like a tree drying up by the roots. But no. One day my man was showing Johann's little Friedl how we used to make bitter-grass dolls and the next he was in the hospital. There was one in Campo Grande now so it was only ten kilometers. He looked so thin in the bed and pale, though he was sunburned, but he smiled.

"Always it was you in bed, now at last it's me." Then he laughed, not much because it hurt his chest. "When will we be in together?"

His head and beard were all white, like snow, but his eyes were like the first night in Friesens' *sommastov* fifty-four years before in Schoenbach, Manitoba when he just stood there, looking at me, and said, "Well we wanted us, and we've got us, what do we want now?" I just had to laugh with him. Then he said,

"We can thank. Our Lord has been good, here in the Chaco. Two sons ordained preachers, all children married and happy and grandchildren and great-grandchildren, here and in Canada, and enough to eat. And quiet. But they will ask you."

"Yes," I said. "When we first came they did, but not now for years."

"What did you say?"

"They should ask you."

"Yes," he said, and was quiet for a little. "But now they'll ask again, and you tell them. You can tell them that we could be in Canada now, yes, and we'd be rich like Marie and Esther and so many relatives and drive cars and farm with a combine and three tractors. Maybe they won't ask you, maybe they'll just blame us like – like some for moving here and who knew to what land we were going or dragging our children, not even the Elder or the delegation. But you don't bother yourself with that. We were the parents. Maybe we were wrong, maybe we were right, but we thought we couldn't raise our children when they took the German and the Bible lessons away in school. Maybe we were wrong, maybe we were right, but we believed it. Here we have land, we have had quiet here; peace and quiet. They're old enough now; now they can decide."

"Yes," I said.

"And don't let one of them, not one, make it hard for you. We did what we believed."

"Yes my Johann," I said.

After a while he said, "God be thanked if they do as much."

At evening he died. We had sent a truck to Greta and Abram on the south Sixty Legua that he was sick and they just got to *hauptcheuik* in Ostwick in time for the funeral next morning, May 1, 1958. Elder Wiebe the Younger preached, and Kornelius too.

Marie had been writing from Canada for years we should come for a visit and now the children thought it would be good; I prayed long and Marie and Esther sent the money from Canada so I flew to Winnipeg for her silver wedding in September. Three days on planes I could dig up what was left of English; strange, over thirty years and I still knew more of it than Spanish. Marie had a nice house, big and new with everything electric, clean like she wrapped it in this plastic every day, and her man worked eight hours a day by a garage. It was cold but nice visiting all the grandchildren and great-grandchildren too, like bees in a hive, and driving around in soft cars on the hard roads to Winkler and Altona and all the relatives. Heinrich had died from a stroke, always a *betchla* and just over fifty, but two of my brothers came from Mexico; I hadn't seen them for thirty-six years. Blumental was gone, only wheat fields there, and Neuboden where we first lived and had school and our teacher drew pictures on the sand. Schoenbach, Manitoba was just the graveyard, a few crooked stones under the trees.

Esther's man, Dennis Willms, still sold Chevrolets, and all kinds of other things now too. He wrote his name "Williams," but even had some farms. He had taken over to run them while they had the war and now they were his; hired people ran the farms and they drove out to one or the other sometimes for a week in summer. It took them three days to show me everything and it took that long not because his big car drove so slow either.

"Na Muttchi," he said, "you always said like Grandpa, 'it all comes from God.' So okay, but it's not always just sickness and want, eh?"

"Not always," I said. "No."

I went to their church. They prayed and sang and read from the Bible; it was all English and not Mennonite but the most people there came from us and to me it sometimes looked they were stretching themselves around for what they weren't. Maybe they weren't. In the summer of 1959 I drove with Esther and her man in their stationwagon to Saskatchewan, Swift Current and Roads and even north to Hague and Rosthern, Saskatchewan. My, friends and relatives by the hundreds. I could have used a lifetime visiting and never needed the room Willms gave me in their big house in Winnipeg. But I was always cold and my feet got heavy; maybe it was all their cement and pavement. I told them I had had such a good visit but there wasn't need to spend my last few days running like an unheaded chicken and meeting my Lord too tired and old to even say a hallelujah. So on October 17, 1959 they put me on the plane. By the afternoon we were in New York and there they put me on one of those big jets, first class too, where almost 200 people can sit while they're going 600 miles every hour and the next morning it was in Asuncion. Dennis came with me to New York and he said, as I was going to get on, that if it had been so easy in 1926 there sure wouldn't be one Mennonite in Paraguay today. So the last time he saw me I was laughing.

The bumpy mail plane took me from Asuncion to the Russlander Zentrale. The flat Chaco was turning hot and green in spring. Through the little window I saw my young Johann and little Johann and Friedl waiting in the buggy and when the dust from our coming down blew away I got out of the plane and into the buggy and we drove home the sandy road to Schoenbach. Simons Colony. Stopping at all the villages on the way took longer than coming from New York.

ELEVEN

Wash, This Sand and Ashes

Towards evening for perhaps the tenth time they lurched down into the ditch to detour the warped culvert across a dry wash when they saw the seated Indian. David said, "There's Orawané, there he is." The Indian's dark hand moved, an imperial gesture to the ground before him. David stopped the jeep precisely there, not getting out.

Tonight was the last night for them to get the supplies to Mariscal. David said it was normally a one-day trip; they were six days on the road and only two hundred kilometers north out of Fernland Zentrale mostly that day's driving. They had not stopped even at noon since in any case nearly every hour they had to repair flats from the spinas on the overgrown road left by oil companies fifteen years before. And once they stopped to shoot another antelope; David this time, who dropped it where it stood. Still they were over twenty kilometers from Fortin Mariscal where the jeep road, such as it was, ended, where the mission outpost wagon was to meet them as they had arranged six days before when the war-surplus radio made a momentary connection. Six flats and a sand-ruined bearing before they left colony land held them four days, and then the Ayerooas advance war party another. Now Orawané, on his rag in the spotty shade of a bush.

"He wants a ride back there," David said, and slowly

unhooked his door. "Back to the women and children, in the hills."

They both got out. The sun was low and the temperature down to nearly one hundred, John estimated. Almost possible even for a Canadian. One hundred was, given the right preceding circumstances, almost even comfortable. He walked through the sand, around, and they both looked down at the Ayerooa sitting one leg under him, the other straight out like a gigantic black log mottled with fungus. John stepped back and the jeep fender burned him.

"How did – that . . . ?"

David made some sounds and the Indian leaned forward, unwrapped with the same imperial dignity the rag from what had been the foot; the leg was bloated to foot dimension and only the nails, thick and broken as cattle hoofs, gave a hint of toes. David squatted on his hams, as if unperturbed by smell or flies.

"I've never seen this before," David explained in German, "two spinas through the foot – there in the ball and the heel – at the same time. And he was careless, maybe running fast in a hunt. They both broke off inside when he pulled them out, and then later he dug around in the holes – see, trying to get this one out through the top of his foot, about there, where it came through when he stepped on it. Even his system can't take all that poison."

"That's – that's –" he thought, loving god I have no German vocabulary for this; or English.

The Indian was pressing systematically all the way up the limb and from the sequence of holes cut or broken there black pus welled, one by one. David spoke and the Indian answered, their throats clicking as if they gagged and spit.

"He says he can't get it all out, and he wants to go home now."

"Did he know we were coming?"

"Of course not."

"Then what . . . ?"

"He'd have – stayed here, that's all. But we came."

"So . . . ?"

David said nothing.

"David," John said quickly; he was squatting down too, mind clenched against his nausea, "you said it's only twenty more kilometers – we could get the supplies to Mariscal and we load the wagon quick and you go on with Jake on the wagon to the station, as planned. And I, I take the jeep back to Zentrale, as planned, but start back tonight and if I don't have trouble I can pick him up and get him to Zentrale Hospital tomorrow some –" he stopped, heart lurching as David looked up at him.

"No one drives at night. I can't miss those spinas in broad daylight and you don't even know –"

"I know, but we could – try. I can fix the flats –"

"Reimer," David said.

"Well –"

"I'm not talking about that. Sure, you could try. But look at him."

"Well, the doctor would –"

"They'd have to take it off at the hip. Try. An Ayerooa with one leg?"

John looked to the brush. His shot had wounded the antelope, its slender head barely above the campo grass, and they had followed its blood-spoor into the spined brush, knees bent and running hard in the wooden heat, sometimes crawling, sometimes down flat with their bellies twisting on the hot sand, and in two minutes he would have been as lost as he was pronged except for David's infallible direction. When they got out again David peeled off the strips of his shirt and brushed iodine on his hands, his bleeding back. "Here you have to bend lower," was all he said.

"How can we load him?" John said finally.

"And him over there. They don't leave a chief alone." John

had not seen the other man, small and almost effaced against another bush, now coming toward them. "And the dogs, there'll be at least two."

Orawané refused to stir without the dogs and David clicked and gagged away five minutes of falling daylight to convince him the jeep must move so slowly the dogs could easily keep up. They carried the chief, David at the leg. They lifted him into John's seat and placed around him his two spears, bow, arrows, three glass bottles of water stoppered with grass, a hollow gourd also filled with water, and his bag of cactus-fiber. The tires seemed hard still; John got up back and then the other Indian, each on one corner of David's jeep extension box piled tight with supplies under the canvas. There was room for each to stand on one foot. Their hands, pale tan and black, gripped beside each other, below the coagulated blood of the little antelope tossed up on the box, beside the mosquitoes bloated beyond motion when the jeep motor shuddered, started.

The nails beside his were white on black fingers, old-hard as horn, like the young woman's sitting beside the dying fire the night before. Everyone asleep but he squirming from his back in the hammock. Through the mosquito netting he saw her tip a water gourd to her mouth, work the water around a moment, then jet a tiny stream of it yellowish in the dying light into her cupped hands and wash herself as she squatted on her hams: first face, then shoulders, breasts, stomach, hips, thighs, legs. Completely, mouthful by mouthful. He forgot himself, watching that strange ablution, rhythmic and intent as the songs they had sung, first the new war chief, new since Orawané was left behind, a song heaved out with guttural, fierce, slashing gestures, and then the other, quiet and small, his hands clutched about the tall spear erect before him, nails gleaming in the firelight. A quiet repetition, the line rising and dying, the breath taken more heavily and more heavily until there were only great gasps lifting the song between the minor repeating tune, forehead and cheeks glistening as the face, smooth and hairless below the black part of hair gathered in a giant bush behind the neck, gulped for air, sobbed for air and whatever the eye-holes saw in the darkness beyond the three-foot steel prong of the spear wrapped tight with cactus rope to the quebracho shaft, hammered down to needle point out of some American oil company discard. And when the song, tears standing on his own eyelids though he knew no word, was over, the Ayerooas squatting about began to laugh. A girl started, and soon they were all, except the chief and the singer, rolling over, howling. A man seized a woman; she shrieked and jerked away; with a lunge the man knocked her over into the darkness and then all, still laughing, scrambled after them to see. Even the new chief was gone; and the sad singer. He had looked at David; for him this trip was a dream: all day among primitives together with the one white in the world who knew their language, knew them; except for no clothing they had seemed almost like the Christian Chulupis around the colony, almost, but with an aura of something they carried like their smell, a strangeness that in this burst of violence, pathos, raging laughter fingered through him like fear. Not for his own life; the aura he had caught from old Franz Epp that night; or the later night when he had explained how time and again over the years on the cotton field plowing he had turned up tiny bodies eaten past human recognition by busy ants: it is how they keep their families small. A hunter moves; he cannot have more than one small baby. Anthropologically that made fine sense; also while you were scraping your plow clean? He could not believe that. So much seemed to move in so many directions he could not gather together what, except at times seemed simply his own dumbfounded incomprehension about life and people. He knew himself, he thought; he was university trained, a professional who could help people live with the land, help it live for them; living with Christians who felt they had to "evangelize" Indians – they must learn to farm the land, hunting so near its limit – he knew himself broad-minded, perceptive, understanding; he had built his enlightenment so deliberately, so intently careful against his own father's more and more clearly recognized nose-aimed myopia. But it seemed now he still understood nothing. Perhaps he – knew? – even less than his father. Perhaps it was impossible to get at anything at all essential about people by understanding. Perhaps they did need to be saved from hell; the hell of their being born, living and dying? David in his peasant Mennonite voice said, "They have only unmarried girls with them on the wartrail; they can move fast. The last one has a wife and new son, his first, in the hills above the mission. That was what his song was. I think; song words are sometimes very strange, old fashioned." "What's this war they're after?" "With another part of their own people. That group came to these last spring, tricked them, speared one man and took two women. It always goes on, when the rain comes so they can move between waterholes." "Every spring?" "That's even in the Bible: at the time that kings go out to battle. Huh! Kings." "When these get attacked in the hills, what happens to your mission?" "They're not really hills. It's a big valley, like a bowl, and in the middle is a plateau as high as the land around the valley. From below it looks like hills." And having heard that song, he saw from his hammock the Ayerooa woman clean herself in the bowl of her mouth and hands and then, squatting as always on her hams, reach down and wash as carefully down her glistening body, face to feet, with sand and ashes from the campfire.

"All set, Reimer?" David called.

John looked at the face of the Ayerooa dangling with him by one foot on the jeep. At rest against the box. Across the Indian's eyebrowless ridge of forehead and down the high cheek was the same warrior streak of ochre; but it was badly smudged and his black eyes in the dropping light seemed to roll in a yellowish fluid as he stared motionless over the hump of the antelope covered with mosquitoes bulged like plastic sacs.

"Yes," he answered, "I guess."

The jeep began to move. Staggering through the spinas of the ditch. Trying to crawl up again on the abandoned oil road.

TWELVE

The Vietnam Call
of Samuel U. Reimer

"SAMUEL. SAMUEL."

The call came to him sleeping. He was awake suddenly, erect and tensed in bed, eyes wide. The window faced him pale in the dresser mirror with the blob of yardlight in one corner. The kids' bedrooms were along the hall, and anyway they wouldn't – he looked down. The mound his wife made under the blankets was barely discernible. Always breathing through her mouth and in the morning griping again about the humidifier on the furnace –

"Samuel. Samuel."

He couldn't doubt that. Someone had called his name. He shivered abruptly, violently; he felt something had driven down into him to his very grounds. Called by his name in the night. After a moment he realized his hands were up, clenched in fists as for defense; his wristwatch glowed. Cats you don't just hear a clear voice sing out your name in your bedroom at two thirty-five in the morning! Do you? But he'd just heard it. Hadn't he? He put his hand on the mound beside him and shook.

"Emily." She moved in her sleep. "Hey, hey Emily, listen, see if you hear –" she muttered turning, muttering, and his hand, still shaking her, slipped from her shoulder through the top of her nightdress onto one warm breast. She jerked away.

"Sam, for cripesake I wanna *sleep*!"

Anger spurted in him; he hadn't meant a thing to get that usual – he thrust himself to his side of the bed, jerking against her clutch of the blankets. For a time he lay stiff. The bedroom came back to him in the usual night silences; the furnace vent whirred; somewhere something snapped in the cold. That tone of hers took care of his sleep – huh – voices. He swung out of bed on his side and padded to the kitchen. Shrunken meatloaf, carton of Slim-it milk, split celery; not one stupid thing in the whole stupid fridge. Abrupt as a cell bursting in him he craved violence; to swallow and swallow again and again, have green rhinos explode in his brain, ravaging pink trees and playing their horns like golden blazing angels. Crackerjack. He shook his head. One more and I'll stand on my head in the can drooling molasses. He found an apple and slid into the nook bench, munching. The yardlight shone through the frosted window and beyond the length of the barn he could just make out the rafters of the new hoggery. Weather didn't stop the carpenters; they were okay. It should easily be done by –

"Samuel. Samuel."

Thinking about the hoggery, he said aloud before he comprehended,

"Yeah?"

"I am the God of your fathers, the Lord your God. Go and proclaim peace in Vietnam."

Even for a southern Manitoba Mennonite Sam Reimer was known as careful; not always completely slow or stubborn, but careful. He had once heard an agricultural extension lecturer say that in order to keep track of modern farm complexities farmers should use memos freely. Sam's pockets were always stuffed with papers but his groping fingers now found only a clotted handkerchief. He glanced about in the half darkness, saw his wife's wall pad and grabbed the pencil while tearing away the top sheet.

"Cou – could you say that again, hey?"

"Of course." The voice continued at dictation speed, "I am the God of your fathers, the Lord your God. Go and proclaim peace in Vietnam."

"That's what I thou –" he jerked erect, staring.

His head sang; every sense he had seemed tilted forward, vibrating. The same old modern kitchen they'd planned on so long – another twelve years to pay if that July rain doesn't come again, but the pigs – he felt for the switch. Fluorescent staggered, blazed. He had written fast, over a list of groceries, but there were the words. What the jumping green apples. For only the sound he could not have believed it; not even after three calls and the statement twice. But the "of course" too. It was written over "Pork chop lean 4 ls." Emily never knew abbreviations for anything. He sat, staring at his scrawl. Dear Lord Jesus.

Near dawn he switched off the light and went back to lie in bed. The alarm buzzed and he got up with Emily, dressed, went out to feed and milk the cow. When they tore away the old house (built early in 1880 Emily's grandmother, then alive, thought) they of course tore away the old passageway between house and barn. He put the attached garage there, but the neighbors laughed because he built the new house foundations where the old had been and that left room for only a one-car garage. As they laughed at his one cow. It couldn't give enough milk for six, but he didn't like milking three any more than having only a cat on the yard. Farms should have animals, at least a cow. Long ago he had decided that once the pigs got going he'd sell her and maybe tear down the cavernous barn altogether, or convert it – to something (it was a great deal cheaper to build a complete modern hoggery than try to convert that ancient shed, they had said) – he was leaning against the stallhead, watching the cow nuzzle her alfalfa. What time was – he got to the double doors; the kids were already running towards the road. In passing Jamie shouldered Janie into a drift; Sam shouted and the twin glanced about, startled, then whooped happily over his shoulder as he ran,

"Ma's mad! She yelled twice!"

He hoisted Janie, dusted her rear and watched until the yellow bus swallowed them, Sammy, James, Angelica, Janie last by far. Eating he once or twice actually tried to listen and discovered, to his mild surprise, that gaps of sound were blocked out almost as if, sitting in the mod breakfast nook, doors were opening and closing in his ears. When he did not concentrate he heard nothing; when he did, only loud inconsecutive clusters of small words came through, mostly prepositions and adjectives. Yet Emily's mouth continued moving. Standing he could hear very plainly, however. He went to the boys' bedroom.

Emily stood in the doorway. He closed the dictionary, sliding the paper out under his hand and into his pocket.

"Oh, just – thinking about a word, looking it up." Pyjamas tangled his foot and he kicked them aside. "Can't you tell Sammy – you know," he flung out his arm at the littered room. The built-in beds had stained maple drawers under them.

"Well I tell him and *tell* him and that's true, but he's more like you every day, if he hears me I can't tell it from what he does. Just look!" She seized a glove from the chiffonier. "I tell him till I'm absolutely purple, 'They cost 1.98, you're not getting one more pair this winter, you'll just wear those big mitts if you wreck these for Sunday.' So look! Once he wears them to school when I'm not looking when he tears out and they climb the rope at recess and slide down, slide slow and then real fast so you land with a bump and can fall over as if you're shot, and look – 1.98! Kerpoof!"

"I told you right aways," Sam went by her into the hall, "no ten-year kid needs calfskin gloves. For what does he need gloves? Horsehide mitts like we had is what he needs."

"Oh sure. Any old thing is fine so I'm ashamed to show my

kids in church. You don't care what your kids wear but I'm not going to –"

"All right all right," he was pulling on his coat. "Everybody's said everything before."

"Then don't just blame me. If we ever had more I wouldn't have to –"

"Emily." Squared to her, the shabby housecoat shiny at every edge, hair rollers hung about a face he suddenly knew he no more saw in particular than his own shaving – he had once walked eight miles after a day of threshing just to look at a lighted window which might have been hers . . . hadn't he – "It's slow on the land, but wait just a –"

"Slow! Eleven years here with you and it's never better, just worse! When my pa had this land it –"

"We've paid off a lot, and you've had a nice bungalow almost three years now –"

Her face stiffened, "*You've* had a nice bungalow. You'll never get over that, never, 'if you'd only let me wait one year more with the bungalow we could of got the big tractor and that one crop would have paid for it *and* the bungalow and we'd had a good start and –'"

"Everybody's said that too!" and then his tone shamed him. "I didn't mean that now, honest hon. If the crop had got a little different these two years you know it'd be better. Once the hoggery gets done and the sows in –"

"Always it's the hoggery, your Centennial *Pro*ject that hoggery! Borrowing thousands for where there's less than nothing already. Pigs supposed to fix us up forever, some kind of miracle pig or something."

"Miracle?" A door shut and he heard nothing. After a time his glance focused; she was looking at him silently. "No," he said. "No, I can't – I didn't expect that. Just pigs litter so fast. Year round operation, not everything in one – no, not that."

"What's the matter? Sam, you feel sick? You're acting so –

funny." The last word hung between them, and he shrugged suddenly, turning. "At least aren't you going to town?"

The cold doorknob roused him. "Yeah. Sure," and he got out his memo. "I have to – yeah, get nails and plywood for sheeting."

"Get me some groceries. Take the list – huh, where is it? I wrote a bunch of things down."

"What?"

"My list, can't you hear, who tore off –"

"I got it already," he patted his pocket.

"What? When did you?"

"Some time, early this morning."

"Well give it here then, I have to add to it yet."

Something hunched together in him and he did not dare. "You know what's on it, what else do you need?" and to his immense relief she did not insist. He added lettuce and rubber gloves, size ten, and went. A helper was handing up rafters to the carpenters; exactly where, in the old pattern sleeping somewhere in his childhood haze of Russia, of the plateaus of Orenburg edged by a faint line of Urals, the cross-granary would have stood. The village here was gone now, theirs the only well and yard left behind the long rows of cottonwoods. Where had all the people gone? On the road the Ford seemed to shimmy worse than usual, but the road was rutted in snow and he could not be certain. Three miles from town it twisted sharply and something snapped. He trundled nose-down into a drift; the right front wheel leaned at a crazy angle. He walked to the farmhouse across the field and half an hour later the wrecker brought him in.

"Front suspension all shot to – you know," the garage owner grinned in sympathy. "You should of traded for that Impala last fall."

"Yeah. There's lots a guy should do and doesn't. How much this time?"

"Time I've got. Even parts. Around sixty, somewheres."

He sent the groceries along with the lumber truck. At the post office to avoid the talking men he bought, for the first time in his life, a Winnipeg morning paper but one glance at its headline churned such revulsion in him he thrust it into the wastebarrel. He seemed suspended, looking from somewhere through a reversed telescope; there, he saw, the small town world wagged on, but he was somewhere not touching it. What slightest difference did another bill he could not afford on the Ford make. He was walking residential streets staring at squat ugly houses he had never noticed, at familiar faces that had no names and seemed to return his look an instant and duck away. On the narrow sidewalk a mother pulling her baby in a boxed sled approached; he stood aside; she brushed by and his arm rose to her shoulder and stopped her. Her glance came up; a face he knew taunt in the cold suddenly pulsing red; he comprehended himself and stumbled backward, almost sprawling in the piled snow. My God. For several blocks he did not trust himself. He crunched back towards Main Street but his intention waned somewhere and he was staring at a car license; he looked up and above him in gray noon loomed the Mennonite Church. Its sheer modern roof looked almost like an old barn; and as vacant. Only an education wing window showed light.

In the study, where he had never been, books lined three walls to the ceiling. At church they usually sat far back because of the children and so the mobile face was familiarly distant in this suspended world. But after two sentences and reading the note, the face across the desk seemed to hang on balance, teetering between perhaps consternation and laughter. He almost chuckled then, for the first time that day.

"It is kind of – funny, I guess, if you just look at it, cold. But I wrote it down word for word."

"Well," the pastor shifted away in his chair, "yes, what did it

– what were the words again, exactly?" Sam repeated them. After a moment the other said, "You've been following the war quite closely, I suppose."

"No."

"No?" eyebrows lifting.

"I – I guess I don't like to hear about that stuff. We don't get papers."

"But it's all over, radio, TV news."

"I never listen. There's always so much murdering, and things. Actually, I guess I'm not even sure where Vietnam is. In southern Asia, but not exactly. The U.S. is bombing communists there or something, isn't it?"

The pastor brushed his hand over his face before he said, as if dictating, "Yes. They are bombing communists in North Vietnam and also fighting Viet Cong – communist guerillas – jungle fighters – in South Vietnam. There are over 350,000 American soldiers over there now, and more going, with an average of one hundred killed every week."

"There's no Canadians?"

"Canada is one of three nations trying to administer the – no, no Canadians are fighting."

"That's what the voice meant, then . . ." Sam began heavily and stopped.

"What?"

". . . proclaim, 'announce or declare publicly,' peace to Americans and communists."

The pastor started forward, "My dear brother, what in all of –" their glances met and after a moment he continued, calm again, "What did it sound like, this voice?"

"It was – just a voice."

"Well, was it like a man's, child's, or what?"

Driven to the thought Sam realized that the sound of it was with him still, perhaps more than ever; as if he had been saturated, soaked in its possibility and he was tiptoeing about trying to avoid the match. But the voice itself? "The voice, it wasn't anything particular, just an ordinary voice with very strange . . ." He could not find a word.

"But no voice is 'ordinary'; they're very distinctive. Did it sound like anyone you know – like mine, for instance?"

"No, not like yours. It was just – quiet, and really clear."

"I was thinking, perhaps my sermon last Sunday on what our Mennonite Church, as one of the historic peace churches, had to say on Vietnam and how we as neo-pacifists must share and restore the dignity of man to an afflicted . . ." The familiar voice flowed on; Sam watched until the mouth stopped. He said then,

"I never listen anyways." Such a strange expression hardened on the pastor's face, Sam asked, "What's the matter?"

"You never listen?"

"Oh. I guess not, no. You preached about Vietnam on Sunday?"

"Yes." The silence lengthened, then Sam heard the other, probably repeating a question, ". . . why to church at all?"

"Why?" He thought a moment. "Where we live – you're new here but it used to be a farm row village, Gartental, long ago, but now there's just our yard left because Emily's father bought the other places to make his land and the others built new houses out on their quarters – just our yard and at the other end the Sommerfelder Church that was the school too. The Sommerfelder come every Sunday and the preacher in his black coat reads a sermon maybe three hundred years old. They always come, and visit after. We've always come here, what would we want at a Sommerfelder church, and . . ." he understood himself suddenly and stopped. There was a rueful smile on the handsome face before him.

"Doesn't our church, you a baptized member, mean something to you?"

Somehow he had not thought about that for a time. "I can't tell, now," he said finally.

"Then perhaps I can," tone slackening as in weariness. "At least you're candid. And I'm not completely new – almost three years, and I've been past your place. Beautiful trees. Anyway, what will you do now, with this?" There was a silence.

"Well, why not just forget it? People dream funny things every night and forget them as fast."

"This wasn't dreaming. I wrote it while it happened."

"It wasn't a dream?"

"I was in the kitchen eating an apple, in my pyjamas. I –" he could voice nothing of the feeling he had had on first hearing the voice; driving into him. "I – I wrote it down – right here on the grocery list."

The pastor burst out laughing. The sound bounced about the office, then dropped as quickly. "I'm sorry. But it's a little – odd, isn't it?"

"It's more than that," Sam said heavily. "Lots more."

"Well," the tone lifted cheery, "I've been thinking there's two things you could do." The pastor was making a tent of his fingers and sighting over their tips at the bank calendar on the wall. "One, I have a fairly complete file of papers, periodicals on Vietnam, for, against, in the middle. Take some home and read them." At Sam's look he added, "You ought to know something of what's happening in the world."

The weight like sickness, threatening all morning, was soaking up in him. "Yeah." He pulled out his memo. "Two."

"You have to hear it again."

"Huh?"

"My dear brother, what you say is too – you can't believe it if it only happens once. You have to test it – this voice. Make sure."

"Test?"

"Well, if the voice is the – as you said it, then it can surely speak again, can't it?"

"I guess so."

"Right. So don't decide anything till you hear it again.

Tonight try it in the kitchen again, and there you have the tape recorder ready. When it speaks, you record it!"

Sam stared. "That's too stupid," he said finally. "If I can hear it I –"

"No! It's not stupid! It's just plain, factual, repeatable evidence, it's," the pastor was half out of his chair, both arms across the desk, fingers tensed, "it's even biblical! Your voice makes such a – an incredible claim, you've *got* to test it. Like Gideon tested a command he thought came from God, with a sheepskin; it stayed dry when everything else was wet with dew – well."

"That's pretty funny stuff for the Bible."

"Funny? No funnier than what –" it was a moment before the stunned look cleared the pastor's face. Then, "Don't you ever read it?"

Sam said slowly, "Not for quite a –" and then he laughed, violently. "We haven't got a sheep, only a cow and a cat!"

The answering laugh cut on a flick of hysteria. "Well, well, okay, it's a modern equivalent of sheepskin. You can use this portable; it's the church's anyway, so you helped pay for it; perhaps."

He paid $67.83 by check at the garage and drove home. In the sunken livingroom the four children sprawled a yard from the TV watching a spineless father being duped by his daughter about a date. Despite Angelica's screams and knowing Sammy or Jamie would switch back the instant he left, he turned to a travelogue and went out to milk. After supper he began with the papers. When the pictures of sprawled naked men and napalmed children were too much he got Emily to find the Bible. He did not hear her; once she was shaking him, pointing to the clock and he said, "Okay, go; I'll read some yet," slowly reading the pastor's Bible references, one after the other. It was exactly like it had happened to Abraham; a couple of times. When he looked at his watch it was nearly two; so was the kitchen clock. He went into the hall, listened to Emily and the children breathing in sleep, then closed all the doors and got the tape recorder from the Ford's trunk. He set up the mike, checked the tape, then tripped the light switch. The recorder sat in light filtered through window ice.

Next morning from the tape came Sam's voice, stumbling a little over Gideon's words, "Let not thine anger be hot against me, and I will speak – ask but this once with the fl – ahh – tape recorder. Ahh – tell me again, just so I'll have some evidence, then shall I know that thou wilt save Is – want me to go to Vietnam. Okay?"

The reels turned on and suddenly the pastor hunched forward, "Sam listen, I –"

"Just listen, it's just almost done," Sam looked at Emily, huddled head down, motionless in her chair. Perhaps he should have explained more about the voice while they drove in. But the pastor would help do that. It was finished and he switched it off. "There's the scientific evidence," he said, "everything."

"How did you get – this?" the pastor was staring at his fingertips.

"Just like I heard it the night before. I was in the kitchen around two o'clock and set the rec –"

"Emily too?"

"Emily? No, she was sleeping. It was around two, maybe a little after, and then I read that and the voice came, right away like you heard, like the night before: 'Go and proclaim peace in Vietnam.'"

"Then you asked more?"

"You notice it even explained that 'proclaim' doesn't just mean announce, it means 'show them, tell them it's necessary'?"

"Well. What did the voice say when you asked what you'd do there?"

"Just like you heard, when you get there you'll know. If I can hear it here I can over there, that's for sure."

"Sam," the pastor said after a long pause, his face as if in a vice, "Sam, I – I – Emily, you –"

She raised her head for the first time. She was crying. "Yes," she said, "tell him."

"Sam, there's no voice. Just yours on the tape."

"Huh?"

"Just your voice on the tape. You ask something, then everything's quiet, absolutely, then you ask another question. There is no voice."

He stared at them, dumbfounded. A terrifying conviction about them flamed up in him and he was jabbing at the machine, fumbling and jabbing. "Listen, there!" he twisted the volume and heard the voice thundering in the room, "Listen. Hear that," and he whispered words already, forever, seared into him, "I am the God of your fathers, the Lord your God. Go and proclaim peace . . ." He stabbed at the switch. "There," he said, dashing the sweat from his forehead with a flung arm, "There."

The pastor faced him like stone. "There is no voice but yours. Emily?"

"No," she whispered. "Just his."

He looked at the pastor, then his wife. It was as if something sealed, something once flickering and then lost beyond consciousness in a lived-over infancy had been pried open, and he was becoming aware at last of something that in his somnolent life he had never known he had: an unbelievable comprehension for pain, for despair. "Please," he said, "please. How can you deny it, how can you? Look, I've got the evidence. All the time it was recording I watched the needle, like you said. Look." He switched the tape on; the needle vibrated with his own words and kept on; he let it run to the end, and the needle never rested.

The pastor started back, fumbled in a drawer, pulled out another, larger, machine and strung the tape in it. They all stared at the flickering needle.

"There has to be some – electrical mistake – some –"

To Sam the world where the two hunched together, bowed before the recorder, was slowly retreating to insignificance.

"It's not the electricity," he said, despairing for them. "Admit it. Man, I won't ask you for a thing, that's for sure."

"Reimer!" The pastor stood, facing him. "I don't care what that needle does! Before God, Sam, I can hear only your voice!"

"Oh." He paused; Emily's look, too, was not quite possible to deny. In the long distance from them that became absurdly plain also. "Yeah, sure. It's for me, so why should you hear it. So, now I can go."

He meant Vietnam and he began to order his affairs. Next morning, after a tearful Emily had left for church with the gawking children, he spread his accounts and mortgages on the breakfast nook. They were orderly, and not too much computing made it clear that if he sold out completely for a minimum price and settled all obligations, he would have somewhere between one and two thousand dollars. Plenty to get to Vietnam. The family? They were in Canada. There were many relatives, and welfare was everywhere. On further thought, however, he decided welfare might be unnecessarily problematic, so after dinner he drove to Emily's younger brother's farm a mile away. He had always gotten on in complete equability with his brother-in-law, a man as mild as Emily was occasionally the opposite, and now his further and further queries were a little unexpected. Finally nothing was left but both drive back and talk to Emily. She had already shifted from tears and the noisy upshot was that her brother not only refused to accept responsibility for either farm or family but concluded, his round face black and disturbed,

"Sam, I don't know, but this is crazy, just plain crazy. If you don't quit it we'll get you to a doctor. There are some like you need, in Winnipeg."

"Oh Sam," wailed Emily, "what'll people say!"

He considered them in their little world, silently. Next morning he informed the building foreman he would pay them two weeks extra wages but, as of now, he was not completing the hoggery. The carpenter was furious but Sam remained adamant and since – as between Mennonites – they had signed no contract the men finally gathered their tools and left. Sam drove to town and talked to the lawyer; the land had been in the Hiebert – Emily's – family for eighty years; when they married he had signed the mortgage for a major part of it, but some of it was also her inheritance and it would be impossible to sell, the lawyer said, if Emily refused; even if she didn't, December was a bad time. Sam decided he would have to face Emily when an offer came; he left explicit instructions and drove on to the hogbreeder whom he had paid a large deposit on ten broodsows. Despite the hard low drifts of a night blow, the Ford steered beautifully.

In the three weeks before Christmas there were no tentative offers; not even inquiries. Emily hardened in her indignation and he stopped talking to her about it and simply had the farm listed in Winnipeg. He read through the pastor's files on Vietnam and war, was working on through the Bible, subscribed to a daily and his letters to Mennonite, Quaker and other peace groups were beginning to draw pamphlets, brochures, requests, explanations, statements on marches and demonstrations and war atrocities. Paper deluged him. He shooed the girls out of their bedroom to sleep with Emily; Angelica howled and went, but Janie refused. Often while she sat on her bed dressing and undressing her dolls all in a row or while she slept, Sam read. He did not know if he had been living until the voice spoke; if, it had been like a melon, an underground tuber. He felt flayed: skinned to the agony of the world before the words, the yet more terrible pictures, but above all before the humanness of children, women, men who must endure living. And what could be thought when you saw little ones broiled in napalm? Jesus had said, "Do good to them that hate you that you may be children of your father which is in heaven," but what did that mean when you weren't hated, rather someone across an ocean and you knew about it? He would clamber up the cavernous barn and labor violently repiling hay in the loft, his sweat indistinguishable from his tears. One day two strangers found him there; the bale-hook hanging in his hand, he climbed down and they retreated to the open door. He went with them without re-entering the house; the kitchen curtain twitched as he got into the ambulance. When they were not giving him tests he lay on the bed thinking it through again, step by step. The pastor visited him once; he was reading the Gideon Bible, which they had not thought to remove, and the pastor could not stay long. He reported that an electrical expert had stated there was definitely something defective in the tape to make the needle jump so oddly, that the church peace committee had passed his project on to the larger Inter-Mennonite Church Service Society, Peace Section, and it had ruled his plans were too likely to raise derision and suspicion among both church members and government agencies for the Society to be able to support him, in any way. But they had enclosed more information on Vietnam Christian Aid. Sam could hardly doubt the pastor's sincerity; his recovery was being prayed for by the church at every Wednesday Prayer Service, but when he asked what they meant by 'recovery,' the pastor could only smile in pain.

"I'm happy to tell you," the psychiatrist flipped a folder shut, "you're one of the healthier men I've run through the mixer. Your head is usually clearer than mine," and he laughed. Smiling, Sam liked him. "Except for the voice. You've been thinking a lot – you have any idea yet why perhaps you hear it?"

"No-o," he hesitated, feeling such an impossibility and longing when he remembered the voice, the order. "I didn't ask for it, I couldn't even have imagined it, not living like that, farming. There must be some things it's even impossible for some people to dream, eh?"

"Dreams are very difficult. Till now I'd tend to agree with you, but I don't know. We'd need more time, and some of your childhood –"

"It came and there it is and I have to do it."

"You're sure?"

"That's all."

"Concern for your family, what will –"

"That's all I lived for. The kids, yeah, they're ours, mine and Emily's, and they've got to be cared for, yes. I know that, that's how my parents lived too. Care for the children God has given you. Sure. But –" he struggled, a kind of ferocious clarity opening in him, "maybe they wouldn't be such brats if I hadn't always been just working for them so much. They're not *every*thing in heaven and on earth. Compared to some things, they're maybe nothing much at all. I don't know.

"If," Sam continued after a moment, "they could see, when they're old enough to see, that I was doing something needed. You know, that had to be, for others, not just so our family has it softer."

"You grow wheat."

"And store it till I get a high price, and all over people starve."

"But that's the way the world runs. You have to pay, you can't change the world."

"Yeah?"

"Not alone, no."

"But we're so way better off than most; we could – pay it ourselves, and give it to the starving. Why not spend tax money like that, why to blow people apart?"

"True."

"When you read what's happening all over, it makes you go . . ." he stopped, gesturing blindly.

"You're sensitive, now, and sometimes one man sees but –"

"You see," Sam went on, oblivious, "if my kids knew, since before they could remember, that I had been something for others – I've been thinking about this and last week I got a letter from my brother in Paraguay. I've been thinking but," he shook his head. "If a guy could know so well what to do."

"Your brother is in Paraguay?" the psychiatrist asked.

"For two years, a agriculturalist in the Mennonite colonies there, for Inter-Mennonite Church Service. He went a month's trip into the bush with a missionary to the wildest Indians there; they've maybe killed a dozen Mennonite farmers in the last twenty years, but this missionary, David Epp, is working with them, trying to write their language, teach them, you know, about Jesus Christ. He lives with them with his family most of the year. And while my brother John was there he found out that this David Epp's father was our dad's cousin and had helped get a whole village of Mennonites out of Russia into China, away from the communists in the thirties and from China they got to South America later, but his father, instead of coming with them, went back into Russia after they were out. Can you imagine that?"

"He went back?"

"John says yeah because they escaped illegally. They weren't supposed to run off and when they did, the Mennonite people that stayed behind would have got it for the ones that got out. You know, sent to prison camps."

"So he went back, to explain?"

"Yeah."

"What happened?"

"They never heard. Mrs. Epp got one letter from him written before the police knew he was back, but they never knew anything more."

"What about the others, the other Mennonites. What happened to them?"

"They all got out of China."

"The ones he went back to? Then he really –"

"No, not them. They don't know about them. They never heard."

"In thirty-five years?"

"No."

The psychiatrist said after a pause, "So what did his going back help?"

Sam was staring at his hands. "Okay," he said finally. "But John says about the son, the missionary now, and we were talking about caring for your kids, that father has had more effect on the son than anything you'll ever see."

"How do you mean?"

"This David Epp never saw his father, our cousin, that he can remember; he was only a few months when it happened and his father's friend took care of him and his mother. But he's made his whole life around what he knows his father did, John writes. Just that, knowing his father went back when no one in the world could say he had to."

They sat in a long silence. Sam said:

"In Vietnam a kid is being fried into a cripple. And I worry about mine don't have a Chrysler to come to church in. Hey?"

"True," the psychiatrist shook himself and sat erect. "But your example is extreme. Many tests have shown that it's not the savagery of what happens, but *how* children experience it, that matters. Never having the proper clothes, acceptable clothes, may be as traumatic for a child's development as going through a war."

"Yeah?" He thought a moment. "So what difference does it make?"

"Does what make?"

"Anything. If a small thing can be as bad for them as something big, forget it. You can't keep them from everything; like you say, maybe one man can't change the way the world runs. But can't he do something, anything, just some little thing maybe about what he thinks is worst? Can't he?"

"Of course, that's the way all reforms begin. Of course. But a voice from – and war has always been –"

"You were in the big war and you say it's terrible. Okay, I wasn't. I was a Mennonite C.O. In 1943 the church worked it out for me and I worked in a camp, but that doesn't mean I'm not really a C.O."

"I didn't mean to imply, I certainly didn't, that –"

"Okay okay, I did, well, mighty little then – dirt jobs, that was the way to live for others in World War II; I guess. I'll never be sorry for planting a tree rather than shooting a man. Anyway that's the way I did, then, and less ever since. Nothing really. But now – now –" he guffawed humorlessly, "now such nothing isn't enough. You see? For me war, mutilation, starving people, that's the worst, now." He thought another moment. "Besides, I've been called," he said.

When he got home that evening after five days in Winnipeg, the children were before the TV. He watched with them; pictures of misshapen monsters and criminals attacking equally misshapen humans. The children coiled tight, laughing in what seemed to him mad release as again and again pieces sprayed into the air and formed together again, apparently unhurt and as hideous as before. "God in heaven," he groaned, and suddenly he seized the machine and hurled it through the picture window. The pane was too strong; the set, though smashed, caught in the glass as the children yelled. He taped several layers of plastic over the hole and Emily got a bigger set on credit next day. Christmas was quiet. The children had never before seen their favorite shows in living color.

The letter from Ottawa was at the post office the day after Boxing Day; he might have spared himself the waiting and gotten the form there immediately, had he known. The postmaster peered through the wicket a moment, then bent and pulled out the passport application. "Making a trip, eh. Overseas?" his tone hung in the air.

The lobby was full as always, farmers laughing and ripping papers but now the boots on the gritty floor ceased and Sam, half turned away, paper under his hand, saw them all motionless, looking. His brother-in-law entered at that moment with the garage owner; when they saw him their talk broke off, faces so suddenly red they had obviously been talking about him. He shrugged, moving, "Who knows," and then the evasion hit him.

"Yes," he said, "overseas." He walked past them all.

"Yep," the notary public levered his seal into the paper, "we was just talking at the folks just the other day, everybody home for Christmas and everything." Sam could not see his face. "You really figuring on – going, there?"

"Where?"

"Well somebody said maybe – but that's dangerous there, and you can't believe everything you . . ."

"Yes," Sam said. "Vietnam."

"That's a dollar. Yep. Well Henry's wife was just saying –". the voice faded. "Yeah, that's right, one dollar."

Sam said, "It'd save me going somewheres else, maybe you'd sign this too, right here."

The other, looking where Sam's finger pointed, laughed uncomfortable, "I've already signed it officially, maybe –"

"It's okay. It says 'notary public' here in the list for character references."

"Yep, I know."

"Well?"

"You know, Emily and the kids, they –" Sam stared at the bent head a moment before he caught the tone.

"They'll be fixed up, fine."

"Well, somebody just said at the folks that Emily and her family – and that you was in Winnipeg five –"

"What?" Sam said, much too loudly and the other laughed louder still, face coming up, hand striking his shoulder.

"Sam, you know me! I'd never believe nothing a Winnipeg doctor –" Sam jerked the form away and went out.

But the contagion was everywhere; he had suddenly exposed the pest. Finally the bank manager, who was not a Mennonite, said without evasion, "It's your family, that's all. Personally, I think you should be allowed to do whatever you want, though – well, but everyone would know in two hours. It'd be worth my job, here."

He was butting a rubber wall, in the place where he had lived eleven years of his life; this too Sam would have found impossible to dream. The banker was looking at him, face drawn in sympathy. Sam said, finally,

"Nobody'll take me to Vietnam, without a passport."

"That's right." The other laughed a little. "There's nothing left – but to go to Vancouver and swim."

Sam rose and the laughter shriveled. "Before you tell that one again," he said, "look at a map. Victoria's closer."

He sent the form to Ottawa anyway but in four days it was back, a great yellow circle around the blank. On a sudden thought he drove to the Sommerfelder Mennonite farmer who, when he was building the house, had without hesitation loaned him $2,500.00 on his word to repay in one year, without a signed note or expecting interest. The Sommerfelder took him to the Elder, who signed in the blank. After three weeks he had another letter from Ottawa: would he report in Winnipeg concerning his application at his convenience, address and room number given. When he drove down Portage Avenue the next morning he discovered the address housed the Royal Canadian Mounted Police. He circled and drove past several times, but there could be no doubt and he finally parked at the Parkade downtown. He wandered around Eaton's, staring at acres of shirts and suits, and children craning at water fountains; bumping into people who stared back at him. By late afternoon he was before the room;

it was bare inside: five books on a shelf, a bank calendar on the wall and a desk behind which sat a young man in a business suit. Someone had been informed of something; that was plain soon enough, though Sam could not deduce exactly what from the sharp-nosed young man's questions. There was a great deal of repetition concerning sensitive areas of the world where Canadians were playing a major role in working for peaceful solutions under very adverse conditions, as in Cyprus for example, and where private travel by persons with – ah – vocal, strong opinions about any – ah – perhaps radical unilateral approaches to the problems in these areas might perhaps militate against even minor hopes of success by the proper international tribunals negotiating there, be misunderstood even by friendly powers, though Canada was a free country and wanted its citizens to travel where they pleased, but it had to also think of their safety, of protecting them, and therefore. . . . He explained, as asked, why he wanted the passport and went home without hope. His heart leaped when the package arrived; inside was the passport. He riffled the pages, leaning against the post office desk in the lobby, ignorant of the people around him, he saw on the second page, in indelible letters, THIS PASSPORT VALID ONLY IN CONTINENTAL UNITED STATES OF AMERICA AND THE FOLLOWING EUROPEAN COUNTRIES and could not read further. He became aware of a desperation building then. He drove to Winnipeg again and a newspaper agreed to interview him but the editors said nix to such a story about a minority religious group; the Mennonites had pretty well lived down the problem of their pacifism in World War II, and some were now big-business advertisers. A TV station did interview him thoroughly, for half an hour, but they cut it to a one-and-a-half minute news capsule when that night an eager reporter thought another sex scandal could be just breaking in Ottawa. Sam received two letters: an old man near Brandon wrote: "I been talking with Gott every night sixty-tree years . . ." and the freshman student organizer at the University of Manitoba wrote he was working on a demonstration or protest parade to the Legislative Buildings. Nothing came of that; a week later the organizer apologized in a formal letter, stating that student apathy had hit an "astronomic low." Even while he was in Winnipeg that second time, Sam realized that these tactics were not the way for him. Nor the way the Quaker in Washington took in showing the world by fire. He was beginning to see something terrifying about his way, about what he found within himself he could, and could not, do. No buyer had come to see the land.

"Sam, Abraham and Isaiah, Hosea ordered to marry a harlot – they lived in primitive times, when everybody heard their gods talking, Assyrians, Greeks, Hittites, everybody," the pastor gestured helplessly to the books behind him. "Then."

Sam looked at him.

"A vision isn't *impossible* – of course not, nothing is. But it's not just me – our church leadership, the moderator, the people here, everybody, and then trying to publicize it – it's so – Sam, I didn't sign that petition, I'd help you get a proper pass –"

"They signed a petition, about me?"

"Well, there was some talk but I told them I wasn't having anything to do with that, to just forget it. But if they did they wanted it just for your good, to help you and your family." There was a short silence. "And now," the pastor went on, "that TV thing and in the university some of our students say a communist agitator was trying to start something for you. It didn't work, thank God, but Sam –"

"You ever met a communist?" The pastor stared. "I mean a live one?"

"I – I suppose, sure, when I was at university –"

"When I was about five I met some where my parents were hiding in Moscow. One night I heard them in the hall, saw them all through a window take a father from his family. I was little then, but lately I've remembered all that real clear. Clearer than I see you, right now. When I think of that, when I read of what communists do in the papers, man, I shake. I can't help it."

The pastor said nothing.

"You've got all these books," Sam said, "why don't you read the Bible? Like you told me. In Jeremiah chapter 25 God talks about 'Nebuchadnezzar, the king of Babylon, my servant.' A heathen, and God calls him his servant because he was going to kill Jews to help them remember what they forgot. They'd been just content, soaking up the fat of the land, not doing their job, and don't you think that if you, like you said once, historic-peace-church-neo-pacifist Christians – whatever that is I don't want to be it – sit around and talk big, saving our own skins because we don't like to lose it any more than anyone else, just shut up when it counts and if we're quiet and make enough money there'll always be somebody else to do all the dirty sinful killing and dying, don't you think maybe sometime God's going to start talking about 'Stalin, Ho Chi Minh, Mao Tse-tung my servants!' Hey?"

"But your idea, it's so wild, just desert your family and –"

"I'm not deserting my family! What are all you here for? Fat Christians. Anyway," his voice sank and he was in memory. "Old Mr. Epp, he was a little shrunken man with a big son and he just said to my father standing there with his mouth open, so thankful they hadn't taken us, 'Samuel,' he said to my father, 'I think Mrs. Friesen was praying too.' As quiet as could be."

The pastor looked at him blankly and Sam continued, "All those young Americans being killed in Vietnam, what's so baloney precious about one middle-aged Mennonite like me?"

"It's just – all life is sacred and to save even one life, no matter who –"

"Okay. My kid deserves to live more than a Vietnamese?"

"Well, in theory, of course – no but –"

"Anyway there's no question of them dying, not here. I know you'd all care for them. So it's just me, and so what about me? Probably nothing would even happen to me, and if by some silly chance there did, so what? I'd have been doing a Christian's job – not sitting here just talking, growing fat on the land; not fighting but trying to reconcile, not killing but trying somehow to proclaim peace in Vietnam for the God of my fathers, for the Lord my God."

"Sam," the pastor said, so quietly he could barely hear him, "what does it mean, 'To proclaim peace in Vietnam'? What does it mean? What would you do? Where would you even go, to South or North Vietnam? Would you talk to Viet Cong or Americans – peasants? In the jungles, the mountains?"

A little man nervous behind a tiny polished desk. Sam felt the corner of the useless passport in his shirtpocket and he understood himself like this little man, too little even for a desk, who thought finally when prodded and comprehended too late to do, at each step when he had already botched too carefully what he had to build next. Each step. "Nobody'll ever know," he said. "Never, never." Then his terrible bitterness lurched in him to hopeless conviction, "I think you are the Devil."

The pastor smiled painfully. "Wouldn't 'servant of the Devil' be enough?"

"No," he got himself to his feet and felt for the door. "Then you wouldn't have been so helpful – and understanding, right at the start."

He drove home. The scrap of paper, the tape: he needed them no more than a man shot point-blank must see the bullet to know his wound. At the end of the week he drove to town, then to Winnipeg for several days, and returned to the land for good. Evenings he read a little in the papers that kept arriving. Sometimes he played silently with Janie and her dolls; the other children avoided him and when they quarreled, which was no more often than before, he let Emily separate them. Every day while he could he walked past the skeleton of the hogbarn; he had driven the tractor through the double doors into the barn aisle and was overhauling it there, bit by bit. He had sold the cow.

When the snow began to melt in early April he could no longer work; two weeks later he had no strength to feed himself. The doctor insisted on a hospital where specialists could study the case, but Sam said no and Emily agreed; the doctor kept on giving him different colored pills at each call and shaking his head. Emily cared for Sam in her invariable, efficient way and his father wrote from Saskatchewan what was loose over there and to phone if it got serious. On Sunday her brother took the children to Sunday school.

"Emily," he said on the Sunday before Easter, "I made a mistake."

She turned from the spring air at the window she had slid aside; a bird was singing itself dizzy in the cottonwoods.

"It was a mistake. When I heard the voice, I should of gone. Left a note and gone. When you know like that, are chosen, you shouldn't wait, talk. Go."

"Sam," she said, "Sam, what would it have helped? What?"

"Maybe not a thing, nothing. Like that Epp that went back." He thought a little. "Yes. It would have helped nothing. But do it, that's it. Some of it, just do it," he added heavily.

After a time he was aware of her kneeling by him, shaking, face buried in the blankets. Far away he heard her: ". . . Sam . . . Sam."

"Sure, sure," he said and moved his hand on her hair. "That's all gone and finished. It wasn't for you, or the – no, you can tell them all that. It wasn't any of you. Not really. Emily! You'll tell them? Hey? You hear? You hear?"

For a time after the funeral they feared for Emily's sanity. She refused to leave the farm and one evening her brother found her trying to fire the hogbarn wall; another time it was all a neighbor, who was relieving her brother that day, could manage to coax her out of the barn where she was trying to put together the tractor which, as Sam had dismantled it to the last screw, lay in neat patterns the length and breadth of the long aisle. About that time John returned from South America – he had not received the telegram until after the funeral – and with him to help in time Emily's symptoms slackened and disappeared; finally the doctors said the will could be read. The will contained several surprises. Besides the family plan insurance of $10,000.00 in effect since marriage, insurance on all loans, debts, and mortgages and a $100,000.00 term life insurance contract had been in effect since February. The estate was worth not quite $150,000.00, left entirely to Emily and the children except for $5,000.00 after taxes to John. The lawyer apologized privately to the two men later about the ambiguity of the last clause, but Sam had insisted on the exact wording: "I would like to leave part of my estate to the Inter-Mennonite Church Service Society, Peace Section, but I cannot because that would be hypocrisy."

Though the insurance companies threatened, they knew they could not risk fighting the claim of a widow and four orphans; they had to content themselves with firing a doctor and an underwriter or two. By the end of June Emily was strong enough to drive to Winnipeg to talk with investment brokers. When she returned the neighbors watched her drive by. It was a hot summer and there was too much dust to tell for certain whether she had moved up to a Chrysler or a Cadillac, or Thunderbird.

THIRTEEN

On the Way

I

ELIZABETH HAD perhaps ten minutes to plane time when she noticed the old man in difficulty. She sat too far away to hear them, but the man's clothes, beyond the obvious distress of the two airline agents, left no doubt he was a foreigner; probably – oh, most likely Iron Curtain. She didn't much relish getting up; Toronto International Airport no less and it would be doing well if at any given moment it could officially muster someone who spoke French; a few years ago she would already have been over there – she smiled; admit ten. In any case too long now to glory in her knowledge, at least until the helplessness reversed to smiling gratitude; too long to anticipate before the fact. And the fact was Canada was almost as bad as the United States, which at least had some world-status excuse for being oblivious to the forty-odd languages of the civilized world. That would have made a good centennial article for some centennial issue or other: Canada's greatest threat from the U.S.A. is not political, economic, even televisonic – televisional? – yes, that was – relatively better than the first, at any rate, and one should have about three – better four – refuted points before the striking, new, subtly devastating insight: the real – gravest, profound – quintessential? – yes, "the purest" – U.S. danger to Canada was its blatant North-American-centricity (could you build a proper parallel on "ethno-centricity?" – then "northamericano-centricity," with acknowledgements to TV Spanish and an apologetic obeisance to Professor of English T. J. Jones wheeling once again in his grave) where even cartographers centered North America and split Asia at random somewhere through Tibet and Burma; where English was the only civilized language because it commanded the most competently deliverable megatons and if anyone was going to get vaporized it would be most likely an American-speaking voice that – heavens, to be scholarly she'd have to bring in Russia, certainly now the up-and-coming Chinese – she'd never place it anywhere, except perhaps the *Fish Street Love-In* and that wasn't exactly her style – she was laughing to herself, watching a jet slant into the sky. Once going, her thoughts were as consequential as a kangaroo; a noon hangover from the morning conversation with Rachel, begun by the paperback she discovered just then in the dresser of the Spenders' spare bedroom.

"This certainly wasn't around when I was here at Christmas," she tossed the book in Rachel's lap. "Placed for my consolation?"

"Heavens!" Rachel was sitting on the bed, laughing, "I'm almost embarrassed!"

"Why aren't you completely? It doesn't at all look like something left by the Gideons. If you keep up such thoughtfulness next time in Toronto I'll have to retreat to a hotel."

"I read it here because I didn't want Alex to see me," Rachel's face was slightly red but her eyes still laughed. They had known each other too intimately for too many years to be embarrassed for themselves.

"Has it? Well, I'm the usual professor's wife, about two years behind. Lydia Fern says it's the latest thing for us 'older women' to read."

Elizabeth picked up the book and looked again at the woman on the cover. "Did you like it?"

"Me? It's just to read so you can look around brightly, in all your worldly wisdom. Half the first half I can't believe and three-quarters of the last is repetition."

"Quintessentially quartered. Who are all these older women he praises, how old are they?"

"That's the trouble! They're mostly about thirty, or thirty-five."

They laughed together, seeing themselves; women well enough taken care of but too close to fifty to expect a passing male's notice, unless they smiled hard.

"It has at least wit?" Elizabeth said, folding her blouses carefully.

"Yes," Rachel hesitated on the word, "but not really. There is one rather funny spot, I think. He's – the overpowering-animal hero – rolling in the grass with this semi-reluctant wife who can't quite make up her mind – or whatever she has to make up – and at the great moment the husband comes snorting along in the dark and he has to finish business more or less in his pocket."

"Wit?"

"Well – wittier than soap opera. But with the children on their own and Alex finally at that text, so tied up with committees too, and there isn't that much to do in the house –" Rachel stopped, suddenly sober. "Liesel, do you have enough, living by yourself?"

"Do I – get enough?"

"Oh you!"

The familiar childish name had caught at Elizabeth in annoyance. They had been such honest friends for so long because they never asked about intimacies unless the other began by offering her own, and at that moment it seemed to her Rachel had overstepped in their laughter; she continued, tone bright and sharp, "I had quite enough of marriage five years with José, thank you." Rachel was looking away; "Sorry,"

Elizabeth said. "I guess that reveals something; even after twenty-two years I unearth that rat."

"Everybody makes mistakes when they're young."

"Of course. And some just learn for life. Well, if you like dirty books that are witty, so-called, have you seen *Beautiful Losers*?"

"I've seen it – in the University Library and it looked like such a lovely title I picked it up. Heavens!"

"If you can stomach it, it does have wit, of a kind. But literally rather more – to avoid the obvious Anglo-Saxon – excreta. Some 'great' Canadian critics say it's 'the great' Canadian novel at last."

"Really? Somehow I couldn't get started."

"There is a martyred Iroquois – Huron? – princess in it who mutilates herself with thorns, which is rather unoriginal but –"

"Perhaps she rides them," Rachel suggested with interest.

"That's good, I wonder if Lennie – but that's not too clear, along with everything else. Lucidity today is strictly for morons. And the girl is truly most pure but there are these lecherous old men who – ahh – shall we say are 'adlingulating' her toes, one by one –"

"Ad – what?"

"Adlingulate? I just made it up. English needs such a word; like 'osculate' for 'kiss' – sounds much more proper for us older, rather oldest, women. Come now, remember your Latin: 'lingua'?"

"The tongue?"

"One hundred percent. There are all these old men –"

"The priests?"

"Correct again! Rachel, you really –"

"And there must be a sexy Jew. Maybe homosexual or at least ambivalent, but fighting his Jewishness, or better, a WASP dreaming he's a Jew and – yes, that's it – a WASP as Jew burning himself on the martyr fire of the princess, you know, a faggot for the fire still 'adlingulating' her metatarsal extremities as he transpires to symbolize repentance for all the horrid things Christian bigots have –"

"Good heavens, Rachel! And 'transpires'!"

"Use your Latin! Wonderful! It's The Great Canadian Novel at last! Hasn't it got an Eskimo? A Presbyterian and a dirty RCMP?"

"No. That part is in 1680, there weren't RCMP or Jews in Can –"

"It doesn't matter, a Presbyterian is enough. It's still the great Canadian novel even with just the priests and the Indian toes. It's got everything: race, sex, Freud, religion, and inhibited Canadians: the frustrated priests working off their childish oral-oriented perversions on the pure-beautiful-twinkling-sexy toes of the sexless Indian maiden. Whoopee! I have to read it."

"Oh don't, Rachel. The book will simply confuse all your brilliant clarity! Alex must find a place for you at York; I must write him as soon as I get home; you must give a lecture on –"

"Liesel!"

"– to avoid all Anglo-Saxon again – on The Intercourse, Excreta and Adlingulating School in Canadian literature. Fantastic! Our own literary Group of Seventeen or 'Layteen.'"

"You absolute witch!"

"The Princess Tekakwitha is not sexless. That exactly she is not."

"You've ruined my great Canadian novel," Rachel sat up where she had collapsed on the bed. "Keep your half-hearted recommendations to yourself; you won't let me have my moment of brilliance; just when you compliment you wreck it all by topping me."

"Watch that very complex word 'top.' It's Anglo-Saxon too!"

They literally tumbled together with laughter. Finally they sat up, and Elizabeth said, "See here, you crushed all these blouses, contorting yourself in so un-matronly a manner. That is a fact, like the fact of the pulchritudinous princess. And I did not wreck your startling insight into the Canadian male, old men who've leaked away their zip. . . ."

The old man at the airline counter was no Canadian, though at the moment he looked frustrated enough. Not by toes. Still laughing to herself she got up, went over and said, in Russian, "Excuse me, may I help?"

His slow turn and the look – perhaps gratitude – emerging on his face told her she had been correct. But whatever the problem, he seemed not as involved as the chattering agents; and from the back he had not appeared so old; his face was incredible; worked granite.

"Madam, thank you," she could not catch his accent. "Thank you. Could you, please. My ticket is not valid." It was not a question; his tone expected only confirmation and was perfectly resigned.

"He speaks Russian," she said to the agent. "What is it?"

"Well thank you!" the older agent turned. "Take it, Joe."

"Yeah, I figured that, his ticket's from Moscow and he just come from Montreal," Joe shook his head. "But gee – not a word English or French. Thanks a lot, Ma'am, for your help. Who knows Russian?" He looked at her and they laughed. "You see, it's just his ticket was marked wrong; the flights changed June 30 and the one he's marked for goes to Calgary only and then Vancouver, but he wants to go to Edmonton. There's no fare difference, but the Edmonton flight is later – 7:45. If he goes now and transfers to a local at Calgary he'd get to Edmonton by 5:30, at the latest. I was just trying to explain that for a through flight, and the number's wrong anyway, he'd have to wait another eight hours here. You see?"

"Perfectly, thank you," she was grinning at the youngster,

and he blushed. He was really a most solicitous young man and she should not have said it that way. She explained to the old man.

"I cannot get to Edmonton then." Again like a statement; asking nothing, accepting immediately the worst possible possibility.

"No, no, of course you can," Elizabeth repeated. "He says you can get there more quickly than your ticket is written out or. And the flight number is changed but that does not matter."

"They told me," he said slowly, "that I had to follow these flights, exactly. No others."

"That is no problem here," she smiled. "There is no Intourist here. If you have a ticket, as you have, you go, and change as it suits you."

"You know – Intourist."

"I have traveled in your country, also in the past years."

He must have been very tall as a young man; even the erosion of age had not worn him to her eyelevel. Then she heard her flight. "There," she said, "they are announcing the Calgary departure – the one the agent says you could take. I am going on it too, to Calgary. We could go together and I could help translate, help, if you wish?"

"You . . ." he was looking at her a long moment, and almost it seemed he would ask a question. His tone hung, he looked, a wide veed face with eyes drooping at the corners, eyes grained in brown, the right barely awry under a bluish film like blindness. She laughed suddenly.

"I live in Alberta too, I'm just going back. From a – a conference here." His unmoving look held her distant, so appraising it nearly frightened her. "Yes," she said.

Suddenly his head moved back slightly. "Yes," he echoed her, but with hard decision, "Thank you, that is good. There are only my bags. Two."

In a moment they had arranged the ticket and bags and

were outside, walking side by side across the tarmac; the heat shimmered layers in steaming air laced with grease and jet-fuel. O beautiful Alberta, dry and high as the everlasting hills of Judah. After each Learned Society meeting she vowed, "Never Again!" with all those picayunish belly-mole-centered papers and bulgy garter-belted women who can't take care of themselves or dig up even a five-minute casual male escort; hanging about, wanting you to have a drink with them so they can case the bar; Toronto on the scum-fondled shores of Lake Ontario the end of July! Certainly this year but for Rachel and Alex – Rachel was diabolical! – and none of those ancient mul-tilingual harridans would envy her this ancient, that was cer-tain. His face was almost historic, but his body must still be very strong, carrying that satchel and all those heavy clothes after a long flight so erectly. Perhaps he was one of those unbelievable Georgian peasants who lived to a hundred and sixty – his accent wasn't Georgian. And his strange, foregone-conclusion kind of talk: she did not remember Russians that spoke so, any more than Canadians. Anticipating the worst not to be disappointed? But he was, of course, polite; standing aside for her at the ramp, it was just as well she had not put on the nylons with the run up the inside of – good gracious – she was laughing and the stewardess laughed with her in wel-come, quite without guile. She had nothing to be guileful about, that blonde *maedele* trim to a turn of the lathe, not from an iron-haired woman professor. Almost forty-eight.

She urged him to take the window seat. "The flight may be clear, and I have seen all this, many times," and he accepted with his curt thanks. He stowed his leather satchel, that indeli-bly declared him eastern European, between his feet. Sitting was lovely cool; she looked out past him into the wavering heat. She thought he might comment on something, but he did not; she must continue the friendly Canadian host; at the moment that appealed to her. And to get beyond those eyes –

"It is so good," she said, "you could come visit this year.

Canada is celebrating its birthday; many interesting things are happening, everywhere. Celebrations."

"The embassy told me, in Moscow."

"One hundred years," she continued warmly, "in Europe is not very much, but in North America everything's so new, especially in the west where we are going, that one hundred years is ancient. And then of course –"

"In the Soviet Union everything is less than fifty years."

She had been so caught up in the serenity of her laughter with Rachel and returning home to a month's quiet work before preparations must begin for the known university year, so sans gene because she could, and had, helped understand someone, though perhaps a little strange, that his quiet countering startled her at last. It happened occasionally, in the classroom; prodding and levering out proper questions to scaffold up the big insight and suddenly, out of nonentical agreement, moved a barely perceptible drift, nudging for recognition: we are not only sheep; perhaps none of us are, except you expect nothing but what is sheepish stuff. He was surely a peasant, his profile – she herself had been born one – and his white hair, thick despite its fineness, lay back straight from a low forehead. Heavy eyebrows, long straight nose slightly bulged at the end, a wide mustache covering his entire upper lip, and a jaw line broad and heavy. Seams overlaid his face, chiseled in the tight dark skin. He moved his head and looked at her again; she smiled, his eyes – his mustache lifted a little as she said,

"Yes, of course, yes the newness, factories, buildings, bridges, that was what every traveler in your country sees, what I saw two years ago when I was there four weeks. But out here," she gestured for all Canada and Canadians, "we always think of Europe, and with it Russia, as old. Very old. For most Canadians it is 'the old country,' somewhere over there."

He said, "Russia is old. My people – those from whom I come – have been there nearly two hundred years."

His voice held no strange shyness; the accent, well, at least she had her opening. "You are not a –" but the blonde stewardess was in the aisle, arms full of papers, smiling and helpful. The old man was reaching for his satchel and she said, "It is nothing, she is offering papers to read, while we fly," accepted the morning daily for herself and wanted to continue. But immediately behind came the other stewardess, face smiling above her clipboard,

"Your names are, and are you flying through to Vancouver?"

"Dr. Cereno," Elizabeth said, "to Calgary. And this gentleman doesn't speak English, he's going to Edmonton via Calgary. I can translate – but I don't know his name." She looked at him and he was opening his satchel. Two fingers on his right hand were mangled. "She wishes to know your name: I told her you were going to Edmonton through Calgary."

The dun exit-card – they had not given him a passport – was in the crippled hand, offered past her, its lettering – it looks like swearing some bright little twirp once said in class, and it was that for most western eyes, but never for hers, thank you pappa may your innumerable other good works follow after you as your Good Book says as this one had done – bright and new. "She does not want that, only your name; the agent saw that, and your name is on her list."

"Jakob Friesen."

"What?"

He gave no impression he had heard her exclamation; his voice was quiet as he said past her again to the stewardess. "Jakob Friesen."

"Thank you," and the stewardess was gone. Elizabeth tugged her seatbelt as the engines outside began to roar. Really, the name should not have surprised her; not that much. She had heard that they were coming now, long separated family members, one here, one there, for short visits. A few months usually. But this man; he looked nothing at all one would expect; more like a – there was only an apprehension; she could not articulate in her thoughts what she had thought he was, or why for her he did not fit what he might or should be – and then she remembered her rudeness and said,

"Excuse me, Mr. Friesen, but your name – it was a surprise. My married name is Cereno – my husband is – dead, many years – but it is a Spanish name, Argentina, but my family name is Driediger. That's why..." she stopped. He was looking at her without any expression still.

"I came from the Mennonites," he said finally. "Perhaps they are easier to find in Canada than the Soviet Union."

"Yes, the name," she said. Easier to find in Canada? "I teach languages, and the name often shows exactly –" she stopped; opening lecture, introductory freshman linguistics. She laughed a little, pushed quite off-balance now by his expressionless silence, by the impossibility of now speaking to him as a complete stranger. "Cereno is ambiguous enough, anywhere southern European, but if you know anything about Mennonites a name like Driediger, or Friesen, can't be hidden in –" The jets screamed outside, they were moving; after a polite moment as she paused he turned to the window. Even the revelation of their Mennonite names left him immune; impervious; like the stone he looked. Why had she blurted it out, anyway? For years now she simply let "Cereno" carry her disguise and what she had learned about Mennonites and their actions when they had no idea they were being observed by someone who was – well, had been – one herself, had always been, to say the least, revealing. But faced with his face she had suddenly not only blabbed all, she'd even thought once again, "Before I knew, did I do anything, say anything, that was bad, that was –" as she hadn't thought since she could not remember when, and she jerked to thinking awareness. It was like reverting to childhood; at very least childish adulthood. It must be his face, his unquestioning rock-like silence.

With her thoughts, one would almost have to say "second-childhoodish" – geriatric? – and her suddenly obtuse tongue wandering and leading around the world and into history, it was very well indeed that the jet had moved. With a Mennonite, even one met casually – you never knew who they knew or might someday meet – she had not had such an ungirdled need for expression for it must be decades. Pappa had had the word for that: typical Lowgerman gut-language: *woat derchfaul.* "Frequent fluid verbal evacuations" somehow doesn't suggest quite the elemental picture of the literal: "word through-fall?" – umm – "freefall?" That's certainly startling, if you know anything about parachuting. Too esoteric; the curt Anglo-Saxon children use is appropriate; again. That packing with Rachel must have left her feverish! Smiling, in control, she leaned her head back; the jet wheeled and drove forward without pause; lifted. Her stomach fluttered; she had known it long enough not to bother anticipating that. O God, anticipating still.

"That is very nice," the voice said beside her. "Canada is very nice; the cities about the lake. And all the cars on big roads."

She opened her eyes, leaned forward and looked down past his ear. Back to friendly host: that played easily enough. "Those factories are the city of Hamilton, large iron mills, and the highways lead around the lake to the United States. And Niagara Falls. Many are now on holidays, driving."

"I do not know that, 'Niagara Falls,' but you have large lakes. Like Lake Baykal, but several in a row."

It was truly curious the way he spoke: even concerning the tickets he made statements, and seemingly when he could not do that, he said nothing whatever. If she could work his confidence to ask a question – he must have been in Siberia to know Lake Baykal. A Mennonite in Siberia; that meant only one thing. She said, leaning back,

"The large lakes here are in a chain, yès, but this one – Lake Ontario – is dirty. Not as bad as Lake Erie – over that way, one cannot quite see it – but dirty enough. Too many careless factories. Lake Baykal would be bluer?"

"Yes, it is bluer. And very cold."

"Perhaps like Lake Superior, the largest of our lakes. You can only swim in little bays there in summer, never in the main lake." He nodded, still looking out. "We will be flying over it, soon," she said. He was silent and abruptly she knew nothing how to continue. Her stomach told her the plane had reached cruising altitude. Almighty God don't poke around there, just be thankful not to know to have to think, just be thankful. . . .

"I once knew a Driediger." Her stomach and the vibration had dreamed her away, as always, and at his Russian she was fully aware. He had begun; she could hold back nothing.

"My father was Helmut Driediger. From Molotschna – Orloff, near the big river where in spring the ice broke open and you could . . ."

"Of course." His voice was almost inaudible. "Teacher Driediger from Orloff," he said in Lowgerman, "our *fiera* in Moscow."

"Were you in Moscow? In '29?"

She had answered in Lowgerman but he said in Russian, "Yes."

"He died in Paraguay in 1946," she had to say finally. "Asuncion."

"Ah-h." After a moment he went on, still in Russian, "And you are his daughter. There was also a son – ?"

"Yes, he is in Vancouver, with his family," she smiled as he faced her. The question at last, it hardly seemed important.

"All in Canada, and he died in Asuncion."

"He never left Paraguay, he or my mother. There was too much he thought he – he had to do there."

"For the Mennonites."

"Yes." Clearly he had caught the implication of her hesitating; she must be certain of his attitude; he was old and she did not want to hurt him. And then, very quickly, before she was quite aware of what was happening, he asked her hard:

"Where do you teach your languages?"

"The University of Alberta."

"Do you know my daughter, Mrs. Peter Klassen, Katerina?"

"No."

"Are you still a Mennonite?"

"No. I – not any more."

Questions like a police tribunal, a swearing allegiance! Tone demanding, brooking only facts; he would have them and do with them what he would. Well. What would he do with them? His old rock face and eyes in their peculiar slant rigid on hers; almost the way he had decided in the airport to – to trust himself to her translation. To her? Was that what he had been doing?

"Your father taught you Russian well," his face had shifted almost to a smile.

"Yes. He was a teacher."

He turned to the window an instant: they were above level clouds; then he looked straight ahead, against the table clipped there to the seat. "I believe you are your father's daughter," he said in his curiously flat Russian, not emphasizing any word, "and you have helped me, very much. I will tell you about myself in short, all that it is necessary to know of me."

She looked at him, totally amazed. He did not turn but must have sensed her look because he said, "That is the way I have always traveled, in the Soviet Union. In certain situations you must trust one person and it is always best to choose that person before you are desperate. Sometimes I have been wrong, and when I was wrong –" he shrugged, smiled for the first time. "You pay for poor judgment."

"There is nothing desperate to traveling in Canada, in 1967."

"No?"

Her smile ended. "Why trust me?"

"You speak good Russian." And suddenly they laughed quietly together.

"I will tell you," he said after a moment, looking ahead again. "I have seventy-eight years. In 1929 in Moscow, when your father was working for passports for those thousands of Mennonites that ran together there, I was there in Cliasma with my family – that is, my wife and five daughters – and I was taken by the GPU and sentenced to ten years. I survived. In November 1939 they let me out, go where you want without a ruble. I was on the Lena River and got to Irkutsk when they froze all travel during the war and worked there till 1946. Then I worked west again, along the railroad, and in 1956 I got back to the Ukraine where once our village had been. Karatow Colony, village Gnadenfeld. There is a collective farm there, the whole valley. In 1958 I had a letter from Paraguay; my wife was dead, one daughter living in Paraguay, married, and one in Canada. Two died as children on the way in Germany, one of typhus in Paraguay. Katerina in Edmonton has been sending me parcels and trying to have me come; in 1965 I applied, and Katerina and her husband bought the ticket so now I can visit three months. My other daughter may come from Paraguay."

A lifetime in nine sentences. It sounded so heroic, so pathetically heroic in what he did not mention that Elizabeth felt something move in her beyond tears.

"Then you," she hesitated. "And then you go back?"

"Yes. I have a room in a place for old people."

"You look very – strong – for your age, what you have been through."

"Yes, I have a strong body. That is why I survived. And because I believe nothing."

"You believe . . ." for an instant she doubted her knowledge of the word.

"Yes. Like you, I have no longer anything with the Mennonites."

That was not what she had meant, but she understood his expression exactly. Like some little grandmother who had never seen beyond her *darp* street, despite his lifetime wandering there was for him still only one thing to believe or not believe. Well, she did not believe it any more, either. In that one and only way.

"Would you like to have lunch?" The stewardess was in the aisle, smiling her guileless smile – the nonsense verse rhyme twisted a grin in Elizabeth; a nonsense rhyme before her and an old man at her side believing now his nothing, going back to his one room in a place for old people.

They ate lunch enhanced by wine. They practiced Lowgerman: it was decades since he had spoken it but the sharp turn of mother tongue returned easily. He told her of learning a little of the Evenkis language during the years he was in the Tunguska-Lena region of Siberia. She had only once before met anyone who spoke a Samoyedic language and she worked out some of its structure from the sentences he knew. His face relaxed at her quick analysis of a language totally foreign to her, and she enjoyed herself as she did with children who do not try to mask wonder, with the playful magic of language knowledge. By then they had passed the overcast and below them, clouds piled and turreted in pure princess castles, they saw Lake Superior, heavy blue, he said, like Baykal. They were content then, tilted their seats back together; dozed.

She awoke before he. She had been so engrossed she had noticed no one else on the plane. It was as well; the woman across the aisle slept with her mouth hung slack. Unfortunately, there are no flies on jets. She picked up her paper and began to read; she turned pages quietly, not disturbing Friesen, his white head turned into the pillow on the wall.

On a rear page a headline stopped her; the short news item held her attention for several readings. Friesen awoke suddenly, sitting erect with eyes wide. She said, "Here's something about a Mennonite in Canada, in our biggest daily."

"What?"

"From Toronto; here," and she translated:

MENNONITE CARRIES CROSS

Calgary: While the canoe race and other centenary caravans move east, a young Mennonite walks along the Trans-Canada Highway going west. He is carrying a plain wooden cross. "It's not really a centennial matter," says John Reimer, 28, of Nabachler, Manitoba. "I began it as a personal concern, a kind of walk of repentance you might say.

"But walking along in the ditch, people looking, stopping, talking, it's become more than that, I guess. What I don't know.

"And one lady in a Buick told me it was most fitting on Canada's hundredth birthday. She thought more Canadians should carry crosses."

Reimer has been walking since the last week in June. He says he can make up to twenty-five miles a day and for supplies carries only a blanket, canteen, and a change of clothing. He accepts no money but eats when someone gives him food. He insists that in over a month he has not yet been really hungry.

"Not the way people all over the world are hungry," he says.

His hair is neatly cut and he is clean-shaven. "It's a real problem, shaving after nights by the road. But beards get at certain people and I don't want to annoy anyone. Not more than necessary anyway."

When interviewed Reimer was resting a day outside Calgary at the junction of the Trans-Canada Highway and Alberta

Highway 2 which goes to Edmonton. He said he had not decided yet whether he will continue west into the mountains, or go north.

"I'm happy. I live like the grass," he says. "No institution to maintain. I don't decide anything till I do it. I feel the land."

None of this is typical of Mennonites, he says.

The wooden cross he carries weighs about forty-five pounds.

After a long pause Friesen suddenly asked, "What was that he said, why he started, at the beginning?"

"Ah –" she looked again, "'personal, a kind of walk of repentance you might say.'"

"What is he repenting?"

"It does not say."

"That is strange," he murmured. "Do Canadian Mennonites – do such things?"

"I've never heard of one, before," her thoughts phased blank, empty as a machine drone lifting her away, a limbo thoughtlessly afloat, empty – his eyes were on her. "No, it's like this, Reimer, says, not at all." She shook her head hard. "About a month ago there was a little bit on him, in the Edmonton paper. He was starting then, and it made him sound like a crack-pot. There was nothing since and I thought it had just died out, like these things do. But I suppose not."

"What is that, 'crack-pot'?"

"Oh, when someone is sick, cracked in the head. Does this sound like that?"

"No," he said. "It is merely strange."

"Yes." Strange as a lifetime reeling back; of Edmonton a quiet refuge at the end of everything she thought, known to no one; of the Alte Aula at Tuebingen with poled boats sliding by the island on the glass-green Neckar below the castle and the Hoelderlin Tower, beamed gable facades like the Dark Ages walled up from the creneled walls; of translating for the Americans because she already spoke most of the languages and quickly worked out smatterings of every other: Russian, German, English, Spanish, Polish, Dutch, Americans with heavy hands and direct easy needs for long hair and long legs, their obscenely easy money available if available by the purseload for years and years of classes wherever you wanted to take them, or give; translations begun innocently enough through the refugee work of Inter-Mennonite Church Service after the war in Europe where she fled because then she knew, as everywhere else in the world, only the Mennonite contacts of her father there; strangely innocent still despite Buenos Aires University and the unknowing watched-over years in Asuncion where he refused to leave because the Chaco colonies needed a man in the capital: we'll send you to Argentina, you'll get all you want and can learn, but we're not going to North America, ever; there they have leaders, here who? who will talk to business, politicians, the President? you will get it all, study till you're old enough and you go to Buenos Aires; and in Buenos Aires, such a white-skinned, long-limbed girl of the free world at last; such a long free fool. Slim quick hands, quick dark body over her and through her and half the world away half a life-time later waking from dream in a single bed to the sweat cold over an empty body. Strange; indeed.

"Did you say," she pushed away, "your daughter Katerina lives in Edmonton?"

"Yes, since 1957."

"Trienchi Friesen, almost my age?"

"Yes, we called her Trienchi, yes."

"We were on the same ship, Group 4, *S.S. Hindenburg* from Bremerhaven to Buenos Aires, July 4, 1930."

"Is that so?"

"Yes, your wife and three girls were just down the hall. I did not know she was, in Edmonton." Their looks met; shoulder to shoulder in the soft padded seats, both seemed suddenly naked. "You are that Jakob Friesen?"

"Yes. That Friesen. And you know, of our son."

There was no way to deny it. "A little later, in the colonies, I heard, yes. Only a little." He was looking away, granite face without expression, and she rushed on, "Your one daughter is married there, in Fernland?"

"No, Simons. A Kanadier they call them there, and they wrote he is distantly related. A Friesen too."

"Oh." Again her mind would not move, hanging, clipped to the drone.

". . . four healthy children," he said, and then his expressionless voice went on without hesitation, "there wasn't one building left where Gnadenfeld was, it was collective farm over the whole valley. In 1956 there must have been some Mennonites still left, not all could have got out with the German Army, but they all had Russian names and not one said anything, to me. I believe nothing."

Able to face his carved old face, she knew it was a lie. She wanted to groan in pain for what she understood of him, of herself, and at the same time rage flared in her at the guilt and agony and regret covering, soaked through and through people while the "great" poets and novelists of the western world mucked around wading and parading their own mighty organs and viscera, posturing like puppets, shooting themselves off at the moon and inflating themselves the magnificent modern crusaders of humanity, seers and prophets of the sixties, because they "discovered" Stalin and Hitler, because they "discovered" Dachau, "discovered" Vietnam. Dachaus are everywhere; who could number the Vietnams. In people who believe they believe nothing.

"Mr. Friesen," she said, "would you like to meet this John Reimer?"

"What?" Then, "No." But the corners of his eyes drew up slightly.

"I am staying in Calgary a few days, and he will not be far. There are many planes to Edmonton. I – I could rent a car and we could drive out when we land. Talk."

"That would be bother, and expensive for you."

"Money is nothing. You cannot believe how much I make, for one woman. But of course you want to see your daughter. Yes, of course."

"After thirty-eight years a few hours are also nothing." He added suddenly, "She will only expect me tonight, on the other flight."

"Well then?"

"What is there to see, with this 'crack-pot'?"

She laughed, at the loosening tension in his face as he tried to pronounce the English word. "Oh, he is young – obviously born in Canada. You must meet all kinds of young Canadians, not only those like us, Mennonites born over there."

They were looking at each other as the jet roared on, soberly into each other's eyes.

"I would like to meet this Canadian Mennonite John Reimer."

"Yes," she said. "I too. All we need to find out is if he carried his cross north, or west to the mountains."

II

". . . which is sufficient exercise bicycle stock for our present operation Period They stand up well and provide satisfaction for our customers Period Paragraph

"And finally may I point out that your invoicing for our Order No. OLW 67-894 was incorrect as per terms you agreed upon Period Price you quoted your file 97862 was 76 1/2 cents per flying saucer less 4.5% for five (5) gross or more FOB Winnipeg and less 3.5% on same amount FOB Calgary Period Your invoice TH 67-8936 bills us 76 3/4 cents per less 3.5% on six (6) gross FOB Winnipeg Period We shall expect a corrected invoice by return mail Period Paragraph Yours sincerely Dennis Williams Senior President Outdoorsman Limited"

He clicked off the dictaphone, thought, pushed the switch.

"Oh, and Doris, add a PS, something folksy about if their salesman in October likes elk, we can get him a few days in the elk country west of Rocky, on us of course, you know how to say it. Okay? Thanks."

He clicked off again, replaced the microphone and slid the whole machine smoothly into its padded receptacle under his arm. He should have had this custom-built long ago; why fight a stomach that had grown up when cars were the miracle; let young Dennis fly the company plane, or whatever others he wanted to; western Canada had roads good enough for a Cadillac. As easy to do letters in a car, easier, tires singing on hard pavement, all those horses humming. Anyway, why should he keep shooting around over the country now; let young Dennis and Jack – the name still stuck, young Dennis; forty this month and a daughter and a son in the University of Manitoba, when he was that old he was on his second – well, close to it. With his shares, the city warehouses rented for fifteen years and the potato chip plant in Nabachler maybe young Dennis was worth almost that much too by now. After the first it was easier. Closer than Jack anyway, which was right as oldest son. Someday the "young" would be dropped; perhaps soon. Too soon for me, he thought; old Dennis. Since I was twenty-one. He leaned back against the soft leather and listened to his heart again.

"Hey o poppo, are you finished already?" Irene squirmed about in the middle of the front seat.

He eased his hand from his pulse. "There's a few yet, but I'll do them after Red Deer, when I can't see the mountains over there . . ."

"Then I'm coming back, you promised," and with beautiful fluidity her young body was over, Charles at the wheel shouting,

"Macaroni, watch those big flying feet! Want to wreck us?" as she laughed, collapsed into a three-way L, her legs slanting up from the seat, her feet against the window, her head in Dennis's lap before he quite closed the drawer on his files. Dennis looked along her, their lovely girl a gift when they thought they were long past such things; he caught Esther's eye, her head half turned from the front seat, and smiled. Neither of them had any idea what their life for fifteen years could have been without Irene growing up as they grew old. He smoothed the long red hair; she would never be this new thin thing, Twiggy, thank the lord.

"Your shorts are too short," he said down into her face. "I told you."

Her eyes slanted to her brown legs. "Aren't they nice?"

"Too nice, you silly little girl," he said.

"And the freckles make them perfectly outrageous," Charles said, reached back beside his ear and twisted a toe.

"Poppo my poppo," moaned Irene, in a fantastic contortion cradling her foot, "you must fire your chauffeur with a monstrous fire for he hath abused me!"

"When Charles is correct he isn't chauffeur; he's nephew, and from that he can't be fired. See?"

"If the president won't, the personnel director of D.G. Williams and Sons Inc. Dennis sure will. I'll telex as soon as we get to Edmonton." She uncoiled and propped her feet against the window again, safely out of reach. "Hey, where's the telex in Edmonton?"

They were all laughing then.

"How'd you ever grow up, Moms," hands weaving invisibly, "without mini-skirts and shorts, always covered up all over, summer too?"

"We didn't have time, maybe, to think about it," Esther said from the front seat. "We worked so much, on the land."

"What did all your brothers do, the girls working on the land?"

"You don't understand, Poops, how it was, pioneering. Being poor."

"But you drove wagons, and even sleighs in the winter. You're forever talking about that. It must be nice, pioneering. If you could wear shorts."

"There's only one thing you forget," said Charles into their laughter, "when you're pioneering nobody sprays the mosquitoes."

"Moms said they made smudges, smartie. It would be just sweet, pioneering."

"Yes," Dennis said. "About one weekend."

"Hey o poppo," her eyes flashed up, "can we stay the weekend and drive to Jasper and swim in the hotsprings and take one of the big motor boats along and go up a mountain, just a little, poppo mine, huh?"

"Who could get reservations now in August, a day's notice?"

"Not a hotel! Of course not, we take one of the trailers from the store and sleeping bags and sleep under the pine trees –"

"Let's see now," interrupted Charles, "a motor boat, a camping trailer makes two, and maybe about two horse trailers with horses so we can trail-ride and another trailer with sleeping bags and extra camping and climbing gear, that should do for two or at most for three days. Think this Cad can pull five trailers, Granpa? Only three-seventy-five horsepower."

"If you're scared, I'll drive myself, chi-hick-en –" Dennis got his wide hand over her mouth then, a peasant's hand sure, and she rolled her eyes in green despair at him. He loved her red-blonde head on his thigh, his hand holding her, but the slight tightness in his chest made him want to stretch his legs; her twisting nagged him today.

"Look, sweet, across there, there's still the mountains."

She sat up, away from him. Red-and-white cattle scattered up the green valley's slope and beyond them shone the Rockies, their snow burning blue against the evening sky.

"Gee–sch!" she let out her breath as the car slid up the incline. "Daddy, why don't we have cattle?"

He suddenly could not think why himself. "Grain's safer and I've always worked with machines," he said finally. "Things men make, I guess. I've always thought of buying, selling them, I guess."

"Why?"

He had forgotten she was listening; but he had no time to remember that decades-old reasoning, and he would have needed time, for at that moment they flashed by a car parked on the apron of the road, Irene twirled to look through the rear window, and screeched,

"It's the guy with the cross! There in the ditch the guy with the cross!"

He twisted too quickly, but not quickly enough; he saw only a blur of figures before the road bulged up and hid them.

"It was him, it was him," Irene bounced, almost chanting. "O poppo, let's stop and see him! It was lying right beside him, in the ditch."

"What?" he looked at her, mind racing. The Calgary dailies had had front page stories on him, one with a picture of him looking sadly across the city to the mountains, the wood on his back. "What, what was his name?" remembering only too well.

"John Reimer, from Nabachler," said Charles. "Sam Reimer was his brother."

"Yes. That's it."

"Do you want to stop?" the boy asked. "It's still three hours to Edmonton if I have to drive the speed limit."

"How else is there to drive? Na, Esther?"

"Oh let's, we have to!" Irene went on and on. Esther was looking back at him; in his young and penniless ignorance he had not really known what a wife he was getting; perhaps no one ever knew till it was much too late to remedy, if needed; she had been headstrong then; if not he wouldn't have faced it out with her family about Paraguay, that horror, but she was mellowed now, mellowed in all the successful years, full and rich to what her mother must have been all her life, her mother whom she had not been named after because, as her mother told it, she had screamed too loud at birth to be called 'Frieda.' So that generation of Friesens, at least, had not had one. Her mother had all her life despite her nothing, absolutely nothing he realized again like a twinge in his chest. Some can be that, he thought, but most people need all the things they can get; some even more than they can get; more things. He had thought of this sometimes, before, but he had not felt then like he felt now. It had seemed more distant, and hardly personal. Mrs. Friesen with her calm, as if she had once had a chance and deliberately cut it off, forever, with her calm nothing.

"You look tired," Esther said. "The directors took too long."

"It won't matter, a half hour," he said, trying for a smile. "Still get in bed by ten."

"In Edmonton it's still daylight by ten," Irene said, bouncing with anticipation. "Com-mon smartie driver, wheel 'er right around!"

"Median's a bit wide; normal drivers use cross-overs." And Charles drove steadily on several miles before he found one and turned back south; Irene perched on the edge of the front seat then and Dennis stretched out, foam rubber cushioning his cheek against the window. He would see the mountains a bit longer across the rising land. Odd; he had never thought much about them, one way or another.

When arriving anywhere he never looked until he was outside on his feet, so he could take in the scene with one careful look; if he had, he might not have gotten out of the car, he realized as he stood on the edge of the pavement soft from the day's unclouded heat, feet shifting on the round gravel. The man sat on the far bank of the ditch, an old man and a woman stood below him, and on the road apron, in front of where Charles had halted, was a car and two yards below it in the ditch a motorcycle. Someone – perhaps a man – with hair straggling below a black trooper's helmet supported the black machine against the ditch's slope. He wore cowboy boots, denims, and an extremely dirty sweatshirt from which both sleeves had been ripped. He did not look around as Dennis got out; none of the people in the ditch looked either.

"Ya got the drift, man," the motorcyclist was saying, very harshly to be heard above the whine of cars whipping by, "a bita okay, but ya gotta push a little. Lay yer hand out occasional, borrow a little if they ain't giving. And the enda the legs is too much like plod, a wheel man, a wheel. Put on the drygoods and forget the lumber. There's mountains a' that, all over the world," and he swung his long arm, bare but for a steel bangle and almost as black as his trousers, in an arc behind him.

"Thanks Hawk," the man sitting on the ditch-bank called. "I'll keep it in mind."

"Yeah man, outside Edmonton under the derrick, leave the sign and we'll draft ya a time, high and mighty. A time. See ya. Kid."

A figure Dennis had not noticed in the shade of the parked car suddenly leaped out with streaming hair as the cyclist kicked his starter, the machine screamed and sprang away all at the same instant. The wheels scrunched, spurted gravel, the rear flapping like a flag, the second figure clamped low and riding the machine's whip to fork its leg astride and they were driving down the dip of the ditch and full up the incline, hurdled the apron of the road, a car swerving wildly as they shot up, and all vanished over the hill, gear changes fading in roar.

"Great god," he murmured in Lowgerman, and then sensed Charles beside him and said aloud in English, "what was that?"

"Like those gangs in California, but these are the home-grown-Canadian kind. A troop of them went north when we were coming back; in Calgary they call themselves 'Flight From Hell,' I think."

"They won't make it," he said, looking east across the ditch to the fields. "They won't."

"Make what?"

"Make it from there. What does he have with them?"

"I don't know."

Dennis glanced over his shoulder; Irene hung across her mother's lap, head out the open window but not yet quite daring. He said to Charles, "Come," and strode down the gentle incline, grass stubble crunching.

"Hello," he said.

The man said, "Hello," but did not move, his head tilted back against the fencepost, his legs hanging down the cut of the ditch. He wore yellow shoes without socks and his ankles were dirty.

"Do you know that – those – on that motorcycle?" Dennis asked finally.

The man said, "It's the highway. Anybody can stop, that wants to."

"In Edmonton you'll meet them?"

The other returned his look, unmoving, not even blinking as silence stretched one impertinence to the edge of another. But Dennis suddenly could not face it out; he looked at the other two: the old man in a squarish brown suit, and tie; with snow-white hair and face brown as a gypsy; a tall matronly woman, certainly too decent in appearance to be standing in a ditch beside a dusty bum, that ugly wood tilted against the bank. They looked back at him. No one said anything; as if the seated man's silence had enfolded them all in its resting serenity. To Dennis it seemed momentarily that even Charles, behind him Irene and Esther in the car, suddenly knew that motionless quiet, rest; were seeing him with the flat unattached gaze of the three in front of him, flat like the land planing down to the prairie, he alone coiled, staring about to – the cars whipped by droning on the road – he had to speak; gently. Be carefully gentle.

"Have you eaten, today?"

"Once," the man moved at last: a nod. "But Mrs. Cereno says she brought food," nodding to the woman; she held a grocery bag in her arms. "Thank you," the man said, whether to the woman or Dennis's tone was not clear.

Dennis spoke rapidly, in Lowgerman, "Reimer, what is this *dummheit*, running across the country, like that? Attracting bike riffraff and such like vultures to *os*, a Mennonite talking to newspapers about it. What's the matter with you? I know your father, a decent old man in Rabbit Creek, Saskatchewan, sold him his first Chev after the war, what's the matter with you, first Sam and that *dummheit* and now you dragging yourself across the country, huh?" Lowgerman was always harsher than English and he was glad for it then, the hard sounds, words blunt as hammers that awoke childhood and direct non-nonsense decency; absolute *dummheit*: "stupidity" was not strong enough because it meant more: not only stupid but deliberate bullheaded foolishness beyond all simple ignorance. He sensed this understanding reflected in the long face before him as he began, but the features softened as he went on and when he stopped he could barely deny its – what was it, surely not – pity?

Reimer said, clear and unhurried, "Oncle Willms, why didn't you take the land off him? So he could go?"

He used the polite form of third-person address; though

they had never met, it was more surprising to Dennis now when a Mennonite did not recognize him than when he did.

"Who?"

"My brother."

"That land, why? I wouldn't have touched his land to –"

"To save your undying soul."

"Huh?" but the other looked steadily at him, face long in, clear enough now, pity, and his anger tightened. "Our people came here with nothing and built up this land and worked for recognition through two wars and we made it, we've got responsible men everywhere now, teachers, doctors, professors, engineers, civil servants, members of parliament, even provincial cabinet ministers –"

"Millionaires," Reimer added in the same tone.

"Yes millionaires, what's wrong with that? And you got a good chunk of your brother's insurance too, everybody heard all about that –"

"I haven't got it."

"Huh?"

"I gave it away; too much to carry," Reimer gestured, almost smiling. "Cabinet ministers," he prompted gently.

"In a few years, respectable and decent starting with nothing in this good country. It gave us the chance, mostly just one or two generations, and now you and your bro – but he's gone may he be resting in peace, we won't talk about him – but you, a university graduate and could have a decent, useful job and three times old enough to know better, what's the matter with you? A *halunk* in the ditch!"

"Which answer do you want?"

"What kind of smart-aleck is that?"

"It's not smart-aleck," Reimer said, and his patient expression did not change. "I'm trying to answer you, so you'll understand."

"You've got *reasons* for this?"

Reimer shook his head, "Perhaps not what for you is

reason. Do you believe that there is a God and he loves all people?"

"Don't start that kind of –"

"Will you answer me, as I answer you?"

"Why should I answer all kinds of –"

"Because we are people, we ask each other what's important to us."

Tires whined to the road's silence.

"Do you believe God loves all people?" Reimer said.

"Of course, the Bible says so."

"I know it does, but when I think of the begging children I saw in Ecuador and Brazil and look at you and your – chauffeur, it's almost impossible. To believe."

"He's my grandson Charles," Dennis said in English, feeling suddenly the fury of his weariness. "He understands, he can't talk Lowgerman."

Reimer's attention seemed to shift completely. "Hello Charles," he said. "You're studying?"

"Hello. Yes, U of M."

"Commerce?"

"Well yes, how did you –"

Reimer laughed a little and abruptly pushed away from the post, dropped the foot to the bottom of the ditch in a trickle of dirt. He was very tall and his terry-cloth tee-shirt, covered with flaming parrots in flight, pulled taut across his shoulders and chest. "It fits," he said. "And good summer work for you, driving around your dying grandfather."

"What!" Dennis jerked; a passing car nearly covered his exclamation.

"We're all dying," Reimer said. He was pulling at the cross. "Please, would you sit?" He propped one end on a stone. "Won't you have a seat, that's the best I've got." No one moved; Dennis could not stir his tongue. "Come Mrs. Cereno, it's quite strong enough to hold several."

"Thank you," the tall woman spoke for the first time; she

seated herself. Dennis watched her; she slanted her legs and pulled her skirt decently over her knees. She wore high heeled shoes. Charles said, behind him,

"Granpa –"

reminding him, but he bent down, knowing he must sit, immediately. A voice whispered in his ear,

"Daddy, that old man, he keeps looking at me."

He sat down, almost missing the wide plank. He waited a moment before he said, for only her to hear, "Don't come behind like that, so quiet, sweet. Let him."

"But he looks so – funny – Daddy – let's go – Moms says let's."

"Maybe he hasn't seen a girl in shorts," he almost managed a chuckle. Then he said aloud in Lowgerman, without looking up, "Reimer, who's that old one?"

"I am Jakob Friesen," a voice answered behind him in Lowgerman and Dennis twisted, again too quickly, staring up, "long ago from Karatow Colony, the Ukraine." The old man stepped in front of Dennis seated on the cross, Irene shifting as if about to run, and squatted as easily as if all his long life he had known only the bare ground. "Are you from Friesens too?"

"No," Dennis pulled himself out of his astonishment finally, still staring at the seamed face, "no, I'm D. G. Williams – Willms – from Winnipeg."

The old man said nothing; his expression did not even flicker.

"Na?" Dennis asked.

"The girl, she isn't related?"

"Of course, she's my daughter, our last."

"And she's Friesen too, twice from my side," Esther stood on the ditch-bank looking down at them; Dennis had not heard her leave the car. "My father and mother were both Friesens."

"Ah-h."

"Na, of course," Dennis said, "I didn't think on that, when he asked."

"The girl is a long, red-blonde Friesen," said the old man. "Like once in our family. Gnadenfeld, Karatow."

Everyone looked at Irene; her tan glowed pink in bewilderment and then, with a twist, she sat beside Dennis as if shielding herself.

"What are you?" Dennis asked.

"I just came from the Soviet Union, these two days."

"Today?"

"Yes."

"This is the first time you are in Canada?"

"Yes."

"How can you be related – her family came here – na, Esther?"

"Sometime in the '70's – to Manitoba, almost a hundred years."

"You can't dig that out?" Dennis asked. "And I know enough Mennonites with red-blonde hair. Lots." O god, he thought, I need a bed; sure not long hard relative sniffing.

"Where did yours come from, what colony?" the old man insisted to Esther.

"How should I know that, there were some from something like Frust – was there some place like Furstland?"

"Furstenland, yes, but that was –"

"Lots of people came from somewhere there, where we lived in Manitoba," Esther said. "When I was younger yet than her, I remember."

"Both the Friesen sides?"

"Well," Esther hesitated. She sat down beside Irene, at the crossing of the plank on the stone. "Maybe. But Grandfather on Muttachi's side didn't have relatives here; in Canada he always said he never had one, but Grandmother, he said had more than enough for them all and if he'd had some too it would have been too much for them, just visiting properly would have worn them to nothing and –"

The old man was smiling, his seamy face pulled tight around his jaw and bunched up at his cheeks. "Like she always said, joking," he murmured. "My mother. He had brown hair, didn't he, and his name was Isaak."

"Yes, it was Isaak, but his hair was white when I knew him. I don't know where he came from," Esther said. "He didn't look – like you."

"I can believe that," Friesen said. "If I showed you a picture from before '29 you –" he stopped.

"The Crash too?" Dennis asked.

Friesen said nothing. Esther said, still looking at him, "He died in 1933, he was paralysed on one side and seventy-three."

"The years would be right," said Friesen; but the trace of joy was gone from his face; it was simply blank again.

"If only Muttachi were here," Esther said, "she'd know. She knows everything like this. And she's even got it all written down, I think, in Paraguay somewhere –"

"Oncle Friesen," the strange Mrs. Cereno, seated forgotten behind Dennis, said. "Paraguay."

"Does everything in this ditch speak Lowgerman?" he stared about, but no one seemed to hear him.

"Yes," said the old man, "Paraguay. Do you know in Simons Colony a young Johann Friesen –"

"Who married a Susie Friesen from Fernland –"

"Yes, my daughter."

"My youngest brother!"

"Well," said Dennis, almost forced to chuckle at the revelation on Esther's face, "she looks happiest about you, the newest. As if she didn't have about a thousand already!"

"But this is so . . ." she gestured at the open sky, wordless, "and coming right from Russia, now, let's see, you would be our . . . our . . ."

"Grandfather's nephew," the old man said, nearly smiling again. "I don't know what that is."

"That's simple enough," said Mrs. Cereno, shifting forward on the plank. "You would be cousin to Muttachi – Mrs. Friesen in Paraguay – because you are brothers' children, and a child of your cousin is a first cousin once removed."

"One and a half cousins?" asked Irene in English, and they all laughed. Esther translated, adding,

"This is Irene, our last, and now we know where it comes from, our only red-blonde Friesen."

"You don't speak Lowgerman?" Friesen asked.

"Understand," she said, shaking her long hair before her face in laughter.

He reached out and placed his hand on her shoulder. Dennis saw the two outside fingers were bent to knobs, withered and useless, into the palm. On Friesen's face, old almost as the hills he realized suddenly, there was a look of compassion, sort of dreadful heaviness – understanding? – totally out of keeping with the lovely girl who was returning his look; but her smile was fading, as if his touch and look had discovered for her what she had never yet known in herself. Momentarily there was not even a vehicle on the highway; silence as before a dedication down the valley to the reaching hills.

"Well," Esther said, "Oncle Friesen we'll –"

"Hold it, hold everything," Charles said very loudly, standing over them, arms loaded. "You better say it in Lowgerman."

"Okay. We thought," Reimer grinned, "if you're digging out relatives, why not do it while we eat? Whatever we've got. I'm hungry, for one."

Irene leaped up, "Got some chips?"

"Just a sec, here," with heavy exaggeration Reimer looked into the grocery bag Mrs. Cereno had brought, "but of course!" He held the box aloft. "But you can't eat *these*, they're not 'Williams Wonderful' from Nabachler, Manitoba!"

Irene snatched the box, contorting her face so grotesquely at him that even the old man laughed, not understanding. A sudden oneness, like a still lap of heat on a breezy day, found them in the dust of August grass. John spread the food upon the paper bag ripped up one side and laid like a table on the stubble between them; the traveling cooler came from the car, cushions, the thermoses, both hot and cold. A bit of wind drifted the oil and tire smell from them now and then, modulated the roar of trucks pounding up the slope away, into the opposite valley. The shadows of their cars above on the highway apron now reaching over their feet, they sat on the ground in the ditch; eating; talking.

". . . he built the best *hof* in Gnadenfeld, maybe all Karatow, they always said. But he would leave it only to one grandson, so Isaak went."

"I remember a little, he joked about the 'second son by ten minutes,'" Esther said, "just joking, like he did, even on his sickbed once, remember Dennis that time? But I don't think they ever had much, where it stayed if he brought money along."

"Maybe he couldn't handle it," said Friesen. "It was good he could joke."

"Better he could handle money," said Dennis. "What was this, sending away the second son?"

"Not to break the farm; they had it law in the Russian colonies. It took so long to build up something. Maybe not like, here," Friesen's eye flicked at Dennis, then back to Esther. "It's a collective farm, the whole valley."

"How does that work?" Dennis asked, "Those farms, does anyone even work –"

"Dennis," Esther interrupted, "we have to get Muttachi back again, quick, while he's still here!"

"She's eighty – something – na –"

"But strong yet, and a overnight plane to New York. . . ."

". . . Jesus never said you shouldn't be happy or have fun," John Reimer said. "What gave you that idea?"

"It's all you ever hear of him in sermons," said Irene. "In our church. When did he ever have any fun, always doing those serious things."

"Well, where he went there were so many hungry and sick . . . he cracked a few quiet jokes, maybe. And he was a grown man with a job; for him maybe that was fun. He wasn't exactly a big laugher, at least what's written down about him," John grinned at her sober face. "They didn't write down everything, they admit it themselves. What's fun for you?"

"Oh-h-" the girl tipped back to the sky, dreamy.

"Have another roll," Charles said. "This'll take till midnight."

"Hsssh, driver! Well, I like music, like the Beatles, and Bob Dylan, and —"

"They're nice and noisy, that's true," said John. "But their songs, and Dylan's too, they're really about sad things, real sad. What's fun about that?"

"But they're fun too, the sound and the swing, real swing, drums and listening to the guitar. Sad can be fun, why not?"

"Sure," said John, the humor wiped from his voice, "curled in a soft chair with a full belly, sure, just listening to sad . . ."

". . . like in the '70's again, because of the Russian laws," said Dennis, "but some of them like my father, saw in Canada it was no use fighting a little more school, running away. What can you do in Mexico? In Paraguay like her uncles and brothers have found out? Heat and bugs!"

"Johann doesn't say anything, at least what Susie writes. It's hard, she says, but where isn't it — hunn . . ." Friesen hesitated.

"Hard maybe, na, but you get somewhere, here. What do they have now, there after forty years digging in that cactus? A sand farm, with luck one each for their children, driving with horses, and one road open to the market, that's when it doesn't rain. What's that to get ahead?"

"They live, and have always enough to eat."

"Yes, but what have they got?"

"More than I," said Friesen.

"Na," Dennis took a swallow of his hot milk, embarrassed. "I should – it's none of my business what another's got. Her mother wouldn't stay here, either."

"Hunn."

"Was here a year after *foada* died, but then back, no holding her. Land all covered up with cement and pavement, her feet ached she said. Too cold, she said. In a house with central heating and the bathroom beside her room!"

"Oncle Friesen, she knew your wife; they lived on the same yard for a few months, just before she died," Esther said. "She talked about that."

"Yes."

Dennis said into the silence, "So many years, those terrible communists, what they've all done to people, what they'll someday be judged . . ." he stopped.

Friesen was fingering the grass against his leg. Two stalks broke off in his hand. "Did she say," he said finally, "did they talk about, our son?"

"I don't think – Dennis, do you?"

"No," he said. "I didn't even know that, you have a son?"

"She said nothing. In Paraguay?" asked Esther.

"Oh no, no," the old man was looking away down the curve of the ditch, the double chain of highway that buckled the hills tight below them, "he never left Gnadenfeld. Now he would be nearly sixty. . . ."

". . . recognize that economics, even if it is your major," John grinned, and was again sober, "economical problems are just the outside of the problem."

"What do you mean, 'outside'?" asked Charles.

"Well, it's plain. Who heads world governments? On the whole, generals or multi-millionaires. Even the United States – maybe not Canada at the moment but wait until the next election – and why? The problems are not about money; the U.S. is not fighting for money primarily, though a good steady war helps; it is fighting for, and nearly all the fighting and intrigue and oppression of hundreds of millions of poor all over the world is for the same thing: so the few who are in power (that's an exact literal statement of the case: in *power*) or want to get into power, can keep widening their basis for power and influence. So they can decide what happens to people when and how. The more people, the more power."

"What about the generals?" asked Charles.

"Power too. They command regiments for a while and soon discover that the persons who can command the greatest number of people are the politicians 'in power.'"

"But it's all tied in with money," insisted Charles, "economics. For nations and individuals to remain rich is to remain powerful."

"Yes, but we're talking about basics, and if you want to study the basics for what happens in the world then you have to study the theology and psychology, not economics. What people are like, what God is like who made them, if you think he did. Why do they want power, to control people; the power of money? Money is just the symptom."

"I never went much for theology," said Charles, swishing his pop in its paper cup, watching bubbles break on the surface. "I never even thought about it."

"It doesn't pay money," said John. "You can't hold it in your hand. . . ."

". . . in Moscow and went on a big ship all the way to South America?" Irene's eyes shone. "That Latin music!"

"The orchestra wasn't exactly the Tijuana Brass," said Elizabeth drily, and Irene flicked a look. "I was a little younger than you now." Elizabeth shifted quickly with a smile, "and I had some fun. Especially crossing the equator –"

"Oh, I've read about that, they throw everybody for the

first time in the ocean, oh, it'd just be the supremes, traveling on a luxurious ship, to Brazil and Rio and Capulco!"

Smiling, Elizabeth did not correct her. "I'm sure you will, soon."

"Daddy's very strict with money, of course. He has to be, he says, with nine of us, though why my oldest brothers need – they're nearly as old as you and – oh," she laughed, her hand over her mouth.

Elizabeth laughed aloud. "It's kind of you, to blush."

"But I've got everything planned," Irene continued, "when I'm twenty-one and get the first part I'll buy a plane ticket around the world – planes are cushy but just going to Toronto or Vancouver – kook! – and stop where I want. Paris – Shanghai –"

"When you're my age," Elizabeth said more or less to herself, "you've done all that and what does it help once in a while on a long winter evening in Edmonton . . ."

". . . once you've got something built up, you don't want to let it end. That's weakness to have to admit, I couldn't make it go, right?"

"That's true," said Dennis. "But I've never fooled around; if something I started didn't go, you know, get off the ground, I either unload or just take the loss and get out. In business you've got to decide. Now you take Outdoorsman, Ltd."

"What's that?" asked John.

"We've started in Saskatoon, Calgary, and Edmonton: just over a year now selling campers, boats, everything for the outdoor vacationer. Complete stock."

"For the life of leisure."

"Na, we checked into it: more leisure time coming for everyone, so what you need is things for people to do, good and healthy, outside. Then we organize, buy property and merchandise, advertise. It takes a lot, but if it doesn't really move in three years, I'll get out, no looking back."

"Three years?"

"That's enough time. If not, sell and get out."

"How do you know what happens in three years?"

"Na, you know what I mean," Dennis laughed, "in business you can't think just one day to the next."

"Leave alone just today," said John. "Such business is sure different from what Mennonites used to do: sell milk separators and build threshing machines or plows, raise cattle."

"You have to stay up-to-date," said Dennis, "that's true."

"Did you mean that?" Friesen asked.

John smiled. "No, not exactly. Actually, we started talking about letting things go once they finished their usefulness. It's hardest of all in churches. There are so many different directions of Mennonite church, and all of them making sure they stay alive, and no significant difference between many of them. Eh?"

"You don't run a church to make money," said Dennis.

"Of course. In business you fly around in airplanes but in church you walk on foot."

"Like you with your – thing, here," Dennis laughed, knocking on the wood under him, and stopped.

"That's right," said John. "But I'm trying to be consistent, if you want to keep the picture straight. I'm not flying at all; I walk in everything."

"I don't know what that means," said Friesen quickly.

"It means probably nothing," Dennis frowned as if a pain had cut through him. "Like a lot of things that look smart at the beginning. I've always kept one thing straight, and you can be smart while you're young but wait till a few start depending on you. Church and business don't mix. You really believe something and you're not going to let it collapse. That would mean what you'd believed hadn't really been true, and how could you look back . . ."

". . . never think you were," said Esther, looking Elizabeth up and down. "From your name, or anything else."

"I never deny it, but usually it's nobody's business. I thought Mr. Friesen was a Russian."

"You don't have children?"

"No."

"That's too bad, children, well," Esther laughed, coloring slightly. "I can't say for others, but for me they were and are everything. With Dennis so much away."

"My husband died long ago."

"Oh, I'm sorry. And you were in Paraguay, for a while?"

"We came there in 1930. My father was Helmut Driediger."

"Was that your father?" said Dennis, turning to her heavily. "You're from that Driediger? I met him once, at the Inter-Mennonite Service meeting in 1945 in New York when we were talking about the refugees. He was a statesman, real statesman, but he wouldn't come, either. . . ."

". . . seven thirty," said Charles. "And there's always the speed limit."

"Yes, yes, I know," said Dennis under his breath. "You."

"And you look – you should be in bed, Granpa. . . ."

". . . the whole idea of Jesus just talking about people being 'saved' and feeling good about it is wrong. Quite wrong. He was alive, on earth to lead a revolution! A revolution for social justice, the terrible question of his day as it is in ours was and is social injustice to the poor, to the racially oppressed, to the retarded and the helpless. Mary said, 'All people will call me blessed because of the mighty things the Mighty God has done for me, he stretched out his mighty arm and scattered the proud people with all their plans, he brought down mighty kings from their thrones, and lifted up the lowly, he filled the hungry with good things.' That's the good news Jesus came to bring and do. And he didn't do it by setting up a church that can never change no matter where on earth or in what century it is, a church that's never as important to us as living, as eating, as making our pile, that's there a few hours a Sunday and maybe a committee meeting during the week to keep our fire escape polished, to keep us decent as our parents all told us. No! The church Jesus began is *us living, everywhere,* a new *society* that sets all the old ideas of man living with other men on its head, that looks so strange it is either the most stupid, foolish thing on earth, or it is so beyond man's usual thinking that it could only come as a revelation right from God. Jesus says in his society there is a new way for man to live:

you show wisdom, by trusting people;
you handle leadership, by serving;
you handle offenders, by forgiving;
you handle money, by sharing;
you handle enemies, by loving;
and you handle violence, by suffering.

In fact you have a new attitude toward everything, toward everybody. Toward nature, toward the state in which you happen to live, toward women, toward slaves, toward all and every single thing. Because this is a Jesus society and you repent, not by feeling bad, but by *thinking different.* Different. This is the new society of 'church,' and Jesus is its Lord. 'The kingdom of God is within your grasp, repent and believe the good news!' That—"

"Mr. Reimer."

A strange heavy voice. A black police cruiser stood behind the Cadillac; a man in a red tunic leaned from its window.

"Yes officer," John said.

"We had an agreement, right? These cars have been here over an hour, and it's getting late. The light."

"Of course, Mr. McLeod," said John, getting up. "We agreed. Look people, I have to move, and you too. The shoulder of the highway is really only for emergencies. I might think this is one," he grinned at them, "but they don't."

They were all standing; Dennis felt so heavy that Charles's arm under his elbow was suddenly not merely thoughtfulness but necessity. "Pick that up," he gestured.

"I will stay with him, a little," said Friesen.

"What?" Elizabeth said; they all looked up at the old man.

"I would . . ." but no words came; the face crumpled in the yellow light like a paper bag. He said, in Russian, "I want to walk with him. You go."

"But your daughter – Katerina – she . . ."

As in the plane, he was staring before him, not moving.

"Of course," said Elizabeth. "Her address, give me her address and I'll phone from Calgary, and say you'll come tomorrow?"

"Thank you."

"The nights are cold," said John in Lowgerman.

"I have a Russian coat, in the car, if I can?"

"I would like it, very much," said John.

"There has to be a better society possible in the world than that," said Elizabeth as the old man went. "There's too bloody much sacrifice in the world already, so many dunderheads all over the place serving others, carving their bloody way up in the World Sacrifice Association. God. We need a world where everybody can live for himself, just be himself."

"You want everyone except you dead?"

"I guess," she said, voice and eyes like iron. He said nothing. "Sez you. I'll pick up the old guy tomorrow."

"Aren't there twelve hours daylight every day? If you walk in the daylight, you don't stumble."

She would not look at him; nor did she move. He said, "Hate your life. Just a little, more."

He watched her go slowly up the bank, open the door; then he climbed up the bank himself, to the other car. He waggled his hand at the police car; McLeod waved back and it pulled away.

"Won't you come with us to Edmonton?" Irene said. "With me in front there's loads of room."

He smiled at her warm small face. "No," he said, "there isn't. Not for my long wood." He looked in at the man on the back seat, white against the maroon cushions.

"I could get you a good job," Dennis said slowly. "Something worthwhile."

"I know."

"Na, we'll see you on our way back, in a couple of days, Charles."

"Who knows," and he raised his hand in greeting as the car murmured, leaving him open across the black pavement to the valley and the mountains against the flaming sky, his hand raised in farewell as if he knew already before Edmonton Charles would find out more than he ever dreamed of driving the Cadillac much too much over the speed limit, could already hear the sirens trying to wedge a way before them into the darkness, could already see the bright lights of the hospital: that would not be nearly bright enough.

III

Wide to their left yellow blobs drilled silently toward them, dividing in twos and sometimes fours as they came out of the fading light; the sounds rose like whistles behind them, rising to a shriek as the blot lunged by under their elbows, sounds fading before the red dots. They walked just below the loose gravel where the grass began. In the ditch there were often driveways or steel culverts or on the hills piled-stone water-catches to get over. That was fine in the morning, John explained, when dew freshened the stubble and you felt your muscles loosening, but in the evening it was plain climbing.

"You learn too what grass is easiest for walking; they have different kinds. There is a big difference. Grass and land."

He paused. Something jerked slightly at his feet. He moved it gently with his shoe to the edge of the pavement, stopped and in the motion, without touching the cross which hung hooked over his shoulder with the long end dragging behind, dropped the end of its crosspiece down with a quick, clean crunch. The light of a passing car caught the brown arc as he toed it into the ditch.

"At first I tried it with my heel," he said, "but it feels very bad. I wash it off whenever I get to some water. Between Swift Current and Calgary there is hardly any water."

"Hunn."

"Prairie, immense, and very many of them. One morning, the sun was so bright, and there was half a mile where I counted over seventy such before I stopped, counting."

"Why do they run there, on the way?"

"I cannot think, why. They sit up like little posts, looking at everything. They move very fast and usually make it, out of the way."

They were walking again.

"Sometimes it is one of a pair. Then the other goes on the road and will not go away. It happens often; it must be a pair. The live one will not go and a new low car comes and if the driver does not want to he drives over with his wheels on either side, you know like this, and the live one feels the shadow over it and sits up. East of Gleichen there was about half a mile."

"Gleichen?"

"It is an Indian reserve."

"Reserve?"

"Where only Indians can live."

"Oh. In the Soviet Union, they have that too, for such like Jews."

"What do they call them?"

"A nice big name: 'autonomous oblasts.'"

"'Reserve' is a nice big name, too."

They walked in single file, the old man following the little furrow of the dragging wood. The sun was gone to a livid orange raggedness on their left, over them to the right the sky sank into gray. Between vehicles sometimes it was very quiet, sometimes for almost a minute.

"Are you tired?"

"A little."

"When there are trees across the road, or brush, we will stop."

"It is, very, empty."

"But in gullies, trees grow there."

They were going up an incline and after some moments the old man said,

"Why, on that side?"

"There are trucks at night, even more than now. If there is wind it comes from the mountains, and that side takes the sound away a little."

"You learn, walking."

"Every little comfort helps."

"Comfort?"

"Usually," with a laugh, "you sleep so sound you hear nothing, in any case."

"Yes," the old man said. He had tied his coat in a bundle on his back and as he walked he unraveled and then braided again the end of the cord with which it was tied. The orange light flickered on his eight good fingers, but he did not look at what he was doing.

"Magpies and crows, they must be in Russia too, they sometimes clean them off the road."

"You do not have vultures?"

"They say, but I have not seen them. In the south farther there are. They sail in big circles, looking. I shot a deer in Paraguay once and we threw what was left of it away. In the morning I went to look at them there. They flew into a tree, just sitting; looking at me."

"In the mountains of central Asia, there are griffons, that eat such things."

"Where, in central Asia?"

"In the mountains of Kazakh, west and north of China, and other places."

"Are they so ugly too?"

"Very. They hunch up their wings, when they sit, and pull

their long necks back, between them. The neck and head is naked."

"Magpies at least look nice."

"I do not know that."

"A black bird with a long black and white tail. You will see it tomorrow. Ah, see that? There is brush down there in that draw, I think. Perhaps the ground is even soft."

It was not soft, but a wedge of willows made fine resting under the whispering poplars growing up the south slope. They had gone in far enough that the lights were gone, and almost all sound. The copse was very dry, but a careful fire was permissible.

"Very small, but nice for coffee, and friendliness."

"I have something here," the old man pulled out a black flask. "Would you?"

"Thank you. But go ahead, it will warm you."

"It is nothing for one to drink alone when there are two by a fire."

"True. I will drink what I have and you drink what you have. And we'll share the two rolls left."

They ate the dry bread. The black coffee tin sat on a rock against the tiny pointed fire.

"Do they often yell at you, like those in that car?"

"A few more now, perhaps, because of the papers. But there were always some. Never when one is alone in a car; they yell for each other."

"Do they stop?"

"Sometimes. They are very loud sometimes, and sometimes angry. When there are enough of them. Or they are older."

"Angry like Willms?"

"For sort of the same reasons, though backwards. They talk about Mennonites not fighting in the war and now doing this to shame Canada when it is a hundred years old. Once two cars came, full of men in old uniforms."

The old man stared into the fire.

"But the police are very good."

"The police?"

"There is no law against walking in the ditch. I have been walking over a month, and probably they know where I am all the time."

"Is that good?"

The other chuckled, lifted the tin from the stone with a looped willow and set it on the ground. It steamed coffee. "It was good then. Suddenly their car was there and after a little the others drove away."

"They always come like that?"

"No! I am usually big enough to help myself; especially with girls."

"Girls? I meant the police."

"Oh, they come too. One drove by, parked her car in the next town and walked back and talked all night."

The old man was squatted by the small warmth of the fire in the cool evening, unraveling the cord again.

"Fortunately I had almost a pound of coffee," drinking. "This seems such a fine rich country, does it not?"

"Yes, in one day it seems a fine rich country."

"When you see more it will seem so even more. For many it all comes so easy, the easy business of staying alive and being comfortable, they get all mixed up living. Before I began I could not have imagined what I would hear, how comfortable and rich people can get mixed up, living."

The old man was braiding the cord.

"They really do not know where it is, up or down."

The old man held the cord against the firelight, studying his braiding.

"Really. Like that girl, she had done everything she could think she wanted to do, worked at it and tried it and suddenly she had tried it all, most of it a few times over, and she didn't know any more, what do I want? Unfortunately her family had enough money she was not expected to work to feed herself and buy her clothes; for most people that helps: they have to do something during the day that makes them tired and at least satisfied when they can do something, anything, else for change from their work. Even just sitting by the TV gives them the impression they are living then. But this one, and unfortunately in a way it is too easy to have enough to eat and stay dressed in this country if you are only one, this one did not *have* to do anything if she did not want to herself, and she no longer knew what she wanted. Everything fit outside, no problems, and she didn't know what to do with herself inside."

"What did you say?"

"At least she knew she was mixed up inside. 'You don't know,' she screamed once, 'how terrible it is to be always only bored.'"

"Yes," said the old man, untying the knot he had just made with equal care, "at least she still screamed. What did you say?"

"What can you say? If a person insists every minute of his life he is bored and gives five hours of example, I guess he is. When she was through I told her what I wanted was to live the concern for others and love that Jesus showed."

The old man began braiding again.

"But she had heard and seen and done and felt and smelled too much about that word 'love' too. It just made her puke, she said. And she did."

"You live this concern, walking the highways with that?" the old man gestured with his cord to the other leaning against the cross leaning against a tree.

"It is – hard to explain. I don't think I have ever explained it at all to a Mennonite."

"I have nothing with Mennonites. I believe nothing."

"It is, in a way, almost easier with men in old uniforms. Some of them remember long ago, what they felt they had to do then, and some of them did it several times."

"I have nothing with them at all," the old man said again.

"Well," the other said, nodding a little, stretching his long bare feet nearer the fire. "I had to – I had done what I thought were good things, studied the Bible, taken agriculture at the university, gone to land-poor countries and tried to show them how to grow things: for Inter-Mennonite Church Service I was in Algeria four years and then in Paraguay one when my brother died in Manitoba and I came back and I felt it had to go different. I had to think different, somehow."

"Your brother died?"

"Sam Reimer. If you were in Canada a few days you would hear about him from our people."

"That Willms said?"

"Yes. Sam thought he was called by God to be a prophet. Like in the Old Testament Isaiah or Jeremiah. He believed God called him one night to go and preach peace in Vietnam."

The old man stopped braiding. "Vietnam?"

"Vietnam. But no one believed him and they worked it so there was no way he could even get a proper passport, and he gave up and died after a few months."

"Of what?"

"He gave up. I was in Paraguay and he never wrote me till the end. Then the telegram got there and I came too late for the funeral; the letter where he wrote me some things came back after I was in Manitoba."

The old man sat motionless by the dying fire.

"He was just an ordinary guy. An ordinary still Mennonite that worked and had gotten started on a farm. He was fifteen years older than I and when they came here from Russia it was depression and so he just had to work at anything; he never could go to school like I, and I never knew him much except in between when he came home from working out. He gave me a hundred dollars to help when I left for Algeria. He just slept and worked his life away till this happened. He sent me this one letter and he put in the note where he had written down what he heard that night."

The little heap of coals glowed in the darkness.

"'Of course I am the God of your fathers the Lord Your God go and proclaim peace in Vietnam.' And under it he wrote, later in ink, 'Samuel, I think Mrs. Friesen was praying too.'"

"What was that?" the old man said.

"A call, like prophets in –"

"No, that praying."

"Oh. That was something when he was a little boy in Moscow. I think I heard some of that in Paraguay from a relative who was there then too, staying in the same house with my parents and Sam, a little boy then, when they were trying to get out in 1929 and one evening the GPU came and took a Friesen there from his family –"

"Samuel Friesen?"

"No, my father, Samuel Reimer. A cousin, Epp, said this to my father –"

"Old David Epp, a short little man?"

"Why yes, David Epp, his youngest son Franz is in Paraguay. He told me."

"Franz Epp, getting signatures for Helmut Driediger in Cliasma. November 1929."

There was a long silence. Finally: "You are that Jakob Friesen."

"Gnadenfeld is a collective farm field now," the old man said.

"Did you see it?"

"Once in 1956."

"Helmut Funk is in Neuheim Colony in Paraguay. He came there after the war."

"He, he –"

"Yes." After a moment the other continued, "We talked one day, and he told me how your son ended, but who would have ever thought . . ."

The old man tied a knot in the cord and put it in his pocket.

He lay down, his head on his jacket, pulling the overcoat around his legs and chest. An ember flared a moment; his long shape lay stretched out on the ground.

"Once you start thinking, you can never think enough, of it all," the old man said up into the air. "You think the years grow over it and it is gone, healed, but all at once one day and it is all there, uglier still. Just when you have decided that three months with your daughter, perhaps both of them, and it will be possible perhaps not to talk about it, to live with them as you have lived now for forty years except you will see them and kiss them a little and touch their children before you go back again to your room for old people. Surely you can do that for them; they cannot understand why you do not even try; they have no idea in ten years of letters why others can come and you cannot, even for a little while. So finally you apply and then you can come to Canada and before you even see your daughter, before you have even settled your stomach in Canada and looked at your daughters once and seen what you can talk and do so that in a few months when you leave they will know only what is necessary for their happiness, no more, before you can be ready first one person and then the second tells you they know that once you betrayed your only son."

"But – Funk said nothing about – that."

The old man lay motionless.

"He told me some had fought against the collective farm, but he had liked it. They went out to work together, and sang, and everyone was told what to do and how much. It was better than Paraguay he thought, but they always kept you afraid. That was the trouble, you were always afraid. Perhaps they did not have to be, but they were. So he said maybe young Friesen had been right when that commissar who was once a Mennonite started cleaning up. He just said Friesen seemed suddenly to – to do just terrible things; he tried to kill the commissar so they executed him. Quickly, in T – T – something."

"Terwoj."

"Yes, Terwoj."

"Suddenly, the end of November, 1929."

"Well, yes . . ."

"Ah-h-h."

It was quite dark. The sound from the old man was like the poplar leaves high above them in wind. From the highway came the rise and pounding roar of transports.

"That is what Sam remembered from a little boy. Mrs. Friesen was praying too. There in Moscow."

"It helped her exactly nothing."

"Somehow he tied that together with being called to Vietnam, and the more I thought about that, the less I could go back to doing what I was. I had to try and think differently, completely; forget about doing something, even about doing what I thought good; forget about getting ahead, building my mind, preparing, about trying to be useful."

"And it helped her exactly nothing."

"So finally it seemed I should walk. But I did not want people to think me a hitchhiker going somewhere. I am not going anywhere; at least not in Canada. That's the whole point, and I have to carry something that shows that. I felt perhaps a bomb or missile would do, because that is what everyone in the world fears. But if I carried that, too many going by it would look as if I was advertising such horrible things. I am a human being, walking. That's all. And for that the best seemed to be the old thing everybody understands something about. Not to advertise a wrong I thought someone had done to me. Just a tired, dying human being, walking the land."

"And it helped us all, all these forty years of lifetime exactly nothing. What is there in this world to understand."

" 'Understand' is not the word; you are right. You can never really 'understand' about someone, anyone, even yourself. It is best to believe in them as human; feel that they are alive like you and need warmth, concern. Like you felt when you did not want to hurt your daughters, or let them know that you now believe you believe nothing."

"If you had been ten years in exile and survived and then dragged yourself back fifteen years and found everything wiped clean like cheap plastic, you would say nothing."

"I have never known that, so I cannot say. But," a wind moved high in the trees, "surely even then I could know, as I know now, that as long as I am alive the possibility can never be completely closed that God is good."

"Ah-h-h. If there is one."

"That possibility cannot be closed, either."

Suddenly behind them, away from the highway, a sound burst at their very ears: a wail, clicks like bones breaking, the hard grinding roll of steel over steel. The sound rushed from loud to explosion as they leaped erect into their shadows, and immediately from the slope above them a voice coughing and almost laughter dying to a wail away.

"What . . .?" the old man whispered finally.

" 'I have set his feet on soft ground; I have set his feet on the sloping shoulders of the world.' "

"What?"

"I am sorry; that was English. From a novel I read. It is said by Coyote."

" 'Coyote'?"

"Yes. That sound at the end was a 'coyote,' a kind of wild dog the Indians believe – well, there are many here. He was on the hill here, above us."

"That was – 'Coyote'?"

"A coyote, yes, just the last little bit; didn't the beginning sound almost like a train – or . . ."

"Train?"

"One of those with one car, a diesel car?"

"I do not know such, trains with one car. Is there a track?"

"There is, but I thought – I – it is miles away, west, at least four."

"Then . . ."

"The wind, the air is so clear it must have been the wind. Coming up the valley. Yes."

"Oh-h," the old man said. They sat down again in their places.

"It is at least four miles. I am sure. The night freights will not bother us."

"Once we sleep, who hears them."

"Yes, we should sleep. The sun is up early."

They stretched out upon the ground, and there was total silence. Then,

"Why didn't you keep going west?"

"The mountains. They look so nice, I thought sitting on those hills outside Calgary, almost like a new world, sharp, beautiful, clean. But usually when you get over there's always more of what you climbed them to get away from. So one morning I started north."

"What is north?"

"After Edmonton and a few towns there are only Indian reserves, Metis cabins, and a few Mennonite settlements, and then nothing but the land, the land to finally the frozen ocean."

"Mennonites?"

"Some very conservative ones; they moved up there to get away from everyone but themselves."

"Aren't they too much for themselves, too?"

"Some. Some keep moving to Bolivia every year."

"Why there?"

"Even some have moved there from Paraguay. They're trying to find a place just for themselves."

"Still."

"Yes. You know the trouble with Mennonites? They've always wanted to be Jews. To have land God had given them for their very own, to which they were called; so even if someone chased them away, they could work forever to get it back.

Wherever they got pushed, or they pull themselves, they try to prove to themselves they are building that land."

"They came close in Russia."

"Closest there, I think. Unfortunately. But they are still trying to find it, and it isn't anywhere on earth.

"That's the trouble with Mennonites; they show it clearer than most other Christians, especially Protestants. They wish they were, if they could only be Jews. On the mountain Moses said, 'Go over that river, there's the land God has given you forever,' but Jesus just said, 'I'm going to make a place ready for you and then I'll come and get you. You wait.' Moses gave his people manna to eat when they were hungry, and Jesus did that a little but then he changed. Then he just said, 'I'm bread enough for you. Remember me.'"

"That's the big trouble with Jesus," said the old man. "He never gives you a thing to hold in your hand."

The other answered, "There are things, many things that you can't hold in your hand."

It was completely dark. The poplar leaves clicked in the wind; the slope rustled as from feet. An airplane was flying, somewhere but in the diffusion of the sky-ed wind it was impossible to tell whether it was moving north or west over the blue mountains.

Afterword

BY EVA-MARIE KRÖLLER

The Blue Mountains of China appeared in 1970, a traumatic year in Canada's history. The FLQ crisis and the implementation of the War Measures Act marked the end of the nation's centennial decade with political upheaval and peremptory violence. These events also put a temporary stop to the euphoric rhetoric of social harmony, national vigour, and cultural excellence. The books of 1970 – Margaret Atwood's *The Journals of Susanna Moodie* among them – might still celebrate ancestral traditions, both personal and collective, but another tone sounded in them as well. They presented a pessimistic, even apocalyptic vision of a future mired in indifference, enslaved to technology, and threatened by nuclear holocaust.

Although Wiebe's novel reflects in several ways the scepticism typical of Canadian literature and culture at that time, it is also resolutely "anachronistic" in its insistence that the world can be made better, that human beings can themselves attain a state of perfection. Thus the individual sections insistently repeat tales of human aspiration and endurance: with God's help, in this book, human beings prevail. When Wiebe satirizes a 1960s cult book and bestseller such as Leonard Cohen's *Beautiful Losers*, dismissing it as pretentious fluff in the closing pages of *The Blue Mountains of China*, he is actively resisting nihilism. When he praises Sheila Watson's 1959 novel *The Double Hook*, he is, in parallel fashion, praising the will to project a spiritual, therefore substantial, vision.

The Blue Mountains of China thus presents a series of stories about the workings of faith, stories that explore tensions between scepticism and visionary commitment. In contrast to its traditional theme, however, the novel is distinguished by its experimental form. The way the novel is organized represents a considerable departure from the one-dimensional didacticism of Wiebe's earlier novels such as *Peace Shall Destroy Many*. His organization – complex and by no means random – makes the 1970 book arguably one of the most challenging in Canadian literature. Yet Wiebe claims that the novel's technical sophistication came about not only because he acquired greater literary awareness than he possessed at the beginning of his career but also because of what happened while he was teaching at a Mennonite college. There, he says, he "encountered men and women of real perception who had thought through a lot of these things, really literate Christians who saw themselves as Jesus' followers and at the same time were acquainted with the thoughts of others and had brought that kind of understanding to bear on what it means to be a Christian." *The Blue Mountains of China* sets out to create a polyphony of voices struggling to formulate what it means to be a Christian.

The book reconstructs the odyssey of several generations of Mennonites who move from Russia to Canada, Paraguay, and across the blue mountains of China. These mountains describe a specific location ("the faint blue straggle of the Great Khingans, distant as a whiff of oriental scent, a world that lay afar and tempted"), but also the ever-elusive goal of their several wanderings. The different episodes of this multiple odyssey are related in thirteen chapters often so discrete as to make the book appear less a novel than the collection of stories it was originally meant to be; indeed several of the

chapters were first published separately. But there is an order
and a coherence to what Wiebe has written. Earlier, in *Peace
Shall Destroy Many*, he used the form of the *bildungsroman* –
the tale of a boy growing up – to follow the growth of faith. In
The Blue Mountains of China, he refuses the linear development and success-oriented ethos of realism that are acces-
sories of the *bildungsroman* and its derivative, the family saga.
He chooses exploratory serial fiction instead. In their versions
of such fiction, Margaret Laurence in *A Bird in the House* and
Alice Munro in *Lives of Girls and Women* are primarily interested in creating a feminine alternative to the male-centred
apprenticeship novel. Wiebe's concern here is an ethnic and
religious community. This revelation does not happen without difficulty. The recurrence of names may be exasperating,
but such confusions of identity are symptomatic of a culture
which places little store in an individual bereft of her people
and her faith. After all, Mennonites have rarely been afforded
the luxury of a safe and stable homeland, and yet they maintain a sense of belonging and family cohesiveness over long
periods of separation.

The most persistent voice – and the one that helps bind the
narrative together across enormous spatial and temporal
disruptions – is that of Frieda Friesen. In four "instalments,"
distributed throughout the novel, Frieda relates, calmly and
unwaveringly, the story of her life: from her early years on the
Canadian prairies to her family's emigration to and settlement in Paraguay, where she concludes her life surrounded by
her many children and grandchildren. Her narrative dwells on
domestic matters, on the rituals of courtship, marriages,
numerous births and almost equally numerous deaths; it
describes, in great detail, the building of houses, the sowing
and harvesting of crops, the digging of wells, the raising of
cattle, and the availability of cash. Sustained by Frieda's unhurried and often awkward cadences, the narrative conveys a
sense of reassurance. At the same time, Frieda relates with

equal calm the many disasters that befall her family and scarcely pauses when her narrative tells of yet another calamity that must be endured. "At evening he died," Frieda starkly announces her husband's death: "We had sent a truck to Greta and Abram on the south Sixty Legua that he was sick and they just got to *hauptcheuik* in Ostwick in time for the funeral next morning, May 1, 1958. Elder Wiebe the Younger preached, and Kornelius too."

Whereas Frieda's narrative may be said to maintain more or less the same distance from events, several of the remaining chapters use the extreme close-up of the restricted third-person narrative and the interior monologue. The second chapter, "Sons and Heirs," relates the few days following Jakob Friesen's return from a Soviet jail to his farm, now half-destroyed and deserted, and his eventual death at the hands of a guard. Although the reader is given a vivid picture of the ruinous state of what was once a prosperous property, the chapter focuses less on external realities than on Jakob's emotional response to them. Thus, his erotic attraction to a young Russian woman is related in impressionist prose that traces every sensual nuance of the experience: "She began coming, to him. The rim of her skirts flickered, slowly, her hips swaying, her neck thrust out of the embroidered blouse like a stalk ending in brief red, tan and swinging black like the hips, but opposite and lapsed in beat."

Or there is Liesel's narrative in "Over the Red Line," which is shaped (and limited) by the perceptions of a rather vain young Mennonite girl on board the ship that is carrying her and her family into yet another exile in Paraguay. Liesel observes the goings-on around her with the detachment of a curious teenager, but she relinquishes all such detachment when she accidentally falls through the railing and almost drowns; here, her narrative conveys the incoherent perceptions of someone about to lose consciousness forever before she is snatched back to life.

Perhaps the most moving and meaningful of such adjustments in perspective, however, occurs in the chapter "Drink Ye All of It," in which David Epp, initially preoccupied with the indignities of a filthy roadside inn – scrabbling lice, no milk for the baby – lifts himself from these concerns and voluntarily returns to the village from which they have just escaped in order to protect from false accusations, most likely without success, those Mennonites who were left behind. Starting with the microscopically observed details of the immediate environment around him, David's perspective grandly pulls back to encompass a narrative of sacrifice so paradigmatic that his grown son fashions his own life around it.

Throughout the book, metaphors help to tie the various episodes together, but at the same time they frustrate any attempts at establishing closure, both in the Mennonites' narrative and in the Mennonites' existence. The most complex and pervasive of these is the house, which serves as an embodiment, always painfully transitory, of permanence and home. Frieda in particular carefully documents the building of white-washed sod-huts in Manitoba and, later, of brick houses covered with galvanized sheets in Paraguay. Each room in these houses – the *sommastov*, the *ackstov* – is assigned a precise function which helps to keep family relations and hierarchies in place and therefore function as a mirror of God-given order. But human order never lasts. Transgressions are regularly signalled by a crossing of spatial boundaries: Jakob beds the Russian girl in the stables, where the partitions have been torn down to be used for firewood, and Liesel almost perishes in her brazen invasion, on board ship, of areas and events that are not meant for her. These transgressions do more than simply declare particular human failings – Jacob's lust or Liesel's pride. More often than not in this novel, the Mennonites exchange a proper house for a makeshift dwelling where order is difficult or impossible to maintain and where a man may not be able even to stand up straight: a jail cell, a roadside inn, the ruins of a cloister. Each one is a reminder that earthly homes are only weak substitutes for their heavenly counterpart.

In her blackened, deserted house, Muttachi spins and unravels, like Penelope, the same small store of wool, and she insists that some of the embroidered table-cloths that are to be carted away with other family belongings stay with her, as tapestries of her existence. Her determination is echoed in Liesel's father's refusal to give up an old shawl to a wealthy passenger, reminding his daughter to "at least leave the shawl" the next time she intends to fall through the railing because "we can't lose everything beautiful at once." But Muttachi's seemingly futile spinning and undoing have, at the end of the book, an even stronger parallel in Jakob Friesen's obsessive tying and untying of the cord around his waist. Joining John Friesen on his eccentric pilgrimage, the old man embodies the wanderings but also the brief moments of respite that his people have experienced throughout their history.

The Mennonite epic becomes an odyssey of *all* human beings who strive to overcome personal and collective hardship and attain redemption. Though stationed so fully in 1970 and its concerns, the book is an accomplished vision of a better place and a timeless future.

BY RUDY WIEBE

DRAMA
Far As the Eye Can See (1977)

ESSAYS
Playing Dead: A Contemplation Concerning the Arctic (1989)

FICTION
Peace Shall Destroy Many (1962)
First and Vital Candle (1966)
The Blue Mountains of China (1970)
The Temptations of Big Bear (1973)
Where Is the Voice Coming From? (1974)
The Scorched-Wood People (1977)
Alberta/A Celebration (1979)
The Mad Trapper (1980)
The Angel of the Tar Sands and Other Stories (1982)
My Lovely Enemy (1983)
Chinook Christmas (1992)
A Discovery of Strangers (1994)

New Canadian Library
The Best of Canadian Writing

M&S

NCL Titles from the Prairie Provinces

Frederick Philip Grove

Fruits of the Earth
Over Prairie Trails
A Search for America
Settlers of the Marsh

Margaret Laurence

A Bird in the House
The Diviners
The Fire-Dwellers
A Jest of God
The Stone Angel

John Marlyn

Under the Ribs of Death

Martha Ostenso

Wild Geese

Sinclair Ross

As For Me and My House
*The Lamp at Noon and
  Other Stories*

Gabrielle Roy

Garden in the Wind
The Road Past Altamont
Street of Riches
*Where Nests the
  Water Hen*

Robert Stead

Grain

Rudy Wiebe

*The Blue Mountains
  of China*
*The Temptations of
  Big Bear*

Adele Wiseman

Crackpot

NCL – A Series Worth Collecting